Doomed to Repeat

Tim Baker

Blindogg Books

ISBN-10 0-9972760-4-5
ISBN-13 978-0-9972760-4-6

Printed on acid-free paper in the United States of America

This book is dedicated to

Harry "Chief" Benn

Thank you for taking me under your wing and teaching me so much at a time in my life when I probably didn't deserve it.

Tim Baker

"Time is the school in which we learn,
Time is the fire in which we burn."

~Delmore Schwartz

Tim Baker

PART ONE
March 27, 1945 – Berlin, Germany

Tim Baker

1

SS Lieutenant-General Hans Gruber had thought the look in Reichsführer Himmler's eyes was frightening until he felt the rage burning through him from the eyes of Adolph Hitler.

"I do not envy you, Herr General," Himmler had said to him. "The Führer's state of mind these days has not been one of tolerance for bad news."

The assessment was no surprise to Gruber. The fuse of Hitler's infamous temper was burning faster and growing shorter practically by the hour.

"Good luck, Herr General," Himmler had added with a somewhat sadistic chuckle as Gruber left.

Now, looking into Hitler's eyes, Gruber was certain the time remaining in his life could be charted in minutes.

Breaking eye contact with the Führer would surely guarantee him a seat on the next train to Russia, or worse, but he wondered if it would be worth the risk anyway. If he were shot, the nightmare would finally be over; if he were sent to the Eastern Front at this stage of the war it would probably all be over soon. The war couldn't possibly go on much longer.

It was no secret that the war was not going well. Germany's once-glorious Third Reich was crumbling. Soldiers were surrendering by the thousands, despite Hitler's direct orders forbidding submission under any circumstances. But these were not the same soldiers who had begun the war. The few who had survived this long were weary beyond human comprehension. New troops were either too young or too old to be expected to fight to the death. Most would rather take their chances with the Americans and British, and some would even prefer dying in a Russian P.O.W. camp over dying of starvation or freezing to death. Many of the newest soldiers were conscripts from conquered nations and the thought of them showing more than a token allegiance to the Fatherland was laughable.

Germany's ability to produce the supplies needed to maintain the war effort had been crippled by constant bombing from the Allies. Hitler's military machine was dying a slow, painful death.

This knowledge combined with Gruber's less-than-optimistic report on the Bell were the fuel stoking the Führer's rage.

Hitler slammed a fist on the desk. The sound echoed off the concrete walls of the bunker.

"Was I not clear, General?"

Gruber noticed the throbbing veins in Hitler's neck.

"Perfectly clear, Mein Führer," he said as confidently as possible.

"Perfectly. Yet you bring me nothing but bad news."

"I am sorry, Mein Führer. But Dr. Spier assures me..."

"If I wanted the assurances of a doctor, Herr General, I would have summoned him instead of you."

The sudden calmness in Hitler's tone was almost more frightening than the shouting.

"Yes, Mein Führer."

Hitler clasped his hands behind his back and walked slowly to the far wall. Gruber remained at attention, eyes forward, while the leader of Germany paced slowly back to his desk. Gruber could feel the hairs on the back of his neck standing as Hitler passed by. In his mind, part of him wished the Führer would shoot him right here, right now.

Instead, Hitler kept walking until he stood face to face with the portrait of himself on the wall behind the desk. Without taking his eyes from his own likeness, Hitler spoke in a very calm and non-threatening manner.

"Inform Dr. Spier I will be there the day after tomorrow and I expect a fully functional Bell. If the Bell is not completely operational, every person in that bunker will be executed, beginning with you. Do you understand, Herr General?"

"Yes, Mein Führer."

Hitler turned to face the general. The slightest suggestion of a smile appeared on his face and then quickly vanished.

"Now I will give you a chance to leave here on a positive note."

"Thank you, sir."

"Tell me about my train."

Gruber felt relief he hadn't thought possible two minutes ago. He snapped up and delivered his report with pride.

"I am happy to report, Mein Führer, the train, has been buried as you instructed."

"And the men who buried it?"

Gruber's eyes lowered subtly.

"They were on their way back to Berlin when their convoy was attacked. There were no survivors."

Hitler nodded.

"This means that you and I are the only two people who know of its location."

"Yes, Mein Führer."

Hitler placed his hands on his hips and nodded again, his smile reappearing.

"Good. This is good. It is my understanding that Dr. Spier believes travel in the Bell could result in temporary memory loss. Is this correct?"

"That is my understanding as well, Mein Führer."

"Make sure the exact location of the train is in the Bell. I will need it in order to ensure the continued glory of the Reich."

Gruber snapped to attention and clicked his heels. The echo bounced off the walls.

"Yes, Mein Führer."

"That is all, General."

Gruber snapped his right arm out and upward in salute and snapped his heels together again sharply before turning to leave the room.

After closing the heavy door behind him, he half-heartedly returned the salute of the sentry and walked away as calmly and slowly as he could.

He closed his eyes and let out a long, slow breath as he climbed the stairs.

The chill of the late-March air was compounded by the light film of sweat on Gruber's face and neck. He turned up the collar of his wool overcoat and walked to his car, the light crunching of snow under his boots the only sound.

His new driver, a young private, snapped to attention and opened the rear door of the waiting staff car. Gruber climbed into the back seat without acknowledging the young soldier's salute. The private closed the door and climbed into the driver's seat. He sat up as straight as he could in order to see over the long hood, forcing Gruber to wonder if he could even drive.

On another day, when it appeared that Germany could not lose, he would have chastised the private for leaving the engine running and wasting precious fuel in order to maintain what little heat the staff car had. Now, with the outcome of the war all but a foregone conclusion, he decided to leave the private alone.

It hardly seemed worth the effort.

Hopefully, in the near future, this boy would return home and live the rest of his days without witnessing the ugliness of war. Provided home still existed, of course.

As the car pulled away from the fürherbunker Gruber caught the eyes of the private in the rear-view mirror.

The private quickly averted his gaze.

"What is your name, private?"

The private tried to deepen his boyish voice.

"Mueller, Herr General."

"Your given name, Mueller."

A brief look of confusion washed over the private's face.

"Eric, Herr General."

"What do you think of the war, Eric?"

"The Fatherland will be victorious. Glorious victory, Herr General."

The private smiled, his eyes probing the general's face for a sign that he had given the correct answer.

"How old are you, Eric?"

Mueller swallowed.

"I am nineteen, Herr General."

Gruber locked eyes with the boy for several seconds.

"I will be sixteen next month, Herr General."

Gruber nodded.

"And your father?"

"My father, sir?"

"Your father. Is he alive?"

"Killed two years ago in an air raid, sir."

"Did he serve in the Great War as well?"

Pride filled Mueller's eyes. "Yes, sir. Injured twice on the Eastern Front, sir."

Gruber nodded. "Undoubtedly a brave man. And you, young Eric, follow in your father's footsteps I see."

"Yes, Herr General. I try."

Gruber sank into the seat and brought his collar around his face.

It wasn't long ago he would have applauded Mueller on his sense of national pride, but now it was only habit that kept him putting his uniform on each day. The habit of a soldier who was once like Eric Mueller, who once believed that Germany was destined to be revered by the rest of the world.

Perhaps it was age, or the inevitable outcome of the war, but that belief had waned significantly in recent months as Hitler's instability grew worse. It was obvious from the beginning that Hitler was unstable, but he parlayed his mental shortcomings with his over-enthusiastic, hate-filled rhetoric, and used it to unite a Germany broken by the defeat of The First World War. The majority of German people listened to, and believed without reservation, his promises of a nation the likes of which the world had never seen. Sadly, the good citizens of Germany failed to consider the possible cost of these promises. Now there were very few left who did not see it for what it was.

The lunacy of a madman.

The man once perceived as the savior of the Fatherland was in fact destroying it. And now as it became increasingly apparent that his legacy would paint him as perhaps one of the greatest villains in history, he wanted to use the Bell as his escape, leaving Germany and its people to reassemble that which he had destroyed.

If von Stauffenberg and the co-conspirators had been successful in their attempt to assassinate him the previous July, millions of lives could have been saved, along with at least some hope for Germany's future.

Gruber gazed absently as the ruins of Berlin passed by his window.

Was this to be the future?

Was Germany's destiny to be written in blood?

Gruber sighed at the realization that the distinction between genius and madman was success or failure.

The two-hour drive from Berlin to Malopolskie, Poland, became a three-hour ordeal of trying to avoid artillery. Several times Mueller was forced to drive the car into a ditch along the side of the road so that he and General Gruber could take cover.

Lying next to Gruber in one of these ditches, Mueller pointed his rifle at the tree line across the road.

Gruber noticed the trembling in the boy's hands.

"Have you ever been in combat, Mueller?" he asked.

Mueller avoided eye contact. "No, Herr General."

"No need to be ashamed, son. There is a first time for everything. Although this will not be your first time."

"Herr General?"

Gruber chuckled. "If the Russians get within range of your rifle, it will be too late for us to fight."

"But the Führer's orders, sir. Surrender is unacceptable."

"I am aware of the order, Mueller. I am also aware of the fact that there comes a time when every soldier must learn when it is time to disregard an order."

Mueller's difficulty in grasping the concept was apparent on his face. Gruber patted the boy's shoulder.

"Come, Mueller. The shelling has stopped for the moment."

When the staff car finally emerged from the trees its driver and passenger were greeted by the familiar odor of the camp.

"Excuse me, Herr General," Mueller said.

"Yes, Mueller."

"Begging the general's pardon, but this is my first...I've never been here."

The young private's eyes were flicking back and forth from the road to the long buildings behind the barbed-wire fence. As the tall smoke stack caught his attention, the staff car drifted onto the grass shoulder.

"Mueller," Gruber said.

Mueller jerked the wheel and put the Mercedes back onto the gravel road.

"I'm sorry, Herr General."

"No apology necessary, Mueller. Over time, you would get used to it, but I don't think you will need to worry about that."

Because we probably won't live long enough, he thought.

"The smell, Herr General."

"That, I'm afraid, you would never get used to. Turn left up here, into the trees."

Mueller turned off the gravel road and stopped at the barricade.

As one of the SS guards approached the car, Mueller rolled his window down.

"Papers," the guard said.

Mueller handed over his credentials and those of the general. As the guard examined the papers, Mueller glanced at the machine-gun nest to his right. The expressionless guard pointed an MG-42 directly at him. He snapped his eyes forward, hoping he didn't look guilty.

"All is in order," the first guard said, handing the papers back to Mueller.

The guard waved an arm at the small shack, and the barricade rose.

Mueller nodded and proceeded along a rutted dirt path barely wide enough to accomodate the staff car.

"Don't be so nervous, Mueller," Gruber said from the back seat. "Routine security."

"Routine, Herr General?"

"Well, routine for locations such as this."

"Yes, Herr General."

During the short drive through the trees Mueller observed three more machine gun emplacements, each occupied by three SS troopers.

After less than a kilometer the road opened onto a small clearing. Having expected to arrive at some sort of military installation, Mueller was slightly confused when he saw nothing in the clearing but a small concrete structure, barley larger than an outhouse, flanked by two more machine gun nests. Two SS troopers patrolled the perimeter of the clearing with German Shepherds at their side. An expressionless SS guard stood in front of the rusted metal door.

The rumble of artillery, closer than Mueller would have liked, shook snow from the boughs of the tall pines surrounding the cleaaring.

Despite the relative warmth of the staff car, an involuntary shiver ran through Mueller's body.

He stopped the car, got out and opened the rear door for the general.

Gruber paused next to the vehicle and cocked an ear toward the sound of the approaching battle. With a sigh, he walked to the small building. The guard at the door snapped to attention, clicking his heels loudly. After examining Gruber's papers he unlocked the door and swung it open.

"Thank you, Herr General," he said, handing the papers back to Gruber.

Mueller noticed that Gruber didn't put them back into his pocket. Apparently he expected to show them again, but to whom?

Gruber nodded at the guard and took a step through the door.

"I will wait here, Herr General?" Mueller asked.

Gruber turned and looked at the young private, who was doing his very best to hide the fear Gruber knew was building inside him with each boom of artillery.

"No, Mueller. Come with me."

Barely able to mask his relief, Mueller closed the car door and followed the general into the small building, past the steely stare of the guard, wondering if there would be room enough for the two of them inside, and what a structure so small could contain to warrant such elaborate security.

The metal door slammed shut behind him, muting the sounds of the approaching war outside.

Inside, the floor was made of steel grating and the lone light fixture attached to the wall provided enough light for Mueller to make out a steep staircase made of the same material. Mueller followed the general down the steps to a landing ten feet below, where they stood in front of another door, protected by another guard, who came to attention and checked their papers before pressing a small button on the wall adjacent to the door. Mueller felt a slight trembling in the floor. After several seconds, the door slid open to reveal another guard standing silently at the back of the elevator car, his eyes locked forward and his machine pistol held tightly across his chest. Mueller glanced back to the entrance above before following the general into the elevator.

Gruber pressed the button next to the door and they began their descent.

A minute later the door opened onto a wide hallway patrolled by more SS men carrying machine guns. Mueller followed the general toward their unknown destination. The bare concrete walls echoed their footsteps until it sounded as though ten men were marching down the hall. So far the only thing Mueller had seen in this fortress of security was SS troopers. His curiosity mixed with a strange fear of the unknown.

They stopped at a door and Gruber presented his credentials to the guard, who glanced at them out of protocol before nodding.

"Thank you, Herr General," he said as he handed the papers back to Gruber.

He removed the key ring clipped to his belt, unlocked the door and swung it open.

Gruber turned to Mueller and grinned.

"Now you'll see what all the fuss is about, Eric."

2

Through the heavy cell door, Abraham Rosen heard the guard insert the key in the lock. He rose from his cot, waited for the door to open and stepped into the hall, falling in behind the lead guard. The other two SS men brought up the rear. As he had done every day for the past two years, Abraham walked with his armed escort along the damp, dimly-lit hallway of the underground bunker. So many times had he made this trip that he knew every stain on the bare concrete walls. He knew how many light fixtures hung from the ceiling, and how many steps it was from his cell to the door to the laboratory.

Why the SS felt he needed three guards was still a mystery to him.

He was sure of only one thing: his education was the only thing making him valuable to the Germans, thus the only thing keeping him alive. Had he been an accountant, a merchant or a tradesman, he would have ended up in the camp just a stone's throw away with the millions of other Jews deemed worthless by the German high command, but his degree in advanced quantum physics from Cambridge made him worth the cost of a cell in the bunker and two meager meals each day. It may not be the life he had given up in England before the war, but it was life.

At the spot he had nicknamed *Piccadilly Circle,* for the way the five intersecting hallways and the machine-gun nest in the center resembled the famous traffic circle in

London, they took the usual route, straight across the circle to the opposite hall.

Abraham was careful not to make eye contact with any of the men in the nest, remembering too vividly the rifle butt to the stomach the one and only time he had had the audacity to look a member of the SS in the eye. Keeping him alive was one thing, treating him like a human being was something else altogether.

On the other side of Piccadilly, with ninety-seven steps remaining in his journey, his mind went back to the night that had led to him being here, and to his losing Sarah...

Abraham squeezed his wife's hand and kissed her cheek.

"Wait here, Sarah. Be silent and wait for me to return."

Sarah nodded, barely able to conceal the fear that had become an integral part of their existence over the past two years. Now at its apex, the next fifteen minutes would either eliminate those fears or justify them.

Before leaving, Abraham saw a glint of light reflect off the gold Star of David hanging from her neck. He tucked the necklace inside her coat.

"I will be back as soon as I can."

Their hands stayed together until Abraham was out of reach. When he was at the edge of the tree line he looked up and down the road for signs of German patrols. Satisfied the coast was clear he crept across the road to the farmhouse. Following the instructions he had received from the Underground, he went to the barn behind the house and knocked softly on the door—two knocks, followed by a short pause, and then three more knocks.

A large hand clamped over his mouth. He was lifted off his feet and dragged to the side of the barn. His abductor whispered in Abraham's ear.

"Say nothing," Abraham was instructed by a voice with a thick French accent.

Abraham nodded.

He was released and told to kneel.

"You have the money?"

Abraham handed the man a cloth pouch. The man handed it to a woman Abraham had not seen a moment ago. She disappeared into the darkness, returned minutes later, and nodded to the man.

"Very good," the man said to Abraham. "You have followed instructions. Where is your wife?"

"Across the road. Hiding."

"Bring her."

As Abraham began to move away the man hissed after him, "Be silent and move carefully."

It seemed to take an eternity to get back to Sarah. Great relief washed over her face when she saw him.

"Are you ready?" he said to her.

She swallowed hard and nodded.

"Move as quickly and quietly as you can, Sarah, but be careful," he said laying a hand on her pregnant stomach.

She nodded again.

He held her hand, stepped out of the trees and crept across the road toward the barn. Halfway there the screech of an owl startled them, drawing a faint gasp from Sarah. Abraham quickly placed his hand over her mouth.

In the field adjacent to the barn they saw the silhouette of the owl swoop down and capture its prey before returning to a perch high in the pines.

Abraham nodded to Sarah, removed his hand from her mouth and led her to the side of the barn.

The French man and the woman led them behind the barn. There, under a moonless sky, they knelt on the damp ground.

"We have twenty miles to cover before dawn," the French man said. "Will this be a problem?" he asked looking at Sarah's stomach.

She shook her head.

"No." Abraham said. "It will not be a problem."

"Do not fall behind, we will not wait for you," the man said. "And be silent."

Abraham and Sarah nodded.

Abraham squeezed his wife's hand. After two years of hiding from the German's, they were finally getting out. If all went well, they would be in Switzerland in a few short days.

"As soon as the others get here we will leave," the man said.

A few minutes later there was a rustling in the nearby brush. The man and the woman turned and brought their machine guns up. A man appeared in the shadows. He walked toward them slowly with his hands up.

"You fool," the French man hissed at him. "Get down."

The stranger stopped in his tracks and glanced over his shoulder. The French man and his partner exchanged a nervous glance.

"Germans!" the newcomer shouted.

The silence was shattered by the eruption of machine gun fire from behind the stranger. His body convulsed and fell to the ground like a sack of potatoes.

The French man grabbed Abraham by the arm. "Come with me."

The woman took Sarah and ran in the opposite direction.

The sounds of gunfire and barking dogs seemed to come from every angle as Abraham followed the French man through the woods. He tried to look over his shoulder for a sign of Sarah in the darkness as he ran to no avail. His foot struck something and he stumbled forward. Only the grip of his guide kept him from falling face first to the ground.

They exited the cover of the trees onto the road. Abraham could see the farmhouse half a kilometer to his right. The French man dragged him to the left.

"Sarah," Abraham said. "Where is Sarah?"

"Forget her," the French man said without turning around. "Forget her and keep moving."

They crossed the street, heading for the cover of the woods on the opposite side.

"Halt!" a German voice cried. "Halt!"

A burst of machine-gun fire sent the French man sprawling onto the ground. A German Shepherd pounced, *clamping his arm in its mouth and shaking it viciously. A second leapt through the air and took Abraham to the ground. Abraham tried to protect himself from the animal's assault, but the dog was too fast and powerful. A German soldier pulled the dog off and commanded Abraham to stand. Almost immediately, four more soldiers ran to the spot and surrounded Abraham leveling guns at him. In the distance, Abraham could hear more gunfire and more dogs barking. He looked to the trees toward the farmhouse and said a silent prayer for Sarah.*

The French man moaned and writhed on the ground. Two of the Germans fired bursts from their machine guns at him until he was still and silent.

Abraham looked at the corpse of the man who was to lead Sarah and him to freedom. Blood flowed along the gravel road into the ditch to be washed away with the next rain.

One of the soldiers shoved Abraham and ordered him to walk. He followed the soldier and the dog along the road, flanked by soldiers on three sides, leaving the body of the French man by the side of the road.

By the time they reached the farmhouse, the gunfire had stopped and the dogs were silent. Four more Germans, along with two dogs, joined them on the road.

There was no sign of Sarah or the other woman.

The quiet returned, broken only by the sound of footsteps on the gravel.

The sound of the guards' footsteps echoed off the walls and snapped Abraham back to reality as they arrived at the lab entrance.

The SS guard at the door removed the keyring from his belt and opened the door. Abraham's escort stepped aside and motioned with his machine gun for Abraham to enter the room.

Once he was inside, the guard, who remained in the hall, slammed the door shut and locked it.

Eric Mueller stood beside General Gruber, gazing around the room as though he were standing on a strange planet. The harder he tried to comprehend the facility, the more confused he became.

Compared to the hallway, this room was bright and warm, and cleaner than any room he had ever been in. Men in white smocks performed tasks Mueller couldn't even begin to guess at. Some sat at desks, writing and consulting pages from the stacks of paper scattered about. Others conferred with each other in front of consoles containing a myriad of lights, dials, and switches. Eric shook his head to eliminate its annoying buzzing, only to find that the sound was not in his head but in the room. At the far end of the room was a large window flanked by banners bearing swastikas. Through the glass, Eric saw something that could only be described as an enormous bell.

Light grey in color, except for a dark red stripe and black swastika on the face. It stood taller than two men and nearly as wide at the base. Around the top was a ring of lighted panels. At the bottom, a series of vents released a steady flow of vapor. On the catwalk surrounding it, more men in white smocks made notes on clipboards and conferred with each other.

Even though he had no idea of the purpose of the facility, Mueller was certain he did not belong here. For some unknown reason, General Gruber had brought him into an area that would ordinarily be off limits to anyone of his rank. Eric assumed even the SS guards throughout the facility were unaware of what they were protecting.

"Mueller," the general called from five steps ahead of him.

Mueller realized he had stopped in his tracks at the sight of the strange object. He snapped his head around to face his superior.

"Yes, Herr General."

Gruber grinned at him. "We will be here all day, Mueller. You will have plenty of time for looking. You may even bear witness to an event that will alter history."

"Alter history, Herr General?"

His confused curiosity was growing more with each passing second.

"All in good time, Mueller. Come with me."

The general walked across the room to meet with a man who appeared to be in charge.

"Good morning, Dr. Spier," Gruber greeted the man.

"General Gruber," Spier said.

"I have come from Berlin," Gruber said. "The Führer was not pleased with my report."

"No. I imagine he would not be. I'm sure by this time next week we will have better..."

Gruber shook his head. "No, Doctor. There will be no next week, the time has come. The Führer wants to hear only one thing when he arrives in two days. That the Bell is ready."

"Ready? Two days?"

Gruber nodded. "And your life, along with the lives of every man in this room, will depend on your progress."

Mueller could see Spier's face drain of color.

"Herr General," the doctor said. "We are very close to the testing phase, but two days? I don't know if that will be enough time."

"You have two days doctor. I suggest you accelerate your efforts. He wants a test today."

"Today?"

"As I said, Doctor, you should not waste any more time."

Spier nodded. "Carl," he called to a man standing at a nearby workbench, who immediately reported to Spier's side.

"Yes, Doctor."

"Our timetable has been adjusted. Inform the staff that we will be conducting a test today."

"Today?"

"Today."

Carl looked from Spier to the general, who looked at him blankly, then back to Spier.

"That is all, Carl," Spier said. "Get on with it."

Carl began circulating the room spreading Spier's message. Within minutes the room took on the appearance of a bee hive.

"We will not be ready for a test for several hours, Herr General. Shall I inform you of the results?"

"No need, Doctor. I will wait here and observe the test myself."

"Stay here?"

"Doctor, perhaps I wasn't clear. The Führer expects the Bell to be fully functional in two days. I will be here to monitor the work so that he is not disappointed."

The door to the laboratory opened. Spier glanced over to see an SS trooper motion Abraham Rosen into the room. When the door closed behind the Jewish physicist, Spier turned to Gruber.

"Herr General, I must inform you, there are still some uncertainties. We are not sure how the rotation of the Earth will affect the Bell's trajectory. We cannot accurately determine where it will land. Also, because of the high levels of magnetism associated with the propulsion, we are not certain if the occupants..."

Spier trailed off.

"If the occupants what?" Gruber said.

Spier swallowed. "If they will survive."

"Isn't that why you conduct tests?"

"Yes, General, but..."

Gruber held up a hand.

"The time for buts has passed, Doctor. You have work to do. I suggest you get busy."

The first thing Abraham noticed was the higher-than-normal buzz of activity in the brightly lit laboratory. Technicians moved about with a heightened sense of urgency. On the far side of the room Dr. Spier was being addressed by a German general. The general's message did not need to be heard to be understood.

Time was running out.

Abraham had heard whisperings among the Germans recently. Being underground for so long, with his only human contact coming in the form of guards who would just as soon kill him and German scientists who rarely discussed anything but their work, Abraham tended to forget there was a war being fought two stories above him. Occasionally he would overhear hushed talk about the course of the war and the inevitable fate of Germany. Judging by the general's posture and actions combined with the grave look on Spier's face, the gossip was, at the very least, rooted in truth.

Dr. Spier noticed Abraham and excused himself from the general.

"Herr Rosen," the doctor said.

Compared to the soldiers, Spier's tone was respectful, although he drew the line at addressing Abraham as Dr. Rosen, as his PhD would normally rate.

"Good morning, Dr. Spier," Abraham said.

"Herr Rosen, the priority of our work has changed. We are now on an accelerated time line."

Abraham nodded, not surprised.

"Accelerated by how much?"

Spier's eyes flicked toward the general. "We must conduct a full test today."

Abraham thought he had heard incorrectly.

"Today?"

Spier nodded. "Obviously I cannot tell you more than that, but I will say that this project has been given the highest priority. My orders are to have it ready for use by the day after tomorrow."

This was more than an accelerated timeline. This was an urgency driven by desperation and panic. Germany was on the verge of losing yet another war. Despite his impulse to celebrate, Abraham maintained his professional demeanor, if for no other reason than the possibility his assumption was wrong.

He nodded to Spier. Regardless of the fact that the new criteria came from high up the chain, Abraham resisted his instinctual urge to remind Spier this project was not something that should be taken lightly, nor should the work be conducted in haste. Not only did the limited amount of respect he received in the lab end at questioning orders, it was understood that this particular order carried with it the threat of the ultimate punishment for anybody who considered such action. Even a German.

Abraham nodded again.

"If a test is to be conducted, we have a great deal of work to do."

Spier looked relieved. "Yes, Herr Rosen. We do. General Gruber will be here to observe the test."

"Let us hope it goes well."

"Yes. For all of our sakes."

Eric watched the doctor approach the new arrival. Like all of the others present, the new arrival wore a white lab coat and white pants. The most notable exception, aside from his shaved head, pale complexion and somewhat sunken cheeks, was the yellow band bearing the Jewish star on his right arm.

"Herr General?" he said softly.

"Yes, Mueller?"

"Begging the general's pardon, but what is this place?"

Gruber grinned and nodded. "I suppose I should give you a bit of an explanation. This laboratory is responsible for producing the greatest invention of all time. A device like nothing man has ever before attempted to create, one that will turn the tide of the war in an instant."

"A new weapon, Herr General?" Mueller's eyes went to the strange bell-shaped object.

"A weapon? Not exactly. No Mueller, I would not call it a weapon. At least not in the conventional sense."

"Then what, Herr General?"

Gruber turned to face Mueller straight on.

"What would you think about a vehicle that could transport a man to another time and place?"

Gruber grinned while Mueller struggled to comprehend the idea. The grin grew wider the longer Mueller pondered the question.

"Think of it this way, Mueller. An automobile will take you from one place to another. This vehicle will take you from one time to another."

"One time to another?"

"Yes. From today to yesterday, or tomorrow."

Mueller's eyes went to the bell. "This is...I can't believe such a thing is possible. My father once told me of a book about such a machine, but that was..."

"A story."

Mueller nodded, still fixated on the bell-shaped device.

"This is not a story, Mueller. The best minds in all of Germany are working to make it possible," Gruber said.

Mueller's eyes snapped to the new arrival in the lab. "But that man, Herr General. The one speaking with Dr. Spier. He is a Jew."

Gruber glanced at the two men.

"Yes he is. Before the war he attended Cambridge University in England where he studied concepts that you and I could not begin to understand. Without his contribution to this project it would not be where it is. Jew or not, he is a brilliant man."

The confusion on Mueller's face grew at Gruber's suggestion that a Jew could be of any value to the master race. Eric struggled to make sense of the General's statement. Surely the general was aware that his words, if heard by the wrong people, would be considered treasonous and could lead to a firing squad. Nonetheless, he continued.

"Eric," Gruber said, "a man's worth is not defined by his ancestry but by his contribution to society."

"How can a Jew contribute to German society?"

Gruber felt his heart sink.

Mueller was much too young to fully understand what he was saying; he was merely reciting the dogma that had been fed to him over the past ten years. Youthful passion is a wonderful thing, but Gruber had witnessed the passion of an entire generation get twisted and distorted so it could be used as a weapon of hatred capable of acts he had never thought possible.

As a lifelong soldier, Gruber was not opposed to the war. He believed in Germany. What he did not believe in was *the enemy within.*

Young Mueller, like thousands of boys his age, was a pawn in one man's personal vendetta of evil.

More times than he cared to recount, Gruber had seen and heard acts of hatred and violence that went beyond those normally associated with war.

The fanatical views of Hitler's party had introduced a new facet of war in which there were two enemies: one on the battlefield under the flag of another nation, and one on the home front with no flag and no uniform. An enemy hiding in plain sight and seeking to undermine and sabotage the Fatherland by driving it into financial ruin.

Those who knew the latter was an imaginary foe also knew enough to keep such thoughts to themselves or suffer the consequences.

Gruber watched Mueller's young eyes gaze around the room in wonder. Although he barely knew the boy, Gruber sensed that young Eric Mueller did not accept blindly the rhetoric forced upon him, but at the same time was not sure how to deal with his own skepticism. Gruber could see the potential for good in Mueller despite the short time they had spent together.

With any luck, Mueller would survive the war and learn that the true enemy is the one who would tell you who you should hate.

Perhaps there was a way to give Mueller the time he needed to see Germany from a different perspective and also to stop Hitler from escaping the fate he deserved.

"Mueller," Gruber said. "Come with me. I have an important task for you."

Mueller followed the general toward the large window. Standing in front of it was Dr. Spier and the Jew. They seemed to be engaged in a very serious conversation. The mysterious Bell loomed behind them.

Gruber interrupted the conversation.

"Dr. Spier, may I have a moment of your time?"

3

The shift in Spier's demeanor fascinated Abraham and nearly made him smile, something he hadn't done in two years.

Normally the doctor maintained a presence of confidence and authority when addressing his subordinates in the lab. Today, however, there was fear in his eyes. He was not issuing orders anymore; he was making requests. Requests accompanied by a barely masked sense of urgency.

"Herr Rosen," Spier said. "I cannot stress it enough, we must perform this test today. General Gruber will oversee it personally and report the results to the Führer. Shall we say two hours?"

For Spier to ask for such a hurried test confirmed what Abraham already knew—the situation was dire. He consulted a clipboard and looked through some notes on the bench.

"I wish we had more time, Doctor, but if you want to conduct the test in two hours, we will do so."

Spier nodded. "Good. Thank you, Herr Rosen."

"Have you decided whom to send yet?"

Spier's eyes found their way to Abraham's, and he nodded nervously.

"I think you should be the one to test it, Herr Rosen."

Again, Abraham thought he misheard the doctor's response.

"Me?"

"Yes, Herr Rosen. You."

"Why me?

"It is no secret that your contribution to this project has been invaluable, Herr Rosen." Spier glanced at the general. "And I don't think you should be punished for that."

"Punished?"

Another look at the general.

"I could be shot for telling you this," Spier continued. "Once the project is complete you are to be..."

Abraham sighed. Not because he was surprised, but because he had hoped to live to see the end of man's hatred for his fellow man. With so many around the world joining the fight against Hitler's barbarism, he had allowed himself to believe that the end of the war would bring great changes to the world.

Now, regardless of his assistance, or maybe because of it, he would never know.

"Please understand, Herr Rosen, this is not my decision, nor is it the decision of any of the men in this room. We all understand and appreciate the value of your assistance to our work, even though we are forbidden to express such thoughts. But the high command would never acknowledge the fact that a Jew played such an important role in the creation of the device that will go down in history as Germany's, perhaps man's, greatest accomplishment."

"I appreciate your gesture, Doctor, but surely your superiors would not allow me to be the one to test it."

"I can convince them that you have the knowledge needed for the task. I can also tell them that, as a Jew, it would be a less significant loss if something..."

"If it fails," Abraham completed the thought.

Spier nodded. "Will you do it? Once the Bell lands, you can set the controls to return while you remain behind."

Abraham looked around the room, and his eyes stopped on the Bell. He thought about Sarah and the lunacy of life since the Nazis took power. The world was upside down and spinning out of control. This could be his only chance for escape, his only chance to see how one of the most bizarre chapters in the history of mankind ends.

He locked eyes with Spier and nodded. "I will do it."

"Excellent."

"Excuse me, Dr. Spier," General Gruber interrupted. "May I have a moment of your time?"

Spier nodded at the general. "Of course, General."

"I'd like to talk to you about the test."

"Yes, Herr General, we should be ready in approximately two hours."

"Who will be manning the craft?"

Spier swallowed and glanced at Abraham.

"I thought Herr Rosen would be an ideal candidate. He has extensive knowledge of the project and will be able to provide valuable information upon his return."

Gruber regarded Abraham with a mixture of curiosity and apathy.

"A fine choice, I'm sure. However, when the Führer departs in the Bell, he will undoubtedly wish to take a...companion."

Spier nodded. "Yes, I'm sure of it."

"Then perhaps there should be two passengers in the test, to make sure the Bell functions properly under actual conditions."

"Two passengers?"

"Yes, to make sure that the presence of another person doesn't alter the results. I suggest young private Mueller, here."

Spier looked at the private, whose face was painted with surprise and fear.

"Private Mueller?"

"Yes. He is young and healthy and will not interfere in Herr Rosen's work."

Spier considered pointing out that, unlike conventional aircraft, the number of occupants would not affect the Bell's performance, however if Gruber decided to pull rank, he could order Rosen to be left behind in favor of one of the German scientists.

He nodded with as much enthusiasm as he could muster.

"Of course, Herr General. An excellent idea." Spier checked his watch. "We will begin the launch readiness check shortly. Herr Rosen and the private will need to be in the preparation room in one hour."

"Very good."

"Herr General," Mueller said once Spier and Rosen had walked away. "I don't...what is..."

Gruber raised a hand to calm Mueller, then led him to a quiet corner of the lab.

"Listen to me Eric," he said. "Even though the war goes on, Germany has lost. In a matter of weeks, maybe even days, it will be over. For men like me, death will be a welcome escape, but you are too young to wish for such a fate. I am giving you a chance to not only survive the war but to also make a contribution that could possibly save countless lives."

"Herr General?"

"In two days the **Führer** will attempt to use this device to get out of Germany and avoid the fate he deserves. If he is allowed to escape, there is no telling what the future holds. You must prevent that from happening."

"But how, Herr General?"

"By destroying the Bell once you reach your destination. Do not allow Herr Rosen to bring it back. If you have to kill him, so be it."

Mueller's eyes widened, and he glanced at the Bell. He shook his head slowly.

"Mueller." Gruber placed his hands on the boy's shoulders. "You are a German soldier. It is your duty to serve the Fatherland as best you can."

The boy stared at the general as though he were being asked to kill his own mother.

"Herr General, you are asking me to..."

"Do your duty. That is what I am asking you, Eric. I am asking you, not as a general to a private, but as one

German to another. I am asking you to do something that may seem contrary to a soldier's duty, but you must remember, your duty is to Germany, not the Führer. Putting on a uniform makes you a soldier; following your conscience in the face of immoral orders makes you a man."

After a moment of thought, Mueller snapped to attention. "Yes, Herr General."

"History will thank you, Eric."

In the preparation room, Abraham and Eric sat naked on examination tables while a medical doctor gave each of them a thorough physical exam. The doctor looked at Spier and nodded.

"Neither of these men are the picture of health, but they should survive."

"Thank you, Doctor," Spier said as the physician left the room.

Spier handed each of them a pair of plain, brown pants, a white undershirt, socks, and a pair of leather shoes with no laces. Eric glanced at his uniform folded neatly beside him.

"You cannot wear your uniform, private," Spier said, anticipating the question. "Not only is it important that you look inconspicuous, but there is too much metal in it. It could alter the trajectory of the craft."

Mueller nodded, pretending to understand.

"We anticipate launch in fifteen minutes," Spier said. "It is time to get on board."

Spier led them back to the lab. The faint buzzing Eric had heard earlier had grown louder. General Gruber waited by a console which was manned by three technicians who spoke to each other in hushed tones, consulted gauges on the panel in front of them, adjusted dials and made notations. Spier spoke with each of them in turn. After speaking to the last one he turned to Gruber.

"Everything is ready, Herr General."

"Very good. Carry on," Gruber said.

Spier opened the door next to the large window overlooking the Bell.

"If you would follow me," he said to Abraham and Eric.

The blare of a wall-mounted klaxon halted everything.

After several seconds of stunned silence, the room turned into a flurry of panicked activity.

"What is it?" Mueller asked.

"The alarm," Gruber told him. "The facility is under attack."

Suddenly the rest of the technicians and scientists were scurrying about in blind terror.

"What do we do?" Abraham asked Spier.

Spier looked at Gruber who had drawn the luger from its holster and moved behind the console.

"Continue as planned," Gruber barked.

The wailing of the klaxon seemed to grow louder. Muted machine-gun fire and small explosions could be heard outside the lab.

Spier led Abraham and Eric along the catwalk to the door of the Bell. He opened a small panel, moved a lever and turned a dial. There was a sucking sound as the door to the Bell opened.

"Get inside. I will make the final preparations," Spier said.

Abraham and Eric stepped into the Bell and the door closed with a whoosh.

Eric felt his ears pop.

"What do we do?" he asked.

Abraham pointed to a light on the panel in front of him. "When this light goes on to signify that the roof is open and all is ready, I start the ignition sequence. One minute later, we will be gone."

Spier sat at the console, pushing buttons and turning dials. Light poured in from above as the roof opened.

An explosion shook the lab. Spier turned to see a hole in the wall where the door had been. Smoke poured in from the hall, followed by a group of Russian soldiers stepping over the corpse of the sentry who had been outside the door.

Gruber emptied his luger at them.

"Hurry Doctor!"

Spier glanced behind him at the Russian soldiers moving toward them as Gruber reloaded his gun and resumed fire. The klaxon competed with the gunfire and the all-out chaos of the invasion. Spier slammed his hand on another button. He looked at Gruber, who was still trying to fend off the attackers, just in time to see an explosion of crimson soak the general's tunic.

"General!" Spier said.

As Gruber lay bleeding, he reached into the pocket of his tunic and struggled to hand Spier what looked like a leather cigarette case.

"Inside...," he coughed, "...location of Hitler's gold train," he gasped. "Get it into Bell."

Spier watched the general die then looked at the object in his hand. He had heard rumors of the gold train, but the concept of a trainload of wealth, treasure, artwork, and weapons seemed like the stuff of legend, rather than fact. Now it appeared the rumors were true, and he held the location of unimaginable wealth in his hand. A bullet ricocheted off of the console to his left. The invading Russians would guarantee him a fate worse than death, the case in his hand could be an opportunity to live out his days as one of the richest men in the world. Before he was even aware he had made a decision, he found himself running through the door toward the Bell.

Five or six steps to salvation.

An explosion propelled him along the catwalk until he slammed into the Bell. His back felt as if it were on fire. He opened the door to the Bell and stumbled in. After struggling to close the door he collapsed to the floor.

"Herr Spier!" Abraham shouted over the din.

"Go," Spier ordered weakly.

Abraham returned his focus to the panel, flipped a switch, then pushed a button.

The small cabin felt as if it were spinning, slowly at first, but quickly gaining speed. The three men were pushed back against the wall and pinned in place by the centrifugal force. The buzz of static electricity filled the air.

The spinning and the static grew to an unbearable level until there was a thunderous explosion followed by silence.

The Bell streaked through time and space.

Inside< the three occupants lay on the floor in a semi-catatonic state, unaware of what was happening to them. While outside witnesses throughout history would hear a building of static energy followed by an explosion. They would catch a split-second glimpse in the sky of an oddly-shaped glowing object, which appeared to hover in mid-air for a split second before vanishing without a trace.

Tim Baker

PART TWO

March 27, 2019 - Flagler Beach, Florida

4

Sherry Cote stared blankly at the pages of the text-book, hoping for an epiphany. With an exam facing her at the end of the week, she struggled to digest and retain as much information about *the law of evidence* as she could. She felt confident in her chances on the test, but the amount of studying involved in obtaining a degree in criminal justice was taking its toll on her.

Maybe she didn't want to be a cop as badly as she thought.

"Go back to school, they said," she muttered. "It'll be good for your career, they said."

She closed the text book, pushed it aside and took a pack of cigarettes from her purse.

"I'm taking a break," she told Carmen. "Be back in ten."

As she began to remove her headset the line rang.

"Christ. Perfect timing," she said. "Nine-one-one emergency," she said into the mouthpiece attached to her headset. "What is your emergency?"

"Yeah. Hi," the male caller said. The sound of loud music and the voices of dozens of people could be heard in the background. "I'm at Finn's, on the roof. I just saw, like, this explosion in the sky and something crashed in the water. It was, like, huge. I think it was a UFO."

The man was obviously drunk, but Sherry had to log the call nevertheless.

"So, you're saying you saw a UFO crash into the ocean near Finn's?" she repeated for the sake of the recorded transcript.

"Yeah. That's what I'm saying."

"Okay. I'll have an officer come and take your statement. Can I have your name?"

"My name?"

"Yes, sir. So the officer can find you and get your statement."

"Look, man, I reported it. Ain't that enough?"

"Sir, your name is strictly for the witness statement, you won't be..."

The line went dead.

"Unbelievable. Must be a full moon, or something," Sherry said.

"I don't think so," Carmen said as she perused a copy of *People* magazine. "I think that's next Sunday."

"Well, then this guy is really drunk. Either that or a UFO just crashed near the pier."

"I'll go with A. Drunk," Carmen chuckled. "Final answer."

"I'll send a unit over anyway."

She dropped her cigarettes on the counter and keyed the microphone. "Two-David-nine."

There was a short burst of static before the response came. "Two-David-nine."

"Butch, can you roll by Finn's and take a look around. Some guy just reported a UFO crash in the water near the pier."

"A what?"

"You heard me. Just check it out."

"All right. I'm just coming through Highbridge. It'll take me fifteen or twenty minutes to get there."

"I'm sure the aliens aren't going anywhere."

"Ten-four. Two-David-nine out."

Sherry picked up her cigarettes.

"I definitely need a break," she said.

5

The silence was gradually replaced by the sound of an alarm bell.

Random images flashed through his mind.

Barking dogs. A woman holding his hand, then gone in an instant. Erie shadows cast on the walls of a long stark hallway. A roomful of men in white smocks. Soldiers. Gunfire. An explosion.

Then nothing.

The spinning sensation gradually gave way to a slowly increasing awareness of the here and now. His eyes opened. Wherever he was, the only available light came from a panel of some sort above him.

Struggling to his feet, he surveyed his surroundings.

Although he had no specific recollection of where he was or what was happening, he understood on an instinctual level that there was no need to panic but also that time was of the essence.

The panel in front of him had an array of flashing lights, none of which meant anything to him, although he felt they should. On the floor behind him were two others. One, a young boy, the other an older man, his back covered in blood. The room rocked gently from side to side as if it were floating. When water began to seep in at the base of the door, something told him to get out.

He knelt beside the older man, who was barely conscious. The man handed him a small leather case.

"Gold train," he said.

He stuffed the case in his pocket.

"We must get out," he said.

The older man nodded weakly.

He went to the boy and shook him.

"We must get out."

The boy jolted upright.

"Destroy it," he said.

"Destroy what?"

The boy looked at him blankly and shook his head. "I don't know. Where are we?"

"I'm afraid I don't know, but we must get out. Quickly."

There was a strange familiarity about the room, as well as the other man and the boy, but he knew this was not the time to ponder explanations.

The boy helped him open the door. The night sky offered very little help in identifying where they were. Water flooded the compartment until it levelled off with the sea water outside. In no time at all the level rose to their knees as the vessel began sinking.

"Help me with him. He is hurt."

The two picked up the older man and stepped out into the warm ocean water. Somehow they were able to stay afloat until they reached water shallow enough to allow them to stand. Fifteen minutes later, they waded ashore and collapsed in the surf, exhausted.

He rolled over and looked for the vessel. It was important, but he didn't know why. It had either been swallowed up in the dark of night or the blackness of the ocean. He couldn't tell which.

The boy got to his knees and vomited sea water. After catching his breath, the boy looked at him.

"Who are you? Where are we?"

He looked from the wounded man to the boy and shrugged.

"At the moment, I'm not sure of anything."

A short distance away, a pier extended from an A-framed building into the water. "Let's get under there," he pointed to the dark space beneath the building. "It will give us a place to think where we won't be seen."

They picked up the older man and dragged him to the shadows.

Once concealed from sight under the building, he placed an ear to the older man's chest.

"He is dead."

"What do we do?"

"I don't know. What do you remember?"

The boy closed his eyes and shook his head rapidly.

"Being underground. Nothing makes sense to me. I remember an explosion. I remember feeling like I was on a train. And noise. Loud buzzing noise."

He nodded.

"I remember the explosion also. I seem to also remember something about a cave of sorts. And the sound of footsteps."

"Did we kill him?" the boy asked, pointing at the dead man in the sand.

"I don't think so. The injuries on his back look as if many small objects struck him with great force. More force than we could muster with our bare hands."

"How do you know that?"

"Cambridge."

"What is Cambridge?"

"I'm not sure."

"Eric."

"I beg your pardon?"

"My name is Eric." What is your name?"

"Abraham. It just came to me."

"I remember soldiers."

"Yes, so do I."

The boy looked at the dead man. "I don't remember him."

"I seem to recall owing him a debt. I also think his presence here is a mistake, but I don't know why. Perhaps we should consider moving. We don't know how it will be received if we are found with him."

"Found by who?"

"I don't know; I just have this odd feeling as though somebody will be hunting us."

Abraham looked up and down the dark beach, unsure of what he was even looking for. Bright lights shone at the top of the dunes, accompanied by many noises he was unfamiliar with combining in a cacophony of confusion. Not far away, a set of steps led from the beach to the top of the embankment.

"Let's see where those stairs lead," he said.

Staying close to the tall dune, Eric followed Abraham to the wooden steps. They knelt in the sand at the bottom.

"Let's go. Move slowly, but do not draw attention to yourself. We don't know what is up there, so be prepared to run and hide."

Creeping through the darkness, afraid of what might lie ahead, had an inexplicable air of familiarity to it, but he shook it off and kept moving.

They took the steps slowly until they were able to see the source of the light and noise. Strange looking vehicles lined both sides of a road. Others drove by with bright lights leading their way. Tall poles with light fixtures at the top lit the roadway. Loud music mixed with the voices of many people and laughter came from an establishment across the street. The music stirred a memory; an orchestra in white suits, dancing with a beautiful woman, happiness. The music he was hearing now bore no resemblance to the music in the flashback.

"What do you think?" Eric asked.

"Strange music."

A young couple squeezed past them, laughing and talking as they trotted down the steps to the beach. Eric watched as they strolled along the beach arm in arm until they vanished into the darkness.

"English," Abraham said.

"What?"

"The couple. They were speaking English."

"You understood?"

"Yes. I understood what they were saying. They spoke of high tide. They wondered if the water was warm enough for swimming. The woman made a strange comment I don't fully understand."

"What was it?"

"She asked if sharks feed at night like the one in jaws. Perhaps I didn't translate it correctly. It makes no sense to me."

"They were speaking English," Eric said. "So, we are in England?"

"I don't know. They didn't have English accents."

Abraham looked across the street. A tall sign, brightly lit from within, stood in front of the building. On the face was the image of a lion sitting on the beach beneath the words *The Golden Lion* in English. The aromas drifting through the air triggered something in Abraham. He inhaled deeply.

"I haven't had a good meal in a long time," he said.

"Wartime shortages," Eric replied.

"Wartime?"

"I don't know why I said that."

"Maybe we should ask somebody for help."

"How do we know who to trust?"

"I don't know," Abraham said, "but I think we need to take the chance."

Eric nodded and moved up the remaining steps toward the road. As he stepped between two vehicles, he found himself marveling at their odd shapes and bright, smooth finishes. He couldn't recall ever seeing anything like it.

The sound of screeching tires, followed by a loud horn blast, froze Eric in his tracks. Abraham grabbed the boy by the shirt and yanked him out of the path of a large, black vehicle.

The driver climbed out and charged toward Eric.

"What the fuck? Why don't you watch where you're going, asshole!" the driver shouted. "Jesus! I could have killed you. What are you? Stoned or stupid?"

Abraham stepped between Eric and the man. "We are very sorry," he said in English. "We are new here. Please forgive my friend."

"Dumb ass! Why don't you go back to wherever you came from!"

Abraham guided Eric away from the gathering crowd and back toward the stairs.

"We must be careful. Until we learn more about where we are."

"This is A1A," the man shouted after them. "Not some back-woods-ass country road in East Bumfuck."

A small crowd of people had gathered in front of The Golden Lion looking across the street at them.

"Perhaps we should go back down the stairs before we draw the wrong sort of attention," Abraham suggested.

The courtyard of The Golden Lion was full. Every seat at the outdoor tiki bar was occupied, the beach-like dance floor was full of shoeless dancers moving in the ankle deep sand to the reggae music, and there was a line of about ten people waiting on the sidewalk along A1A for tables.

A pair of motorcycles turned off A1A onto North Fifth Street and parked along the picket fence separating the courtyard from the road. The two riders dismounted and entered the courtyard.

The bartender at the tiki bar spotted them and spoke quietly to two men near the end of the bar, who immediately got up and found another place to enjoy their drinks. The bartender then withdrew two bottles from a cooler and set them on the bar in front of the recently vacated spots. The two motorcyclists dropped onto the stools.

"Ike and Brewski," the bartender greeted them. "What's the good word?"

In Ike's hand, the bottle of Budweiser looked like a miniature. He took a long sip. "How's it going, Tiki?"

"Couldn't be better unless I was you," Tiki said.

Ike's companion downed one-third of the bottle of Yuengling and wiped his mouth with the back of his hand.

"Ahhh," he said. "Just what the doctor ordered."

"How's it going, Brewski?" Tiki asked.

"Not good. Not good at all."

"Really? What's wrong? You can tell me; I'm a bartender."

Brewski shook his head. "I saw a very depressing sight today."

Ike laughed. "Depressing is a bit melodramatic."

"Maybe to you."

"What did you see?" Tiki asked.

"They're tearing down the mini-golf course by the water tower."

"Really?" Tiki asked. "And that's got you down?"

"I happen to like mini-golf."

"You should see him on the big clown head. Never misses," Ike said. "Well, except for that time he got pissed off and hit the ball so hard he embedded it in the poor clown's face. Looked like the clown had a zit. They never could get it out."

"To each his own," Tiki said.

"Whatever," Brewski waved the topic off. "How's everything with you, Tiki?"

Tiki grinned and stroked his beard. Leaning across the bar he lowered his voice. "See that blonde at the end of the bar?"

Ike and Brewski casually glanced at the buxom woman sitting alone drinking white wine.

"I made a bet with her that she isn't a real blonde. Soon as I'm off work, she's going to prove it to me."

Brewski held up a closed fist. Tiki bumped it. "I can't lose," he said.

He left them to check on his other customers.

In the center of the courtyard was a set of stairs leading to the rooftop deck. Under the stairs a man in a wheelchair sat at a table with two other men. Ike made eye contact with the man in the wheelchair and nodded. The man returned the nod then wiped his forehead with his napkin and let it fall to the ground.

"Don't get too comfortable," Ike said to Brewski. "Ralph just dropped his napkin. He may need us shortly."

Brewski looked toward the table. "Who are those guys?"

Ike shrugged and sipped his beer. "Don't know. Could be somebody who lost a bet and doesn't want to pay up. Could be somebody complaining their food was cold. The guy in the suit looks familiar, though."

"Looks like a used-car salesman," Brewski said.

"A used-car salesman couldn't afford that suit. Custom made. Well groomed. Unnaturally white teeth. He's got money, for sure, and he wants everybody to know it."

"Color me impressed."

Ike kept a close eye on the table. Ralph appeared to be speaking only to the man in the suit. The other man, who had the look of a body builder, sat silently.

"Whatever they're talking about," Ike said, "the suit thought he was going to need muscle."

Brewski looked at the body builder and snorted. "That's not muscle. That's just a guy who works out in front of a mirror all day then puts on a polo shirt that's a size too small so he can look like a bad ass."

"Probably true, but I still want to know why the suit thought he needed backup to talk to Ralph."

"Ralph doesn't look too concerned."

"Ralph never looks concerned, but if he knocks the salt shaker over, we go and join the party."

The conversation continued with the man in the suit doing most of the talking. Ralph sat calmly eating shrimp cocktail. The man in the suit leaned in closer and pointed a finger at Ralph. The gesture was accompanied by a smirk.

Ralph nodded, leaned back to restore some distance between them and reached for his glass, knocking the salt shaker over in the process.

"Let's go," Ike said. "You take muscle beach."

Brewski downed the last of his beer. "Roger that."

They walked away from the bar in opposite directions. Ike moved across the dance floor, straight to the table.

Brewski moved to the right and took up a spot a couple of steps behind the weight lifter.

"Evening Ralph," Ike said. "How's everything?"

"Excuse me," said the man in the suit. "This is a private conversation."

Ike looked down at him. "Ask me if I give a shit."

The man in the suit looked at the weight lifter and nodded. As the weight lifter moved his chair back and tried to stand, Brewski stepped up behind him and grabbed his gold hoop earring.

"Easy there, Arnold," Brewski said. "Why don't you park your glutes back down in the chair before I rip your ear off?"

The suit nodded discretely and the muscle man slowly lowered himself into the chair. Brewski sat next to him and unbuttoned his black leather vest to reveal the Glock nine-millimeter pistol in his belt.

"Ammunition is expensive, so don't make me waste a bullet on you."

Ike took a chair from a nearby table and sat between Ralph and the suit. Even seated, his six-foot-six, two-hundred-seventy-five pound frame dominated the table.

"Why don't we start with introductions?" he said to the man in the suit. "I assume you already know Ralph. I'm Ike, and you can call him Brewski. And you are?"

The man in the suit glared at Ike, obviously unaccustomed to being treated with such a lack of respect.

"Leaving," the suit said.

He stood and buttoned his jacket. "Ralph, we'll finish this conversation at another time."

Ike stood and towered over him. "When that time comes, you talk to me first. You follow?"

The man looked at Ike and grinned. "Good night," he said. He turned to the weightlifter. "Let's go, Stuart."

Brewski stood and pulled the weight lifter's chair out. "Good night, ma'am," he said.

As they left the courtyard the man in the suit shook hands and exchanged greetings with several people, smiling widely the whole time.

Ike and Brewski sat down at the table.

"Friends of yours?" Ike said to Ralph.

Ralph shook his head with a look of disgust. "I'd rather be friends with a rattlesnake."

A server approached the table.

"Does anybody need anything here, Mr. Donabedian?" she asked.

Ralph looked up from his wheelchair. "Hello, Malissa." He pointed at Ike and Brewski. "These two need another round. Coffee for me."

Malissa nodded as she cleared Ralph's dinner dishes. "Okay. I'll be right back with that." She flashed a lingering smile at Ike before walking away.

Ralph shook his head. "Ike. Do you know how hard it is to find good help? I've told you before—hands off."

Ike put his hands up in defense. "What? I'm innocent."

"Yeah," Brewski said, "and I'm Evel Knievel."

"Thanks for the support," Ike said to Brewski.

Ralph's cell phone rang. "Hello," he answered. "The Red Sox? You'll be laying eight to five. Five hundred?" Ralph took a small pad from the pocket of his wheelchair and made a note. "Okay. You're down."

He disconnected the call. "Where were we?" he asked.

"Not counting the non-fraternization policy? We were discussing your two friends," Ike said.

Malissa returned with their drinks. Ralph put some sugar in his coffee and spoke as he stirred.

"The man in the suit is Geoffrey Hanson. He wants to buy The Lion."

"And his nose was out of joint because you told him to pound sand?"

"I told him it wasn't for sale, but he tried to convince me it would be in my best interest to reconsider his offer."

"He threatened you? You?"

"It wasn't a threat in the conventional sense. No broken legs or anything like that."

"Then what?"

"He suggested that the FBI might be interested in some of my extra-curricular activities."

"Really? He's trying to blackmail you by saying he'll turn you in to the feds? He's dumber than he looks."

"Maybe not."

"What do you mean?"

"If he was just some jerk with a lot of money, I would have had you two show him to the ocean."

"So, he's not just some jerk with a lot of money?"

"No. He's one of Florida's senators."

"I thought the name sounded familiar," Brewski said.

"A senator is trying to strong arm you out of your restaurant?"

"Not just me. I've spoken with Grant from Finn's, Ed from Friend's Café, and John from Johnny D's. They've all had similar meetings with him."

"He's trying to buy Flagler Beach."

"Pretty much."

"Just out of curiosity, what was his offer?"

"Half a million."

Brewski snorted.

"Half a million?" Ike said. "If this place was a three thousand square foot house he couldn't get it for half a million, let alone the most popular restaurant on the strip."

"That's why he threatened to pull out the big guns, if you will."

"Does he have that kind of clout?"

Ralph nodded. "He's in his third term—all without winning an election I might add. Some say he's being groomed for the White House."

"How the hell does he get to be a senator without winning an election?" Brewski asked.

"Let's say without winning a fair election. The governor appointed him when Senator Mike MacDonald died in a car crash in 2007...a very suspicious car crash. After finishing out the last six months of that term, he won reelection when his opponent, Phillip Harris, was caught in a scandal involving a male prostitute, which Harris adamantly denied and claimed was a set up. Then, less than a month before the 2014 election, his opponent withdrew his name from the ballot, citing personal issues. He was found dead a month later with two bullets to the head. It was ruled a suicide. There was no time to put another name on the ballot, so Hanson basically won by default."

"The ever-popular two-bullet-to-the-head suicide. If I've seen it once..." Ike said.

Over the ocean there was a flash of lightning, immediately followed by an enormous thunderclap.

"Holy shit," Brewski said. "Is it supposed to rain tonight?"

Ike leaned back in his chair and looked at the night sky from under the stairs.

"Nothing but the moon and stars. Not a cloud in sight," he reported.

"Sure as shit sounded like thunder."

"An atmospheric anomaly, maybe," Ralph said.

"Anomaly?" Brewski said.

"Freak thing," Ike said.

"Ahh."

"Back to the subject at hand," Ralph said. "Buying commercial property on A1A is just Hanson's latest venture. Shortly after he became a senator, he began buying residential rental properties."

"So he's also a slum lord."

"Actually, the opposite. Any property he acquires that isn't occupied by a white, nuclear family has the rent raised to an amount which the tenants can't afford. Once they move out, he rents to Mr. and Mrs. Whitebread and returns the rent to the fair market amount."

"Flagler Beach's one-man gentrification team," Ike said.

"I'm afraid so."

"And if he buys up businesses he'll make sure the staffs are as white as the driven snow."

"Naturally," Ralph said. "He thinks he's saving America from the vermin."

"We need to save America from him."

"There's another thing."

"And the hits just keep on coming," Ike said.

"In the next election, Hanson will be opposed by a young man from St. Augustine by the name of Adam Morley."

"I know Adam. He's got a boat in the marina. Runs eco-tours. Owns the fish camp out on Cubbedge Road. Nice guy."

Ralph nodded. "That's him. He's a good man and would bring some much-needed integrity to Washington."

"You want us to make sure he wins?" Brewski asked.

"No," Ralph said. "That would make us as bad as Hanson. What I want is for Adam to have a fighting chance in the election."

"So, we need to prevent Hanson from arranging any bad luck for Adam."

"Exactly."

"Why don't we just take Hanson for a one-way boat ride?" Brewski asked. "We'd be doing society a favor."

"I'd like to see him get what he deserves," Ralph said, "but with as little death as possible."

"Killjoy," Brewski muttered.

"People like Hanson always have followers," Ralph said. "They're dangerous enough when their leader is getting them all riled up, but if you make Hanson a martyr they'd be even more dangerous."

"Why don't we think bigger?" said Ike. "Instead of making him a martyr, let's just expose him for what he is. A racist asshole."

"That would be ideal, but Hanson is smart enough to keep his hands clean. You won't find any proof of his leanings. In fact, he often holds rallies and gives speeches to the very people he is out to oppress. They fall for his bullshit and actually cheer for him. He presents himself as the hero of the little man."

"Okay," Ike said. "So he's not your average dirtbag. Looks like I'll have to get together with Bill Eldredge and see what sort of dirt he can dig up on Mr. Hanson. Everybody has skeletons in the closet, finding them is a matter of letting the right people do the digging."

Ralph nodded. "That's a good way to approach it."

The sound of screeching tires, followed by some prolonged shouting and cursing, interrupted the conversation. Ralph glanced toward the commotion.

"Why don't you guys see what's going on out there? We don't need some drunk jerk scaring customers away."

A small crowd was watching the driver of a van yell at two men. The driver climbed back into his van and gave a middle-finger salute to the two men as he sped off.

"Asshole," Brewski said.

"Let's see who he was yelling at. I don't think Ralph would object to buying them a drink."

The targets of the van driver's rage were nowhere in sight.

"I think they went down the steps to the beach," Brewski said.

At the bottom of the stairs, Ike looked north while Brewski looked to the south.

"I don't see anybody. I know it's dark, but they couldn't have gotten that far."

"No," Ike said. "Unless…"

He took his cell phone out and used its flashlight to peer under the stairs. Two men sat underneath, looking somewhat frightened and very confused.

"Hey," Ike said. "How you doing? Sorry about the commotion. If you'd like to come across the street, my boss would like to buy you a drink."

The two men looked at each other. The older one motioned to the younger one to follow him, and they came out from their hiding place.

"Name's Ike," Ike offered his hand to the older man. As the man reached for it, the younger man took off running north.

"Eric, nein!" the older man shouted.

Ike and Brewski looked at each other. Ike put a hand behind his back and nodded. Brewski sighed and put his hand behind his back.

"One, two, three," Ike counted off.

Brewski's hand came out in a fist, Ike's flat, palm down.

"Sorry, bro," Ike said. "You lose. Get going before he gets too far."

"Son of a bitch," Brewski said as he took off after the fleeing man.

"So. Where were we?" Ike said to the older man. "Oh, yeah. I'm Ike. And who might you be?"

The man offered his hand. "My name is Abraham."

Ike shook his hand. "Nice to meet you, Abraham. Where you from?"

Abraham shook his head. "I'm not quite sure."

"Not quite sure? How about your friend? Did you call him Eric? Any chance he might know?"

"Yes. His name is Eric, but I'm afraid he will not be any help either. We are both unclear as to how we got here and where we are from."

"Amnesia? Fascinating. Have you hit your head recently? Been in a car accident?"

"Car?"

"Yeah. Car. You know? Automobile?"

Abraham nodded his understanding. "Yes. I remember automobiles, but I do not think we were injured by one."

"A little too much to drink, maybe?"

Abraham shook his head. "I don't believe so."

"Well, maybe if you sit down and relax a little things will start to come back."

"Yes. Perhaps."

Brewski returned, huffing and puffing, guiding Eric by the arm.

"Christ. He's pretty fast," he said. "Took me a minute to convince him I wasn't going to hurt him. He doesn't speak English. Sounds like German."

"Yes. German," Abraham said. "We are from Germany."

"Germany?" Ike said. "How long have you been in town?"

Abraham shook his head. "Within the last hour, perhaps."

"You've only been here for an hour? Perhaps?"
Brewski said, indicating their wet clothes. "And you decided
the first thing you were going to do was go night swimming?"

"As I explained to your friend," Abraham pleaded.
"We are having trouble remembering the exact
circumstances that brought us here."

Ike looked from Abraham to Eric, whose youthful face
still showed the combination of fear and confusion.

"All right," Ike said. "We can try to help you. First let's
go across the street. You can get some food. You both look
like you could use a good meal. And I think I can find you
some dry clothes. We'll play it by ear after that."

Abraham nodded and had a brief conversation with
Eric in German.

"Very well," he said to Ike. "We will go with you."

Seated at a table inside The Lion offered them a
degree of quiet and privacy unavailable in the crowded
courtyard.

When Malissa brought glasses of water Abraham and
Eric downed them immediately. Ike and Brewski slid their
glasses across the table, and both were drained in seconds.

"Maybe you should bring a pitcher," Ike said to
Malissa.

Malissa returned with a pitcher of ice water, filled
their glasses, and the two newcomers drank again, this time
a bit slower.

"Malissa," Ike said. "Would you see if there's a couple
sets of cook's linens in the back? They look like they'll fit into
some of Julio's."

Malissa nodded and walked away.

"Okay," Ike said to Abraham. "First things first. You
speak English, but you've got a German accent, and your
friend here doesn't speak English at all, only German. That
sound about right?"

Abraham nodded. "That is correct."

"Okay. So let's assume you're from Germany. You don't remember when you got here. Do you remember *how* you got here?"

"Well," Abraham pondered the question for a moment. "No. I am sorry."

"Maybe by boat?" Brewski suggested. "Since their clothes are wet."

"I suppose it is possible," Abraham said.

"You know your name is Abraham. Do you remember your last name?"

"Last name?"

"Yeah. Surname?"

"I'm afraid not."

"Hold on a second," Brewski said. He went to the bar and returned with a pad and pen which he slid in front of Abraham. "Sign your name," he said.

Abraham looked at the pad then back at Brewski with confusion. "But..."

Brewski put the pen in his hand. "Just sign your name."

Abraham shrugged and wrote on the pad. When he was finished he looked at it, shrugged again, and handed it to Brewski.

"Abraham E. Rosen," Brewski read.

"Is that your name? Abraham Rosen?" Ike said.

Immediately a flicker of recognition crossed Abraham's face. He smiled and nodded. "Yes. Abraham Rosen. That is my name."

"Let's try it with your friend," Ike said. "Give him the paper and tell him to sign his name."

Abraham translated the request. Eric furrowed his brow, took the pen, wrote on the paper and handed it back to Abraham.

"Eric Mueller," Abraham read.

Eric smiled and nodded.

"Wow," Ike said to Brewski. "I'm impressed. Where'd you learn that trick."

Brewski shrugged. "I saw it on an episode of *House,* I think."

"Well, we're making progress. I can have Bill Eldredge run a check on the names, see what he comes up with."

Malissa returned and handed some bundles to Ike.

"Come with me, gentlemen," Ike said, leading them to the men's room.

Once the room was empty he took them in. "Go ahead. Change your clothes. I'll wait outside."

After a few minutes, they exited the rest-room wearing hounds-tooth chef's pants and white, short-sleeved utility shirts.

"Looking sharp, men," Ike said.

Abraham handed their old clothes to Ike. A small, leather case fell to the floor. Ike picked it up. "Wow. Looks like an old cigarette case," he said, handing it to Abraham. "Haven't seen one of those since my grandmother was alive."

Abraham took the case and looked at it curiously.

"This is mine?" he asked.

"It ain't mine," Ike said.

Abraham tucked it in the breast pocket of his shirt.

Malissa met them at the table and asked if they were going to eat.

"Are you hungry?" Ike asked.

As if he suddenly realized, Abraham nodded. He asked Eric, then relayed the answer. "Yes. We are both very hungry."

"Do you have any preferences? The fish and chips here are fantastic."

"Anything is fine, I'm sure."

Ike sensed a certain amount of confusion from Abraham, as if he were unsure what sort of food he enjoyed.

"Why don't you bring us all cheeseburgers," Ike said to Malissa. "Fries, coleslaw. Nothing fancy."

Malissa wrote down the order and left.

"So, let's see what else we can find out," Ike said.

Abraham reached for the pitcher of water. Ike glanced at his arm and reached out to stop him.

"Where did you get that?"

Abraham looked at the inscription in blue ink on his left forearm, A-16081.

He shrugged and shook his head. "I don't know."

"Do you mind if I take a picture of it and send it to my friend?"

"A picture?"

Ike nodded. "Picture. Photograph?"

Abraham looked at him blankly. "If you wish."

Ike took his cell phone out and snapped a picture of the tattoo and forwarded it to Bill Eldredge.

"I have a friend who can find out a great deal of information with his computer," Ike said.

"Computer?"

Ike chuckled. "We'll talk about that once you can remember a little more."

"May I see that device?" Abraham pointed at Ike's phone.

He held it in his hand, turning it over, obviously fascinated. When it vibrated in his hand, he dropped it on the table.

"I am sorry," he said.

"No problem," Ike said. "It was just a notification from my friend letting me know he got the picture."

"You mean it is a camera as well as a communication device? With no wires?"

"That's right. It's wireless. It performs dozens of functions, but its primary function is a telephone. It tells the time, the temperature..."

"Time," Abraham said.

"Yeah. The time," Ike said.

"I remember something about time being important."

"You mean like you're late for something?"

"No. It has more to do with the passing of time."

Malissa delivered their food. Abraham and Eric looked at the huge burgers and mounds of French fries with eyes of wonder.

"Dig in," Ike said.

"Dig in?" Abraham said.

Ike grinned and pressed a few buttons on his cell phone, then spoke into it. "Dig in."

He held it out to Abraham and Eric then pushed another button. "Hau rein," the phone translated.

Abraham and Eric were impressed and confused at the same time.

"Understand?" Ike said.

"Hau rein, in German is..." he searched for the English. "To bury it."

"Ahhh. A bit too literal, I guess. I was just telling you to go ahead and eat."

"Ahh, essen," Abraham said.

"Okay," Ike said. "Essen."

Abraham and Eric looked at the food with curiosity.

"Like this," Brewski picked his burger up and took a huge bite then wiped some ketchup from his chin. "Mmmm. That's the good stuff."

Abraham and Eric followed suit and were soon devouring the food as if it were the first meal they'd had in days. Ike and Brewski shared a look while the two wolfed their food.

Malissa returned to the table. "Sorry to interrupt, Ike, but Mr. Donabedian would like to see you."

Ike took another bite of his burger before standing. "I won't be long," he said to Abraham. "Brewski will stay with you."

Brewski nodded as he chewed. "Not going anywhere."

"You wanted to see me?" Ike said when he arrived at Ralph's table.

"Ike," Ralph said. "Did you find out what all the commotion was?"

"Yes and no. Some guy in a van was yelling at a couple of guys out on A1A. The van driver took off before we got to him. The two guys we found under the walkover, soaking wet, scared, and pretty confused."

"Drunk?"

"Not as far as I can tell. More like they have some kind of amnesia. They're German by the sounds of it. I'm giving them some chow and trying to see if we can't figure out what to do with them."

Ralph nodded. "Okay, but Tiki tells me a cop came in asking if anybody called in a..."

Ike waited. "Called in a what?"

Ralph shook his head and chuckled. "A UFO sighting."

"Really?" Ike said. "That's interesting. I'll see what I can find out."

Ike crossed A1A and walked a block south to the Flagler Beach PD cruiser parked in front of Finn's Beachside Pub. Standing behind the cruiser was an officer almost as big as Ike, talking to two women. Ike stood a polite distance away until they were finished then approached the officer.

"Evening, Butch," he said.

Officer Butch Cabral shook Ike's hand. "How's it going, Ike?"

"You tell me. I hear you're looking for little green men."

Cabral shook his head. "These sorts of calls don't usually come in on Wednesday. They're usually reserved for the weekend. But..." he said with a grin, "it's not up to me to question it. Just doing my job."

"To protect and serve. Right."

"Exactly."

"So, do you have any leads?"

Cabral laughed. "Yeah. About a dozen drunks say they heard some thunder and saw some lightning."

"Yeah. We did too."

"I just shake my head. Thunder and lightning. In Florida. That's so rare it must be a UFO."

Ike laughed while Cabral did his best to maintain his un-emotional, law-enforcement expression.

"I don't know how you can keep a straight face, Butch," Ike said.

"It isn't always easy. I'm going to check out the beach. Somebody said they heard a splash."

"Mind if I tag along?"

"You speak Martian? I might need a translator."

"I got an app for that."

The beach was deserted. Cabral shined his flashlight over the surf.

"I don't see a thing. There isn't even anybody making out. Let's check the other side of the pier."

They walked above the surf line under the pier, Cabral sweeping their path with the beam of his light.

"Oops," he said. "I stand corrected." He shined his light on the shape of a person lying in the sand beneath the pier. "Looks like one of the Martians couldn't hold his liquor."

"Sir," Cabral said loudly when they reached the man lying in the sand. "Sir, can you hear me?"

"Is that a lab coat he's wearing?" Ike asked.

"It wouldn't surprise me." Cabral knelt next to the man and shook him. "Sir. Can you hear me?"

"His clothes are wet," he said to Ike. "And he's cold as a rock."

Cabral felt the man's throat.

"Shit," he said.

"What?"

"I don't feel a pulse."

"Oh, boy."

"You'd better get back to The Lion, Ike. I'm gonna have to call this in."

Ike backed away. "I was never here."

Brewski was downing the last of his beer when Ike returned. The table was cleared and Abraham and Eric were still drinking water.

"There's a bit of a situation on the beach," Ike said to Brewski.

"What sort of situation?"

"I'll explain later. Right now, I think we should get gone. You get the van, I'll pull the bikes behind the building."

Brewski was gone before Abraham could ask "Is something wrong?"

"I'll explain as we drive. I think it'd be best if we found another place to talk. I'll be back in two minutes," Ike said. "Stay right here. You follow?"

Abraham stood up. Ike motioned him to sit back down.

"No," he said. "I didn't mean to follow me. I was asking if you understood. So, just stay here. Okay?"

Abraham nodded. "We will stay here."

Several miles north of The Golden Lion, Ike broke the silence in the van.

"Okay," he said, turning sideways in the passenger seat. "Let's make a long story short. The police just found a dead body on the beach, under the pier at The Funky Pelican. Not far from where we found you."

"No shit?" Brewski said from the driver's seat.

"No shit," Ike said. "So, I'm gonna level with you two," Ike pointed at Abraham and Eric. "If you know anything about it, now is the time to tell me. I might be able to help. But if you lie to me, I'll drop you off on the road and tell the cops where you are."

Abraham's eyes locked on Ike's. There was no deceit in them, only fear.

"We know about the dead man," he said.

"I figured there were too many coincidences for you to not know about him. He was fully dressed and his clothes were wet. Did you kill him?"

"No, sir. We did not kill him."

"Who is he?"

"Spier," Abraham said, almost as if the knowledge was new to him. "His name is Spier. He is a scientist. We were working together."

"So, you're a scientist?"

Abraham nodded slowly. "I believe so."

"What were you working on?"

Abraham pondered the question. "I remember a bell. Underground. Many soldiers."

"Soldiers? Underground?" Ike said. "Like a bunker?"

"I don't know. My memory is very..." With a look of frustration he finished, "...scattered. I see random people and places, but I cannot always piece them together. Then a piece will fall into place, such as Herr Spier's name."

Ike pointed at Eric. "This kid is too young to be a scientist. He looks like he hasn't finished high school yet."

"High school?"

Ike waved a hand. "Skip that. Ask him if he remembers the underground place you worked in."

Abraham and Eric spoke for a minute. At one point in their conversation Ike perked up.

"Yes," Abraham said. "He remembers the soldiers. Many of them."

"Did I hear him say 'SS'?" Ike asked.

"Yes. That is what he said. What does it mean?"

Ike shook his head. "Are you telling me you've never heard of the SS?"

Abraham flinched and covered his head.

"Are you all right?" Ike asked.

Abraham lowered his arms slowly and nodded. "I am fine."

"What was that all about? Why did you cover your head?"

"I'm not sure."

"This shit gets curiouser and curiouser," Brewski said.

"You got that right," Ike agreed.

Twenty minutes later Brewski parked the van in the lot of the St. Augustine Municipal Marina.

"Home sweet home," Ike said.

Judging by the looks on the faces of Abraham and Eric, the sights and sounds of St. Augustine were something they weren't accustomed to. They continually looked around as they made their way along the docks.

"Here we are," Ike said, standing in front of the fifty-foot yacht with the name *The Great Escape* on the transom. "All aboard."

They sat on the rear deck.

"Would you like a beer?" Ike asked Abraham.

"Beer? No, I think I would prefer some red wine."

Brewski laughed. "Nobody forgets what they like to drink."

Ike went inside and returned with beers for him and Brewski, a glass of merlot for Abraham and a can of Coke for Eric.

"Sorry, sport," Ike said to the boy. "But I think you're a bit too young to drink."

Eric looked at him, confused, but took the soda and drank.

"Too young?" Abraham asked.

"Right. Not old enough. We have laws in this country."

"Some of which we actually obey," Brewski added.

"Which country are we in?"

Ike and Brewski shared a look.

"I guess we never did get to that," Ike said. "You're in America."

Eric sat up, eyes wide. "*Amerika. Der Feind!*" he said.

"What'd he say?" Ike asked.

Abraham looked confused. He shook his head. "He said America is the enemy."

"Enemy?"

"This is what he said."

"Whose enemy?" Ike asked.

"Depends on who we pissed off this week," Brewski said.

Abraham looked at Eric, who was still standing, but clearly unsure why. "I suppose he would mean Germany's enemy."

"Shit," Brewski said. "Again?"

Ike downed a mouthful of Budweiser. "I think it's time for bed," he said. "Maybe this conversation will make sense in the morning."

"I doubt it," Brewski said. "I seriously doubt it."

Ike showed Abraham and Eric to their beds. They were sound asleep in a matter of minutes. Ike joined Brewski on the rear deck.

"What do you think?" he asked.

Brewski shrugged, drank some beer and said, "I think I'm going to go home, go to sleep and hope this was a weird dream."

"Good idea, but I think you're going to be disappointed."

"Story of my life. So, on a different topic, how are you liking the new boat?"

Ike swallowed some beer as he looked around the boat.

"Well, it's bigger, faster and more comfortable than *The Mare*.

"Always helps."

"And she was free, so there's that."

"Yeah, you still haven't told me how you pulled that off."

"Can't do it. I'd have to kill you."

"Of course."

"Even with all that, I had her for twenty years, so I miss her."

Brewski downed the last of his beer. "You never forget your first girl," he said as he walked away.

6

From the balcony of his twelfth-floor condo in The Aliki Tower, Geoffrey Hanson looked out over Flagler Beach. The small beachside community was probably the last vestige of unspoiled coastline on this side of Florida. With no buildings more than three stories tall—aside from The Aliki, which was built prior to the current zoning ordinances establishing height restrictions—it was truly the best kept secret in Florida.

Had it not been for a defective fuel light on his Beechcraft Baron forcing an unexpected landing at the Flagler County Airport, followed by a two-night stay waiting for repairs, he may never have discovered Flagler Beach. In his heart, he knew the unscheduled landing was fate. Flagler Beach was his destiny.

In less than ten years he had gone from an accidental visitor to the single largest property owner in the town, and his empire was growing now that he was branching out to commercial investments.

When people recognized him they displayed one of two reactions; respect or fear. Either one was fine with him...they both allowed him to get what he wanted from people.

"Excuse me, Mr. Hanson."

Carla, the cute little thing who cleaned the condo once a week, stood in the doorway.

"What is it, honey?"

"I'm all finished." Her polite way of asking to be paid.

"When are you gonna let me take you out?" he asked, holding the cash slightly out of reach until she answered.

"I'm engaged." Her usual reply.

"I told you," he said with a lecherous grin. "I won't tell him if you don't!"

She smiled and extended her hand.

"Fine," he said. "But one of these days..."

He slapped her rear-end when she turned and then admired it as she walked away.

"Yeah," he said after she was gone. "One of these days I'm gonna make you moan."

A knock on the door interrupted his fantasy.

"Yeah," he called.

Stuart stuck his head in. "You ready to talk?"

"Yeah. Come on in. Bring me a drink, and get yourself something."

Stuart handed Hanson a glass of scotch then sat in one of the other chairs on the balcony with a bottle of water.

"Okay," Stuart said. "We're ready to move. Where do you want us to start?"

Hanson drank half of his scotch and put the tumbler on the glass table between them with enough force to spill most of the rest of the drink.

"You start with The Golden Lion. Not only am I tired of that crippled bookie acting like he owns this town, but after the way his goon talked to me last night I want to show him who he's fucking with. Nobody treats me like that."

Stuart nodded. "Okay. He's got a cook named Julio. Been working there more than ten years. Tomorrow's not going to be a good day for him."

Hanson nodded. "Good. What else?"

"There's a bartender there. He's got a real reputation as a lady's man. We can use that. And there's a waitress named Malissa. She's been there since Donabedian opened the place. She's got a kid in high school who is about to have a run-in with the law."

Hanson finished his drink and handed the empty glass to Stuart.

"Good. Once the press gets hold of the sort of people Donabedian employs, it should put a damper on his business."

Stuart left the balcony to refill Hanson's drink.

"Get started today," Hanson told him when he returned.

"Will do. What about the FBI? Are you going to tip them off about Donabedian's gambling operation?"

Hanson shook his head. "That'll be the last resort. If we can't get him to give up The Lion voluntarily we'll call in the big guns. I'll make him wish he had sold the place."

Stuart nodded. "Okay."

Hanson looked at the gold Rolex on his wrist. "It's ten o'clock now. I have to fly up to Washington today for a few meetings. I'll be back tonight. Probably around ten."

"By then the wheels will be in motion."

"Make sure of it."

Ike was startled from sleep by a loud shout.

When he reached the other cabin, Eric stood over a frightened Abraham shouting at him in German. Abraham's frightened eyes flashed to Ike, asking for help. Ike pulled Eric away in a bear hug. The boy's futile attempts to break Ike's hold on him were almost comical.

"What's going on?" Ike asked. "Tell him to calm down."

Abraham spoke to Eric, convincing him to relax.

"Tell him I'm going to let him go, but if he does anything stupid I'll tie him to a chair," Ike said.

Abraham relayed the message. Once Eric's body relaxed, Ike set the boy's feet on the floor.

"What the hell was that all about?" Ike asked Abraham.

"He was shouting at me about being a Jew. Saying we shouldn't be sleeping in the same room, and no matter what General Gruber said, no Jew is smarter than a German."

Ike looked from Abraham to Eric. The boy's anger had subsided and he was now looking more confused than anything.

"He said those things to you?"

Abraham nodded. "Yes. It is not uncommon for German's to speak to Jews in such a way."

"Not uncommon? Maybe seventy-five years ago it was common, but it's pretty uncommon now."

"That is the problem. What is now for you, I'm afraid, is not the now that Eric and I know."

Ike's eyes widened. "I take it you remember more than you did last night."

Abraham nodded. "There are still blank spots. As though I am looking through a window, and I see things but then the light in the window goes out. Each time I look, the light stays on a bit longer, so I do remember more. Yes."

"I assume he remembers more, too," Ike pointed at Eric.

"It would appear so."

"Why don't we go out to the deck and talk about it over some coffee? Brewski will be here soon. No point in going back to sleep."

"Coffee sounds wonderful."

Eric and Abraham savored the coffee.

"Okay," Ike said. "Why don't you tell me what you remember?"

Abraham drank some coffee. "As you know, my name is Abraham Rosen. I graduated from Cambridge University in 1935, where I studied advanced physics and engineering. I saw what was happening in Germany at the time..."

Ike held up his hand. "Hold the phone. Did you say 1935?"

Abraham nodded. "Yes. 1935."

"Jumping Jack flashback," Ike said. "I have a feeling I might need more than coffee."

"You may have trouble believing what I am about to explain."

"I'm already having trouble, but go on."

73

"As I was saying, I wanted to stay in England, but Sarah, my wife wanted to return to Poland. When the war started the Germans began rounding up Jews for 'temporary relocation'."

"Yeah. I know that part. Basic twentieth century history."

"We were able to hide for a couple of years with the help of friends who were not followers of Herr Hitler, but once Sarah became pregnant, we knew it was time to escape. The thought of bringing a child into that world was frightening, to say the least. We paid the underground to get us out of Poland, but we never made it. I was captured." He looked away and wiped a tear from his eye. "I never saw Sarah again."

"I'm sorry."

Abraham shook the memory off. "The Germans found out about my education and forced me to work on a top-secret project for them. It was called *Die Glocke*."

Ike held up a hand. "Hold on. Die Glocke. That's the Nazi Bell."

Abraham nodded. "You know of the Bell?"

"It's mostly a myth, but I know a little. Some believe it was a weapon of mass destruction. The other theory is that it was meant for space travel. Are you telling me it was real?"

"That is exactly what I'm telling you. However both of your theories are incorrect."

"Jesus on a jump rope," Ike said. "According to the stories, it's never been found."

"I can tell you exactly where it is."

"You can?"

"Yes. It's in the ocean not far from where you found us last night."

"You mean..."

"The Bell is how we got here."

Noticing the disbelief in Ike's eyes, Abraham continued.

"For two years I lived in a bunker and worked on the bell. My education was the only thing that kept me alive. I'm afraid I can't remember the specifics of the work yet—perhaps it will come back to me soon—but I remember Dr.

Spier telling me that testing the bell was my only hope for survival."

"Wait. Wait," Ike interrupted. "Are you telling me that you and Eric here were the test pilots for the first time machine in human history?"

Abraham finished his coffee and shrugged. "I suppose that is true."

"But why would a bunch of Nazis send a Jew and a kid who is barely out of puberty on such a mission?"

Abraham shook his head. "I'm afraid I can't quite answer that. As I said, there are still blank spots in my memory."

"This is...I don't even know what it is."

"Yo ho," Brewski called from the dock. "Everybody's wide awake, I see."

"Hey," Ike said. "Just in time. We need to go get some breakfast."

Brewski patted his belly. "You read my mind."

Brewski's fork, loaded with home fries, hung frozen, inches from his mouth. He rolled his eyes up to look at Ike.

"You said what?"

"Time machine," Ike said quietly.

Brewski looked longingly at his home fries for a few seconds before putting his fork down.

"Time machine...as in Sherman and Peabody. The Way Back Machine? Set the controls for I-don't-friggin-believe-this. Time machine."

"Probably not quite as sophisticated, but, yes, time machine."

"That's what I thought you said."

"Have you ever heard of the Nazi Bell?"

Brewski shook his head and resumed eating. "Nope."

Ike took his cell phone out. "Hang on."

He handed Brewski the phone. The internet browser was open to a page about the mythical device. Brewski skimmed the article.

"Says here," he said through a mouthful of Spanish omelet, "that it was probably a weapon, but nobody knows for sure."

Ike pointed a thumb at Abraham, who was devouring a stack of pancakes. "He knows."

"Really?"

"Really. He was working on it."

"Working on it? Come on. The guy is what? Thirty-five? If he were working on a time machine for the Nazis he'd be about ninety. Unless..."

Ike nodded. "Now you're starting to get it."

"What about the Boy Wonder here?" Brewski nodded toward Eric.

"We're still trying to figure that out," Ike said. "We know he came with Abraham, but we don't know why."

"Has anybody asked him?"

Ike furrowed his brow and looked at Abraham who was still engrossed in his breakfast.

"Oh," he wiped his mouth. "My apologies, but it has been a long time since I've had such a meal."

"Yeah. Apparently about seventy-five years," Brewski said.

"I will ask Eric what he remembers."

After speaking with Eric for a few minutes Abraham turned to Ike.

"He is Private Eric Mueller of the German army. He was enrolled in the Hitler youth at the age of thirteen then made a soldier in 1945 at the age of fifteen. His father was killed in an air raid two years ago, that is to say, 1943, and he does not know what became of his mother or his sister. His first assignment was as a driver for General Hans Gruber. On his first day, he was brought to a bunker. It was heavily guarded by SS troops. The general seemed to take a liking to him because he took him into the bunker and convinced Dr. Spier to send him under the pretense of guarding me. The last thing he remembers is being attacked by Russian soldiers and getting into the Bell with me."

Ike looked at Brewski. "Do you appreciate the significance of this story?"

"I need more coffee."

With no warning Eric snapped up to attention and extended his right arm in the air. Ike and Brewski looked at him, then tracked his gaze to the big-screen TV where the news was broadcasting a story about a neo-Nazi rally in Georgia, which had resulted in a near riot.

Trying to draw as little attention as possible, Ike casually guided Eric back into his chair.

"Just what we need," Brewski said. "People thinking we've gone over to the dark side."

"Abraham," Ike said. "Tell him he can't do that here."

Their conversation began calmly but escalated to the point where Eric's anger was attracting more looks from nearby patrons. Ike put his hand on Eric's arm and made a calming gesture.

"He says it is his duty as a German soldier to salute the flag," Abraham explained.

"Great. It was hard enough explaining to him that he was in America; now we have to explain to him that it's seventy-five years later than it was when he left Germany."

"Seventy-five years," Abraham said looking at the television, "and the Nazis are still in power?"

Ike shook his head. "No. Not at all. They're mostly a fringe element. The Nazi party died a long time ago. Hitler and Eva committed suicide in a bunker in Berlin in April of forty-five."

"April of nineteen-forty-five?"

"That's right."

"We were visited by General Gruber in late March of that year and told to accelerate our efforts. I remember now. He told us the Führer was anxious to use the Bell."

"He saw the writing on the wall and wanted to get the hell out of Dodge," Brewski said.

"So, you and Eric were supposed to test it and...what? Bring it back?" Ike asked.

"That is correct, but Dr. Spier warned me that if our test was successful, and I returned with the Bell, I would surely be executed."

Ike nodded. "That's consistent with Nazi logic. So you were going to send it back unmanned?"

Abraham looked into Ike's eyes. Ike grinned.

"At least that was the plan," he said.

"Those were my instructions," Abraham said.

Ike downed his coffee and took out his phone. "Bill Eldredge has a friend who teaches history at Flagler College. I'm going to see if he can get her to come and talk to us."

"Hell," Brewski said. "We might be able to teach her something."

The staff at The Golden Lion had just finished preparing for the day when Ike and Brewski showed up. Customers were already drifting in, and a steel-drum player was setting up in the gazebo. Ralph was drinking coffee and doing paperwork at his table.

"Morning, Ralph," Ike said.

"Good morning, gentlemen,"

"Ralph," Brewski greeted.

"Where are your friends?" Ralph asked.

"We took them to a thrift store and got them some clothes and such then took them back to the boat. They need some rest."

"Yeah," Brewski said. "You might say they had a really long day yesterday."

"Are you in the mood for a story?" Ike asked.

Ralph picked up his coffee cup and sat back in his wheelchair. "Always," he said.

Fifteen minutes later Ralph took his half-glasses off and set them on the table next to his empty cup.

"It's a few days early for an April Fool's joke, Ike," he said.

"Ralph, I couldn't make that up if I wanted to."

Ralph looked at them for several seconds, waiting for one of them to crack. "You're serious. Aren't you?"

"As a heart attack."

"And this device is in the water out here?"

"That's right. I'm going to talk to Hap Cameron and borrow his barge. I'll bring it around tonight so we can haul the Bell up and get it out of the ocean. We'll take it over to the Hammock and put it in Pete Duggan's boat-building barn. Pete's in the Bahamas for a couple of months building a sailboat for somebody. I'll let him know we'll be renting his facility for a while."

"And then what? You're going to hide one of the biggest mysteries of the twentieth century in Palm Coast like it's a stolen car?"

"I don't know. But we can't leave it in the ocean. Even if nobody else finds it, the salt water will destroy it."

"So let it be destroyed. I don't see any good coming from it. Even if it were used with the best intentions, the unpredictability of it all leaves too much to chance."

"I think whatever is done with it should be thought about long and hard. Like you said, it's not a stolen car."

"Have it your way," Ralph said.

Two Flagler Beach police officers approached the table.

"Good morning, sir," one of them said to Ralph in a very professional tone. "I'm officer Browning. This is officer Clancy. Is there a Julio Esperanta here?"

Ralph looked at them with curiosity. "Yes. He's in the kitchen. Why?"

Officer Browning held up a piece of paper. "We have a warrant for his arrest."

"Arrest? For what?"

"Can we see him, please?"

Ralph motioned to Ike, who led the policemen to the kitchen.

"Julio," Ike said.

The cook looked up from his work. "Morning, Ike."

"Julio Esperanta," the cop said, moving around Ike. "You're under arrest for car-jacking, kidnapping, armed robbery, and assault with a deadly weapon. Would you put the knife down and step around the table please?"

Julio complied with the order despite the bewildered look on his face. The officer grabbed Julio by the arm and bent him over the stainless-steel table, knocking a pile of shrimp to the floor.

"What the...is this a joke? Ike, what's going on?" Julio said.

"I don't know, Julio. I'll find out. In the meantime, don't say anything to anybody. I'll have Vincent look into it."

The officer read Julio his rights as they slowly escorted him from the building, through the courtyard, past the curious stares of a dozen patrons and the staff.

"What the hell was that all about?" Ralph asked.

Ike was already making a phone call. "They arrested him for car-jacking," he said. "They wouldn't tell me anything, but I'll find out."

"Hey, Butch," he said into his phone. "I need a quick favor."

A few minutes later, Ike stuffed his phone into his pocket and shook his head. "According to the warrant, Julio jacked a car last night, beat up the woman driving it and made her take him to an ATM to withdraw cash."

"Last night?" Ralph asked.

Ike nodded.

"That's impossible. Julio was working for me last night. He was making collections until midnight."

Ike watched the police car drive away.

"Supposedly, there's a witness."

"Find out what's going on Ike."

"You got it, Ralph."

Ike made a phone call to Vincent Lyon, Ralph's attorney, and explained the situation. Vincent assured him that Julio would be out of jail by the end of the day.

His next call was to Butch Cabral at the Flagler Beach PD.

"Okay," he said to Brewski after he finished the call, "We need to go to the Hammock."

The roar of their Harley Davidsons broke the grave-like setting of the trailer park. They rode along a gravel road, under a neglected canopy of old oak trees. Spanish moss hung low from the trees and the ground was covered with brown leaves. The original colors of the trailers were hidden by layers of dirt, mold and rust. Most of them displayed confederate flags.

Ike stopped in front of a trailer with some dilapidated wooden steps and a screen door being held together by habit. A sign in the window to the left of the door read *Home Security by Smith and Wesson.*

"Nice neighborhood," Brewski said as they dismounted their bikes.

"Yeah. According to Butch, the victim of the car-jacking lives here."

Before they reached the steps, the door of the trailer opened. A pregnant woman pushed the screen door open with the barrel of a shotgun.

"Whaddya want?" she demanded.

Ike put his hands up. "Easy now. We don't want anything. Just want to talk for a minute."

She held the shotgun with one hand while she adjusted a stray bra strap with the other. "Talk about what?"

"Are you Constance?"

"What if I am?"

A pickup pulled to a stop behind the motorcycles. Chained in the back was a pit bull weighing at least one-hundred pounds. Three men climbed out. One had a Winchester rifle over his shoulder. Brewski's hand went beneath his vest and gripped the Glock nine-millimeter in the waistband of his jeans.

"There a problem here?" the man with the Winchester asked.

"No problem at all, partner," Ike said. "Just wanting to have a conversation with Constance here."

"I don't think she feels like talking."

Ike nodded and smiled as he closed the distance between himself and the man.

"That's cool. Last thing we want is..."

Ike grabbed the Winchester, twisted it out of the man's hands and slapped the side of his head with the butt, knocking him to the ground. The man looked up at Ike past the barrel of the rifle which was inches from his nose. Brewski pulled out his Glock and covered Constance and the other two men.

"I'm afraid I didn't catch your name," Ike said to the man on the ground.

The man stared back at him defiantly. Ike placed his boot on the man's throat, covering a tattoo of a black widow spider.

"Speak up. I didn't catch that."

"Rick," the man croaked.

"Well now, Rick, here's the story. My friend and I are here to talk to Constance. Not you. So, why don't you, Mutt and Jeff here get back in your truck and go find a nice quiet place where you can take turns burying your bones in Fido over there. You follow?"

Rick stared at him. Ike applied more pressure to his throat. Rick nodded rapidly.

"Good boy," Ike said.

The pickup left a cloud of dust as it disappeared into the trailer park.

Ike turned to Constance, who still had the shotgun levelled at him.

"Constance, either shoot that thing or set it down," Ike said as he pointed the Winchester at her.

She looked from the Winchester to Brewski's Glock and leaned the shotgun against the wall. Brewski tucked the Glock away and Ike placed the Winchester next to the shotgun.

"Good," he said. "Now we can have a civilized conversation. Why don't you tell us where you were last night?"

She swallowed. "I was home. Why?"

Ike grinned. "Well, now we have a problem. We heard a different story. You want to see if you can guess what it was?"

Her eyes telegraphed her indecision. "What did you hear?"

"No hints. You tell us."

Constance looked at Ike, trying to determine what he knew, Ike grinned at her.

"Come on," he said. "It's an easy question."

"This about the carjacking?"

"Alleged carjacking," Ike corrected. "Now, which one of your stories is true?"

There was fear in her eyes now. "I ain't saying nothin' else."

"Are you sure? Because I don't see a car here, so I'm pretty sure you weren't carjacked. I'm guessing you look this rough every day, so it doesn't look like you've been beaten up, and you damn sure don't have any money to take out of an ATM."

"What business is it of yours?"

"Constance, I don't know why you decided to single out Julio, but it would be in your best interest to reconsider this bullshit accusation, or the next time I come here I won't be so nice." Ike raised his eyebrows and smiled at her. "You follow?"

A police car skidded to a halt where the pickup had been. The same two officers who had arrested Julio climbed out.

"What's going on here?" the driver asked.

"Officers Browning and Clancy," Ike greeted them. "Long time no see. Nothing going on. We were just admiring Constance's fine collection of firearms there, officer. No need for concern. I'm sure she has all the necessary paperwork."

"I think you should be going," Browning said.

Ike nodded. "I think you're right. Goodbye, Constance."

Ike and Brewski fired up their bikes and left, leaving Constance and the cops in a cloud of dust.

Tiki had two beers waiting on the bar when Ike and Brewski entered the courtyard.

"Can't chat, fellas," he said. "Got a real live one over here. She says she needs a new bikini and wants to model a few for me."

"Go get her, Tiki," Ike said.

"What's your take on this whole thing with Julio?" Brewski asked Ike.

"I smell a rat. We've already established that Constance was full of shit. Then there were the two cops who just happened to show up and who just happened to be the same ones who arrested Julio. I'll ask Butch about those two." He drank some beer. "And did you notice the bumper sticker on the back of that pickup?"

"Nope."

"It said 'Hanson, Good for Florida, Good for America'."

"Hanson? Our boy from the other night?"

"That's the one. And unless I miss my guess, having Julio arrested was a shot across Ralph's bow."

"What's it going to accomplish?"

"Aside from throwing a wrench in The Lion's gears, it lets Ralph know that Hanson has reach."

Ike's cell phone rang.

"That was Bill," he told Brewski after the call was through. "He'll meet us at the boat in half an hour with his historian friend."

"Cool. This should be interesting."

7

"I think I'm in love," Brewski said as Bill Eldredge and the slender blonde woman walked along the dock toward Ike's boat.

"With Bill?" Ike said.

"Funny. You're a funny man. You think she's married?"

"I think she's out of your league."

"Why? Because she's a college professor?"

"No. Because she can spell *professor*."

"Good afternoon, guys," Bill said as he and the professor climbed aboard.

Brewski offered his hand to the woman. "Allow me," he said.

"Why, thank you kindly," she replied with a Southern lilt.

"Ike and Brewski," Bill said, "this is Mabel Tarrington."

"Mabel?" Brewski muttered to Ike.

"Pleased to meet you," Ike said.

Brewski nudged his way past Ike. "Hi, I'm Brewski. How do you like me so far?"

Mabel laughed politely, pushing a blonde lock off of her face.

"I love the new boat," Bill said. "Must have set you back a few bucks."

"Not as much as you'd think," Ike said.

"What did you do with *The Knight's Mare*?"

"Long story."

"Yeah," Brewski said. "And if he tells you he'll have to kill you."

Bill held his hands up. "I don't need to know."

"Let's have a seat," Ike said. "The guests of honor are inside. I'll get them."

Brewski arranged enough chairs on the deck for everybody, waited for Mabel to sit and dropped into the chair next to her.

"If you need anything, anything at all, just ask," he said.

"Thank you, Brewster. That's sweet."

"Brewski," he said.

"Oh," she said with a soft giggle. "I beg your pardon."

Ike appeared carrying a tray with five bottles of beer and a bottle of white wine. Abraham and Eric trailed behind.

"Chardonnay okay?" he asked Mabel.

"Just perfect."

"Okay," he said. "Bill and Mabel, meet Abraham and Eric."

Abraham translated the introductions for Eric. They all shook hands and sat down.

"Eric is German. He doesn't speak English," Ike told Bill and Mabel. "Abraham will do the translating."

"I speak some German too," Mabel said. "I'm not what you'd call fluent, but I can get by."

"Okay. Feel free to help with any miscommunications between Abraham and me."

"I'm afraid I don't have much for you," Bill said. "Try doing a search for Abraham Rosen and Eric Mueller without a date of birth or a social security number. It's like looking for a needle in a stack of needles."

"Don't beat yourself up," Ike said. "We've got plenty of information to go on now."

"What kind of information?"

"Let's start at the beginning," Ike said. "Brewski and I found Abraham and Eric on the beach last night. They were soaking wet and had pretty bad memory loss. We brought them here, and bits and pieces of their memory began coming back but nothing really solid. By this morning, they had regained fairly substantial chunks of their memories."

"Good," Bill said. "Were they able to remember their dates of birth?"

Ike grinned and drank some beer. "Oh, yeah."

Bill pulled a laptop from the leather briefcase he carried. "Great. Let's have it."

"Okay. But it's not as simple as you might think."

With his fingers poised over the keys of the laptop, Bill looked at Ike. "What's the problem?"

Ike looked at Brewski. "Where do I start?"

"About seventy-five years ago," Brewski answered.

Ike sighed. "Bill, this is going to be...I mean, you may have some trouble with..."

"Come on, Ike," Bill said. "How difficult can it be? Month, day, year."

"Give it to him straight," Brewski said. "Just like ripping a Band Aid off."

Ike nodded. "I think you should get this straight from the horse's mouth. Abraham, would you mind telling Bill your date of birth?"

"Not at all. I was born on August twenty-second..."

Bill tapped away at his laptop. "Eight, twenty-two..."

"Nineteen oh-nine," Abraham finished.

"Nineteen oh..." Bill stopped typing. "Nineteen what?"

Brewski tapped Mabel on the arm. "This is where it gets good," he said.

"You heard right, Bill," Ike said.

Bill looked from Abraham to Ike, his mouth slightly agape, and shook his head.

Ike pointed at Eric. "And our young friend here was born in what year, Abraham?"

Abraham spoke to Eric. "Nineteen twenty-nine," he relayed.

Bill sat back in his chair and grinned. "You guys are screwing with me. Right?"

"Afraid not, buddy."

"Listen, if they were born when they say, that would make them..." Bill did some quick math in his head. "...one hundred ten, and ninety, respectively. Now, unless they discovered the Fountain of Youth I'm just not seeing it."

"Look at the tattoo on his arm, Bill."

Abraham extended his arm. Bill examined the tattoo.

"Mabel," Ike said, "what's your opinion of that tattoo?"

Mabel snapped out of her disbelief and examined Abraham's arm.

"Unless I'm mistaken, that's a tattoo from a Nazi concentration camp."

Ike looked at Bill and raised his eyebrows.

"He could have gotten that in Daytona last weekend," Bill said.

"This looks genuine," Mabel said. "It also looks fairly new, which can't be. I'm afraid I just don't understand any of this."

"Have either of you ever heard of the Nazi Bell?"

"Yeah," Bill said. "It's an urban legend. According to whichever theory you believe, it was either used for space travel, or possibly some sort of secret weapon."

"I've heard of it, too, and I agree with Bill," Mabel said. "There aren't enough facts to support any of the theories."

"You're looking at the only two facts you need. They are proof the Bell exists."

"Proof is a strong word, Ike," Bill said. "What proof do you have that these guys are telling you the truth? I could tell you I was born December twenty-fifth in the year zero, but that doesn't make me Jesus."

"Work your computer magic," Ike said.

Bill hesitated briefly before tapping away at his laptop.

A minute later, he pointed at the screen. "Okay. I've got Abraham Rosen, same birthday, but that doesn't mean..."

"Quiz him."

Bill looked at Ike, then at Abraham.

"Okay," Bill said, consulting his computer screen. "Let's start with an easy one. Place of birth?"

"Lublin, Poland," Abraham responded without hesitation.

"Mother's name?"

"Ellie Meyer."

"Father?"

"Joshua Rosen."

Bill asked several questions, all of which Abraham answered correctly.

"Okay, can you tell me who Dr. Reinhard Furrer is?"

Abraham paused. "I'm afraid I don't recognize that name, but..."

"They still haven't gotten their complete memories back yet," Ike said.

Bill waved it off and sat back with his beer. "No. That's not it. It was a trick question. Dr. Furrer was a German physicist, but he was born in 1940 and didn't earn his doctorate until 1972."

"Here's the long and the short of it, Bill," Ike said. "Abraham and Eric here left Germany in the Bell in 1945. They landed here last night."

"Are you telling me that the Nazi Bell is actually a time machine?"

Ike touched a finger to his nose, then pointed at Bill.

"I don't believe it."

"You don't have to tell me it's hard to believe; that's a given. But if you'd like to join us on a little midnight mission, you'll see the all the proof you need."

"You don't mean..."

"I do. We're going to get the Bell and move it."

"Where is it?"

"In the ocean not far from the pier. Abraham told me enough to get us in the ballpark."

Bill nodded. "What do you think, Mabel?"

"I wouldn't miss it," she said.

"I'll make the arrangements," Ike said, taking out his cell phone. "I'll call you later and tell you where to meet us."

Ike turned the ignition key off, killing the power to the twin three-hundred horsepower Evinrude outboard engines. Moving around the excavator in the middle of the barge, he dropped an anchor overboard.

"According to Abraham, we should be pretty close to the spot where the Bell went in," he said to Brewski.

"This from the guy who had trouble remembering his name?" Brewski said.

"It wasn't tough to figure out. They came ashore between the pier and The Lion, and he figured it took them about twenty minutes to get to shore, so that puts us about here. It was almost high tide when they landed," Ike looked at his dive watch. "And it'll be high again in about an hour, so the conditions are almost the same."

"Good. Get down there and find it. It's two in the morning and I'd rather be in bed. Preferably not my own."

"I'll be as quick as I can," Ike said while donning his SCUBA gear.

"Keep an eye out for nosy fishermen," Ike said before stepping off the deck into the ocean.

After twenty minutes of scanning the ocean floor, a large, dark object appeared at the far end of his flashlight's beam. Lying on its side in seventeen feet of water was the appropriately-named Bell. The diameter at the base was about twelve feet, tapering to less than five at the top. From top to bottom, it was about fifteen feet. The surface had a greyish-black patina. As he approached it, the first thing to catch his eye was the embossed swastika. An eerie feeling crept over him as he got close enough to touch it. His hand hesitated, hovering inches away from the mottled surface. A smile crossed his face when his hand finally made contact.

Aside from Abraham and Eric, he was the first person to see the Bell in over seventy-five years.

Putting aside the historical significance of the moment, he reached into the net bag hanging from his waist. He secured the nylon line to a handle next to the Bell's door then pulled the cord to inflate the bright-orange marker buoy. He followed the sphere to the surface and flashed his light toward the barge.

Working as fast as possible, Ike secured three tow straps to the Bell, then connected them to the bucket of the excavator.

As the excavator took on the weight of the Bell the barge dipped, allowing ocean water to wash over the deck. "I hope this thing isn't too heavy," Ike said to Brewski.

Once it was sitting on the deck they covered it with tarps for the trip to the barn. Two hours later, the Bell sat on the floor of the boat-building barn. It looked somewhat tiny in the massive space, but its significance made up for its lack of size.

They stood next to it in silence for several minutes.

"This is just unbelievable," Bill finally said.

There was a palpable level of anticipation as Ike opened the hatch. They peered inside.

Without saying a word, the four of them stepped inside the Bell and gazed in wonder at every inch of the space.

"I'd be impressed if I knew what I was looking at," Ike said, breaking the silence.

"I've taught history for ten years," Mabel said, "but this is the first time I've ever been this close to it."

"I can't believe they actually pulled it off," Bill said.

"This is, without question, the find of the century," Mabel said. "Somebody is going to be famous."

"If this thing makes anybody famous, it should be Abraham," Ike said. "He helped build it, and the people who forced him to do it killed his pregnant wife."

"I'll second that," Brewski said.

Bill and Mabel nodded.

"All right, folks," Ike said. "It's been a long day. Why don't we get some sleep and discuss what to do about this later."

8

Somewhere in his mind he knew he was still asleep, but the incessant buzzing told him he was moving toward being awake. At first his hand reached for the snooze button on a non-existent alarm clock, but after several unsuccessful attempts to silence it he opened his eyes and picked up the cell phone.

"What?"

"Ike," Ralph said, "where are you?"

He rubbed some of the sleep from his eyes and sat up.

"Ugh. Ralph. What's up? What time is it?"

"It's almost noon. We have another problem. Two of them to be specific. How soon can you be here?"

"Less than an hour. On my way."

Abraham and Eric were sitting on the rear deck looking bored.

"Did you guys eat yet?" Ike asked.

"I'm afraid I couldn't figure out how to operate any of your equipment," Abraham said.

Ike rubbed his eyes. "Shit. I'm sorry. We have to go. Give me ten minutes to shower and we'll hit Dunkin Donuts on the way. Get you some coffee and something to eat."

Abraham and Eric, coffee cups and donuts in hand, trotted to keep up with Ike as he made his way to Ralph's table at the Golden Lion.

Ike pointed to an empty table nearby. "You guys have a seat. I need to talk to Ralph for a minute."

"Sorry, Ralph," he said, sitting next to his boss. "It was a late night."

"No apology necessary, Ikey. This is sort of an unexpected matter."

"What's going on?"

"Hanson has upped the ante."

Ike shook his head. "Now what?"

Ralph sighed. "Malissa's son was arrested at school today for possession of a firearm."

"Kyle? A firearm? The kid's on the damn chess team."

Ralph held up a hand.

"Obviously a frame to get my attention. But there's more."

Ike fell back in his chair. "What else?"

"Last night Tiki was being Tiki, hitting on women and such, and apparently one of the women he flirted with is claiming he molested her. She is raising a fuss with the press and spreading a lot of malicious stories on social media."

"Hanson."

"No question, but what do we do about it?"

Ike thought for a minute, then shook his head. "I don't know off hand, Ralph, but I'll come up with something."

"I don't care how you handle it at this point. Just make sure it doesn't come back on us."

"Goes without saying."

Ike took out his cell phone, called Butch Cabral, and left a voice mail. Ten minutes later Ike's phone rang.

"That was Butch," he told Ralph. "He's out front. I'm going to go talk to him."

Ralph nodded. "Good luck."

The driver's window of the cruiser slid down. Conditioned air escaped the car and washed over Ike. It felt good against the heat of the day.

"Get in," Butch said. "What's up?" he asked after Ike closed the door.

"I'm hoping you can help me out with something."

"I'll do my best. You know that."

"This morning a kid named Kyle Douglas was busted at the high school for possession of a firearm. I'm telling you, Butch, I know this kid, and as sure as I'm sitting here, he was set up. His mom works here. I've known him since he was about five. Anything you can do to help would be greatly appreciated."

Butch nodded. "I'll see what I can do."

"Thanks, buddy."

Ike reached for the door handle.

"Hang on a sec," Butch stopped him. "You might be interested in this."

"What's that?"

"I shouldn't be saying anything to you, but..."

"I never heard a thing."

"Remember that body we found on the beach the other night?"

"Of course. I rarely find dead bodies I wasn't responsible for."

"Hey," Butch said. "Don't joke like that. I'm a cop, for Christ's sake."

"Who's joking?"

Butch shot him a look. Ike held his hands up and chuckled.

"Okay. Dead body. Yeah, I remember. What about it?"

"Jesus. You wouldn't believe it."

"Try me. At this point very little would surprise me."

"I don't even know where to start. First of all, his ID."

"What about it?"

"It was German."

Ike took a deep breath. "So?"

"German from, like, World War II."

"Say again."

"He had these papers on him that were really old German identity cards. Seriously old shit."

"Wow. That's pretty odd."

"That's not even the weird part."

"Really? There's more?"

"The guys back was peppered with shrapnel."

"Shrapnel?"

"Yeah. Fragments. Like from a grenade or something."

"That's definitely something you don't see every day."

"Naturally the body went to the medical examiner, and naturally the M.E. sent the fragments out for ballistic testing."

"Naturally."

"Usually it's days, weeks even, before we get the results of a ballistic test back."

"You got this one back already?"

"Not exactly."

"What do you mean 'not exactly'?"

"This morning, a federal agent called. Said him and his partner would be here tomorrow morning and he wanted everything we had on that corpse. Every piece of paper, every recording of every radio transmission...everything."

"Really?"

"And they wouldn't tell us why. Told us they would be taking over the investigation, When Captain Doughney asked why, they told him it was a matter of national security."

"National security? That seems a bit dramatic."

"You bet it is. There's something weird going on."

"Certainly sounds big. Maybe you'll get a promotion for finding the body."

"Yeah. I won't start spending the raise yet. Hell, I'll be happy if I don't get fired."

"Fired?" Ike slapped Butch on the shoulder. "You didn't do anything wrong. Right? So don't worry about it. It'll be fine. But keep me posted. It sounds interesting."

Butch nodded. "Yeah. I'll let you know what happens."

Ike opened the door and stepped out of the cruiser. "Take it easy, Butch. Whatever it is, it's out of your control now."

He closed the door and returned to Ralph's table.

"Okay, Ralph, Butch is going to see what he can do for Malissa's son. I'll call Vincent and tell him we've got another one for him."

"What about Tiki?"

"I'll talk to Brian from *The Observer*. I'll make sure he knows Tiki is being framed and I'll tell him about Julio and Kyle, too."

"Excellent. The press is the kryptonite of crooked politicians."

"Excuse me for a minute," Ike said. "I need to talk to the boys." Ike nodded toward Abraham and Eric.

Ralph nodded and waved. Ike slid onto a chair next to Abraham.

"Okay," he said. "We need to talk."

"Talk about what?" Abraham asked.

"The night I found you, I asked you about the dead man they found on the beach. You remember that?"

"Yes. Dr. Spier. I remember."

"I know you didn't kill him, but I need you to tell me anything you can about him."

Abraham rubbed his temples and thought for a minute. "I remember a battle. The bunker had been compromised by the Russian army. We were just about to launch the Bell. Dr. Spier was not scheduled to make the trip with us, but when General Gruber was shot, Spier must have panicked. Being taken alive by the Russians was the last thing anybody in that bunker wanted."

"So what happened?"

"He stumbled into the Bell at the last possible moment. He was wounded. If I recall, his back had several fragments lodged in it, possibly from a grenade."

"A Russian grenade."

"Yes. Of course."

Ike sat back in his chair. "If I wasn't part of this whole affair, I wouldn't believe it."

He leaned over and spoke to Ralph. "You know Doc Borque, the county medical examiner?"

"Of course. Richard Borque. What about him?"

"Is he a customer in good standing?"

"He's lost a few bets. More than he's won, actually, but he pays up."

"Do you think if I went to see him he'd be willing to make a little extra cash for looking the other way?"

"I'd give you even money on that."

"Make sure nobody sees you leaving," Geoffrey Hanson said.

"Don't worry," Constance said. "I know the drill. Being caught associating with trailer trash like me would be bad for your image."

Rather than respond to the comment, Hanson lit a cigar and turned the TV on.

"By the way," she said, as she stepped into her zebra-striped stretch pants. "It's almost the end of the month." She patted her belly. "We had an agreement."

Hanson sighed and snatched his wallet from the night stand.

"Three hundred?"

"Three-fifty," she said with her hand extended.

"Christ," he huffed as he slapped the bills in her hand.

"Don't be blaming me," she said. "You're the one can't keep his pecker in his pants."

He puffed the cigar and turned his attention to the TV.

"I'll let myself out," she said as she left the room.

No sooner had the door closed than his cell phone rang.

"Christ almighty," he said. "What?" he answered.

"Mr. Hanson, it's Bill Browning."

"I know who it is, Officer Browning. That's what caller ID is for."

"Oh, yeah. Well, I just wanted you to know. Rick and the boys have been tailing that Ike fella like you said."

"I assume you aren't calling me just to confirm that you and your redneck friends have been following orders."

"Well, no, sir."

"That's a relief."

"Well, sir, he hasn't done much of anything since he left the trailer park."

"What about associates?"

"There's the bald fella he was with, and then there are these other two. This might interest you."

"I'm all ears."

"Yesterday he goes to this restaurant in St. Augustine for breakfast, and while he's eating, one of the guys that's with him, just a kid actually, is watching the news and he sees a neo-Nazi rally in Georgia. Before you know it, he's standing up saluting the flag."

"Which flag?"

"The Nazi flag."

"Is that right?"

"Yes sir."

"Then the other night, Ike and his pal were out on a barge at midnight pulling something up from the ocean."

"What did he pull up?"

"It was too dark to tell."

"Did anybody see what he did after he pulled it up?"

"Well, no, sir. You see, they took that barge around to the intracoastal, but Rick's truck ran out of gas before they got to where they were going."

Hanson closed his eyes and shook his head. "Unbelievable."

"You want us to continue surveillance, sir?"

"Yes, I want you to continue the surveillance. And try to find out what the hell they were pulling out of the water."

9

"Try to behave yourself," Ike said before he opened the door.

"Hey," Brewski said. "When do I not?"

"Well, at least there's not much chance of you killing anybody in here, so there's that."

They followed the hallway until they found the door labelled *Medical Examiner – Dr. Richard Borque*. Ike knocked.

"Come in," a voice called.

Ike pulled the door open and followed Brewski into the small but neat office. A short, overweight man with a Friar Tuck balding pattern looked up from his computer screen.

"Hey Doc. You remember me? Name's Ike, I'm an associate of Ralph Donabedian."

Borque set his glasses on the desk, stood, and extended a pudgy hand across the desk. "Of course, Ike. What can I do for you?"

He gave Brewski a smile and a nod before he sat down. Ike sat in the chair opposite the doctor.

"First, let me say that Ralph sends his regards."

Borque nodded. "Say hello to him for me."

"I will. Now I have a request. It may sound a bit odd, but I guarantee, if you can help me, Ralph would consider it a personal favor."

Brewski crossed his arms over his chest. Borque shot a quick glance at him before smiling at Ike.

"I'll certainly do my best to help," he said.

"Excellent," Ike said. "A couple of nights ago a body was brought in. White male, mid-thirties, had German ID papers."

Borque nodded. "Yes. Yes. I remember. John Doe 16. What about him?"

"Could I take a look at those papers? Maybe get some pictures?"

"History buff?"

"Say again?"

"Are you a history buff? His identity papers looked like vintage World War II stuff. I'm thinking he was probably in some sort of reenactment group or something."

"What makes you say that?"

"Well, the papers may have looked authentic, but they certainly didn't look seventy-five years old, especially when you consider their exposure to the ocean water. Seventy-five-year-old paper wouldn't come away in as good of shape as these did."

"Good point."

"But they really did look like the real deal."

"I can't wait to see them."

"I guess there's no harm in that."

Ike photographed the papers and shook Borque's hand.

"Thank you, Doc." Ike handed him a roll of bills. "I'll be sure to tell Ralph that you were very helpful."

Borque tucked the bills in the breast pocket of his lab coat. "No trouble at all."

They left the building and climbed onto their bikes.

"Now we'll ask Mabel to look at them," Ike said.

"Good," Brewski said. "I'm sure she's dying to see me again."

Ike chuckled as he kick-started his Harley. "Yeah. I'm sure of it."

Richard Borque was focused on his computer screen when the door opened again.

"Forget something, Ike?" he asked without looking up.

Peering around the monitor when there was no reply, he was slightly surprised to see a man standing in front of his desk, wearing a tank top and a camouflage baseball hat. A toothpick dangled from his lip. Behind him stood two other men, looking similarly out of place.

"Can I help you, gentlemen?" Borque asked.

"Yup," said the man in front of the desk. "What'd those two guys want? The ones just left."

Borque narrowed his eyes and looked at the three men before responding.

"May I ask what your interest is in them?"

"No," the man said, placing his fists on the desk and leaning slightly toward Borque. "You may not ask. Just answer the damn question."

"I'm afraid I can't," Borque lied. "It's confidential."

"Well, how about you make it un-confidential?"

Borque stood. "I'm going to have to ask you to leave."

"We'll leave. Soon as you tell us what those guys wanted."

"That isn't going to happen."

Borque reached for his phone. The man grabbed his wrist and twisted.

"I'll break it off at the elbow."

"Get out."

The man moved around the desk without letting go of Borque's wrist, twisting the doctor's arm behind his back. He slammed him face first into the wall.

"You gonna make us do this the hard way, Porky?"

The man lifted Borque's arm. When the doctor's wrist was nearly to his shoulder blade, he let out a gasp of pain.

"All right," Borque said. "All right. They wanted to look at some papers that were found on a dead body."

"Where are these papers at?"

"In the back."

"Well, let's see 'em."

"Fine. I'll get them."

"Why don't you just take us to them?"

Borque led them to the examination room and took the papers out of a locked cabinet.

"This is it. I can't imagine they'd be of any interest to you."

The man looked at the papers as he walked back to Borque's office. "Don't matter what you think, now does it?"

"Okay. I showed you what they wanted. Now get out."

"You sure you told us everything?"

"That's it."

The man picked up a heavy crystal paperweight from the desk.

"Are you sure?"

He slammed the paperweight into Borque's temple. The M.E.'s body collapsed to the floor.

"Jesus, Rick," one of the other men said. "What'd you do that for? We weren't even supposed to come in here."

"It's called taking initiative."

He picked up the papers, then caught a glimpse of the bills in Borque's pocket, which he promptly removed and tucked into his sock.

"Now let's git."

Rick pulled the door open and the three of them shoved past a woman who had been about to enter the office. They bolted down the hall for the exit, hearing the woman scream as they ran.

Ike and Brewski followed Bill Eldredge through the tastefully decorated and well-kept home to the study.

Originally built as two bedrooms, the separating wall had been removed to give Bill ample room for his computer equipment. The room now looked like a computer sales showroom. Every flat surface had some sort of computer equipment on it and two of the four walls were covered with monitors. The windows were hidden behind blackout blinds and the air conditioning was at least five degrees cooler than the rest of the house.

"Jesus," Ike said. "Can't you just use a smart phone like everybody else?"

"Yeah," Brewski added, "and maybe give out jackets to visitors."

"I have five smart phones," Bill said. "Each one with its own number and account. And if you wore a shirt under your vest," he said to Brewski, "you wouldn't be cold."

"He's got a point," Ike said.

"Whatever," Brewski muttered.

Bill chuckled. "What have you got?"

Ike showed him the pictures of the documents obtained from the M.E. Bill plugged Ike's phone into one of the computers, downloaded the pictures, and typed a few commands.

"Interesting," he said after a couple of minutes.

"What?"

Bill filled the screen with one of the documents.

"This is called an *ausweis*. It was basically an identification card for Germans during the war. Back then, people could be detained for any reason, especially by the Gestapo, and if you didn't have an ausweis you might never be seen again. This one is for a Dr. Gerhard Spier."

He closed the image and opened the second.

"This one is permission to be in the bunker. It's the equivalent of a top security clearance. No doubt everyone in the bunker had one."

"Can you do a quick search of this guy, see what you find?"

"Sure."

Bill wheeled his chair to another keyboard. After a few minutes he invited them to look at the screen.

"Dr. Gerhard Spier. Born September twenty-fifth, nineteen oh-four, in Munich. Educated at the University of Gottingen. Says here that he worked on some of Germany's most infamous weapons, but he disappeared before the war ended. He's on every list of wanted war criminals there is, but he was never found."

"Until the other day," Ike said.

"What does that mean?" Bill asked.

"You met Abraham and Eric, but there was a third passenger in the Bell."

"You mean Spier? Where is he?"

"On a stainless-steel table in the coroner's office."

"He's dead? How?"

"According to Abraham, he was hit by a Russian grenade just before the launch of the Bell. He wasn't supposed to make the trip, but he probably didn't want to be killed, or worse, captured by the Russians, so he sort of tagged along."

"Wow. This story just keeps growing."

Ike grinned. "But wait. There's more."

"Are you kidding?"

Ike shook his head. "The police found the body; the fragments of the grenade were sent off for analysis. When the results of the analysis came up with a World War II-era Russian hand grenade, it must have tripped some sort of government alarm, and now the feds are getting in on the action."

Bill sat back in his chair and shook his head.

"You know something? I liked it a lot better when you guys dealt with run-of-the-mill dirtbags."

"Hey, at least we're not boring."

"You did what?" Geoffrey Hanson said.

"He wouldn't talk," Rick said. "I was just trying to find out what Ike and his buddy were doing there."

"So you hit him in the head with an ashtray?"

"It wasn't exactly an ashtray."

Hanson slammed his hand onto the hood of Rick's truck, and gritted his teeth. "I don't care if it was the fucking Holy Grail. You didn't need to hit him."

"How else was I supposed to get the info?"

"There are other ways to get information, you dumb redneck."

Rick's eyes went to the ground. "I'm sorry, Mr. Hanson. I just thought…"

"Thought? You are not paid to think."

"No, sir."

"If you ever find yourself in the same zip code as a dictionary look up the word discretion."

Rick nodded.

"Just out of curiosity," Hanson said. "What did you think the medical examiner was going to give you that would be of any use to me? I want to buy The Golden Lion, not a dead body."

Rick leaned into the truck, grabbed the papers, and handed them to Hanson. Hanson looked them over and tossed them back into the truck.

"A bunch of papers from Germany. Look like they belong in a museum. Worthless to me."

"Yes, sir," Rick said. "I'll get back to following him."

Hanson waved him off and began walking to his car but stopped after a couple of steps.

"Hold on a minute," he said. "Give me those papers again."

Rick handed the papers to Hanson.

"You said the kid that was with Ike in the restaurant stood up and saluted when he saw the Nazis demonstrating?"

"That's right."

"And now we've got some papers from the coroner's office that apparently belong to a very old Nazi."

Rick looked at Hanson blankly.

"Get back to Ike. Don't do anything without calling me or Browning."

"Yes sir."

Rick's truck groaned and creaked as it made its way out of the trailer park. Hanson took out his cell phone.

"Browning," he said. "I need you to look into something for me."

10

Special Agent Doug Freeman held his hand in front of the car's air conditioning vent.

"Christ," he said. "Is the AC even on?"

His partner, Special Agent Mark Bronson glanced at the controls.

"Yeah, it's on."

"Jesus," Freeman said as he loosened his tie and released his neck from the top button of his shirt. "If it's this hot here in March, what the hell is it like in August?"

"To you? It'll probably seem like Hell, most likely."

"How much further?"

"According to GPS, we're only about a mile away."

The nondescript Ford sedan crested a large bridge. Before them lay the heart of Flagler Beach and the Atlantic Ocean.

"Wow," Bronson said. "Looks like a post card."

"If you say so," Freeman said.

At the bottom of the bridge Bronson turned right onto South Flagler Avenue. A block later, he turned into the parking lot of the Flagler Beach Police Department. He smiled at the receptionist as he flashed his badge, then Freeman held his badge up for her inspection but withheld the smile.

"Good morning," Bronson said. "Agents Freeman and Bronson to see Captain Doughney."

The receptionist called the captain then showed them to his office.

After greetings were exchanged, Doughney motioned toward the two chairs in front of his desk then returned to his seat behind it.

"Thank you for meeting with us on such short notice," Bronson said.

"My pleasure. I've got everything you asked for."

Doughney handed a brown accordion folder to Bronson, who passed it off to Freeman without looking at it.

"Do you mind if I ask you why the federal government is so concerned about this case?" Doughney said.

"I'm afraid we're not at liberty to discuss that," Bronson said.

"I see. And you're with the FBI?"

Bronson and Freeman looked at each other.

"Not exactly," Bronson said.

"Not exactly?"

Bronson handed Doughney a business card.

"Central Intelligence Agency,." Doughney read. "Division of Historic Significance? What possible istoric significance does a body on our beach have? Can you at least tell me that?"

"I hate to use an old line like this, but it's strictly 'need to know.'"

"I see." Doughney sat back in his chair and smiled. "I have to hand over my files to you, but I don't need to know why, and you don't need to tell me what you're going to do with them."

"What we can tell you is that we investigate..." Bronson searched for the words. "...special situations."

"Situations."

"*Special* situations."

"But not crimes."

"Not necessarily."

"Well, gentleman, we found a dead body on our beach. Our job is to investigate that crime. How are we supposed to do that now?"

"We are taking over your investigation under the authority of the President of the United States. If you'd like an official order from..."

Doughney held up his hands and shook his head.

"That won't be necessary. You will have our full cooperation."

"Thank you, Captain."

"I guess there's nothing left to say."

"One more thing," Bronson said. "We'll need to interview the officer who found the body."

"I can arrange that. When and where?"

"Can you give us a phone number so we can contact him?"

"Sure. Stop at the receptionist on your way out. She'll give you his cell phone number."

The two agents stood up. Bronson reached across the desk and shook Doughney's hand. Freeman did the same.

"We hope there won't be any hard feelings," Bronson said.

"We all have our jobs to do," Doughney said. "Apparently yours is more important than mine. Good luck in your *investigation*."

"Thank you. Our next stop is the coroner's office. Easiest way to get there?"

"Head west on State Road 100 for about five or six miles. The county offices building is huge. Looks like the Taj Mahal. It'll be on your left. Can't miss it."

"Taj Mahal. Got it. Last thing. We'll be in town for a few days. Can you recommend a good hotel?"

"Sure. The Topaz, right up on A1A. Nice view and a great restaurant."

"Sounds good. Thank you, Captain."

Bronson had to flash his badge at the deputy manning the crime scene tape outside the county offices building.

"What happened?" he asked.

"Robbery," the deputy answered. "Coroner's office."

"Somebody robbed the coroner's office?" Bronson said.

"Yes sir."

"Body snatchers," Freeman muttered.

"This can't be a coincidence," Bronson said as they followed the trail of law enforcement personnel to the coroner's office.

A pair of paramedics were attending to a short, heavy, middle-aged man wearing a white lab coat.

Bronson held his badge up. "You the coroner?" he asked the patient.

"Yes. I'm Dr. Borque."

"Federal agents Bronson and Freeman. Can we talk?"

Borque looked at the paramedic. The EMT finished dressing Borque's wound and said, "He took a nasty blow to the head. The hospital wants us to bring him in for testing."

"Five minutes," Bronson said.

"You're the man with the badge," the paramedic said backing away. "We'll wait over there."

"What happened?" Bronson asked after the paramedics had moved far enough away.

"Three guys came in and wanted the belongings of one of the bodies."

"Just one?"

Borque nodded. "Just one."

"What did they take?"

"Some papers. Identity papers. Nice looking reproductions of old Nazi papers."

"Nazi papers? Why do you say they were reproductions?"

Borque shrugged. "If they were real, they'd be seventy-five years old. Judging by the condition they were in, they were definitely not seventy-five years old."

"Were these papers on the body that was found on the beach the other night?"

"Yes. That's right."

"And these men were after those papers specifically?"

"Well..."

"Yes or no, Doctor. Did they specifically want those papers?"

Borque nodded. "Yes."

"When did this happen?"

"Probably about forty-five minutes ago."

Bronson looked around the hall, and spotted a camera mounted to the ceiling.

"We're going to need all of your video surveillance files."

"I don't have access to those. You'd have to talk to somebody from the Sheriff's office."

Bronson motioned to a nearby deputy.

"Who do I see about getting the video surveillance data?" Bronson asked.

"That would be Sergeant Davis. Second floor, security office."

"Doctor," Bronson said, "we'll need any other evidence, documentation, computer files, et cetera, related to that body."

Borque nodded, obviously a bit put out by Bronson's demand. "I'll have my secretary get you everything we have. Of course, I didn't have a chance to do an autopsy, so there'll be no report on that yet. I can get that to..."

"That's okay," Bronson interrupted him. "There'll be a team here to retrieve the body and take it to Washington. In the meantime, nobody is to go near that corpse."

"Washington? What's so important about this body?"

"They'll be here within the hour," Bronson said over his shoulder as he and Freeman walked away.

Two deputies were sitting in front of the video monitor when Bronson and Freeman walked into the security office.

"Sergeant Davis?" Bronson asked, holding his badge up.

"I'm Davis," a deputy said standing and offering his hand. "What can I do for you?"

"We'll need the video surveillance for the building, inside and out, for the last three hours."

"You caught us at a bad time," the other deputy said, looking up from the monitor. "We've got an investigation going on."

"Not any more. We'll be taking over."

"On what authority?"

"The White House."

"The White House?" both men said.

"How long will it take you to get us the files?"

The room at the Topaz was larger than a room at a typical highway off-ramp hotel. There were two queen-sized beds, a large flat-screen TV mounted to the wall and a beach-themed motif throughout.

Freeman went directly to the thermostat.

"Christ," he said. "I've only been in Florida three hours and I can't stand the heat."

Bronson set his bag on one of the beds then opened the blinds.

"Yeah, but would you look at that view!" he said motioning to the ocean across the street. "I wonder how the fishing is off that pier."

"We don't have time for fishing."

"There's always time for fishing. Our subject was found underneath the pier so we're going to have to go over there at some point to put eyes on the scene. While we're there I'll ask about the fishing."

"I'm going to take a shower."

"I'll check out the surveillance footage from the coroner's office."

A while later Freeman stepped out of the bathroom with a towel around his waist, brushing his thick brown hair.

"Anything interesting?" he asked, standing behind Bronson, looking over his shoulder.

"I'll say. We got great footage of three white males going into the doctor's office, then running out five minutes later like their asses were on fire. Parking lot footage shows them fleeing the scene in an old Ford pickup. I've already run the tag. We'll go talk to Mr. Frederick Turner after we've checked out the pier and canvassed the surrounding area."

"Sounds good." Freeman tossed the towel onto the bed and opened his suitcase. "I hope I brought enough clothes," he said. "I can see I'm going to do a lot of sweating down here."

"We'll go to the drug store and get you some extra deodorant. Take a look at the footage while I shower. See if I missed anything."

"Hey," Freeman said when Bronson emerged from the bathroom. "Did you notice these other guys?"

"What other guys?"

"In the footage. Just before our suspects went in, two guys went in, then left after a few minutes."

"So?"

"Take a look at these guys," Freeman cued the video. "This one is as big as a refrigerator, and the other one looks like an extra from *The Sons of Anarchy*. What do you think they were going into the coroner's office for?"

"Don't know. We'll have to go back and ask the good doctor."

"And check this out." Freeman went to the parking lot surveillance. "The first two guys pull in on their motorcycles and go inside. Five seconds later the three stooges pull in, park their truck far enough away from the bikes to avoid being conspicuous, then go in after the bikers leave."

"You think they were following the bikers?"

"I'd say it's as likely a scenario as anything."

"All right. Any tag numbers on the bikes?"

"No. They were too far from the camera."

"What about using the hallway footage and running facial recognition?"

"I can try, but they didn't look up at the camera on their way in."

"Do the best you can and we'll ask the doctor if he can shed any light on it for us."

Three days' worth of changing tides had rendered the scene where the body was found useless, despite the yellow crime-scene tape strung around the perimeter.

"We won't get anything here," Bronson said. "But take a few pictures anyway."

Freeman photographed the area then followed Bronson up the dune walkover steps to a restaurant called The Funky Pelican. A perky, redheaded hostess, already scanning a map of the dining area for available seats, greeted them from behind a podium when they stepped inside.

"Good afternoon, gentlemen. Two for lunch?"

Bronson flipped his badge case open then closed it quickly.

"Federal agents, miss. We're looking into the circumstances surrounding the body that was found here the other night. Were you here when it was found?"

The girl leaned slightly over the podium and inhaled sharply. "Oh, I know! Wasn't that awful?"

"Were you working that night?"

"No." She returned to an upright position and shook her head. "Wednesday is my night off. My *only* night off."

"Is there anybody here now who was working Wednesday?"

She leaned down and withdrew a binder from a shelf, flipped through a few pages, and scanned it with a finger.

"Wednesday. Who worked Wednesday? Let's see. Richard, not here. Mia, not here. Tonia, not here, and Becky. She's here. The only one here tonight who was also here Wednesday is Becky Pourchot, one of our servers."

"Which one is she?"

The hostess scanned the dining room and pointed. "Right there. The short one with the long, curly hair."

Becky was discussing the power of crystals with an elderly couple who were on their way out. One of her bare feet was pressed against the calf of her other leg.

"Christ," Freeman said. "She looks like a gypsy."

"Be nice," Bronson told him.

"Remember," Becky said to the elderly man, "keep that crystal in your pocket. I promise you'll notice a difference."

"Miss Pourchot," Bronson said, flashing his badge. "Can we have a word with you?"

"Oh. Me?" A hand went dramatically to her chest. "I...well, yes. Of course. But only if you call me Becky."

"Sorry, folks," Bronson said to the couple, who were already moving away. "Do you mind if we step outside, Becky?" Bronson asked.

"Sure," she said. "Follow me."

She led them to a deserted corner of the deck overlooking the ocean.

"You were working Wednesday night," Bronson said, taking a pad and pen from his pocket.

"Wednesday?" she put her hands on her temples. "Yes. Yes. Wednesday was a disturbing night."

"Disturbing?"

"Metaphysically speaking," she said. "I'm really in tune with the vibrations of the universe."

Bronson and Freeman exchanged a quick glance.

"Wednesday night was the night a dead body was found underneath this deck," Bronson said.

"Yes, it was," she said. "It was also the night of a great disturbance in the energy field,"

"Energy field?" Bronson asked.

"You mean like the force?" Freeman added.

"The force," she said dismissively. "That's science fiction. I deal with reality. There is an energy field that surrounds us all. It moves around us and through us. It's part of us. Part of everything."

"Yeah. Like the force," Freeman said.

Bronson held up a hand to his partner.

"So what else can you tell us about Wednesday?"

"Plenty," she said, leaning in to make sure they heard her. "First of all, Mercury is in retrograde, so I don't have to tell you what that means."

"Of course not."

"On top of that, I had been feeling this disturbance building all day. Believe me, Wednesday was not just an ordinary day. There was something happening, cosmically, and it was very big. I came to work and tried not to let the energy affect me, but you can't avoid it. You know?"

Bronson nodded. Freeman sighed and looked around the deck.

"So anyway," she continued. "It was a clear night. The stars were beautiful. Well, they're always beautiful, aren't they? I was standing right here on this very spot, communing with them, when there was a bright flash then a really loud noise, like static electricity from the radio of the gods. You know?"

Bronson wrote something on his pad.

"I nearly passed out," she said. "I don't know how everybody out here didn't feel it, but I looked around and everybody just dismissed it. I asked a few of my customers if they'd felt it, but they either didn't feel it or didn't want to talk about it. Most people will avoid talking about the power they feel, because they don't understand it. It frightens them."

"I see," Bronson said. "What happened next?"

She shrugged. "I went back to work. Unfortunately, I need to work to maintain my Earthly presence. It's a drag, but it's only temporary."

"Temporary?"

"Yeah. Until I move on to the next world."

"Oh. Right."

"So, I went back to work, and maybe a half-hour later there's all sorts of commotion. It wasn't until later I heard about the body. But it's proof. Isn't it?"

"Proof of what?"

"The energy. The disturbance. That poor man was obviously caught in the vortex of a huge energy rift."

"Oh. Yeah. Obviously."

"I'm happy for him, though. He's in the next world now. It's a much better place."

"I'm sure it is. Do you happen to know what time all of this happened?"

"Not exactly. I don't wear a watch because time is an illusion, you know. But I worked from five to eleven on Wednesday, and this all transpired somewhere in the middle of my shift, so I'd say between eight and nine."

Bronson made a note, then handed her a card. "If you think of anything else..."

"If I *feel* anything else, you mean."

"Right. If you feel anything else, give me a call."

"I will." She extended her hands, taking Bronson's right and Freeman's left. She closed her eyes and hummed. "Oh, yes. There is a strong energy here. You gentlemen are on the verge."

They withdrew their hands gently.

"Verge of what?" Bronson asked.

She clasped her hands together and tucked them under her chin with a huge smile. "You'll know it when you feel it. Remember, don't fight it."

"Got it."

They walked away before she could offer any more wisdom. Bronson held the door for a family of five entering the restaurant, then he stepped outside into the bright Florida sunshine.

"Let's go check out the pier," he said to Freeman.

At the foot of the pier there were public restrooms, an FM radio station and a bait shop. The door to the radio station was open. Bronson stuck his head inside, but the small studio was empty.

"Can I help you?" came a voice from overhead.

They looked up to see a thin man in his late thirties on a ladder beneath the high A-framed roof.

"Up here," he said with a wave. "Can I help you?"

"You work here?" Bronson asked.

He came down the ladder and tucked a screwdriver into his pocket.

"You might say that," he said. "I own the station. Vern Shank." He shook their hands. "What can I do for you?"

Bronson gave him a quick glance of his badge. "Federal agents. We'd like to know if you can tell us anything about the body that was found under the pier Wednesday night."

Vern brushed the blonde hair off of his face and nodded. "Yeah, right. Wasn't that something?"

"Were you here that night?"

"No. Wednesday nights Fizz Ed is on from seven to ten."

"Fizz Ed?"

Vern chuckled. "One of our DJs. Ed Velasco. We call him Fizz Ed. You know—it's his DJ name."

Freeman rolled his eyes.

"Right," Bronson said. "How can we get hold of him?"

"You can't. Not until next Wednesday. He went on vacation. Minnesota, I think."

"Minnesota?"

"I know. Right? Who goes to Minnesota on vacation?"

"Did you happen to talk to him before he left?"

"Not really. He called me when the relay went out. That was it."

"So you can't tell us anything about what he may have seen or heard?"

"The only thing I can tell you is that we lost our transmitter and I was here until midnight putting in a new one. I'm just making some adjustments to it now."

Bronson made a note. Vern pointed up to the spot where he had been working.

"You see that white box up there?"

"Yeah."

"That's a relay transmitter. It takes our FM signal from here and sends it to the Aliki Tower." He pointed north toward a thirteen-story building about a mile away. "From there it gets broadcast out. Wednesday night something fried it."

"Fried it?"

"Yeah. Almost like a lightning strike, but not as fast. I replayed the recording of Fizz Ed's show. You could hear the static building for about ten or fifteen seconds, then poof. Signal lost. Dead air. The worst thing you can have in radio. By the time I got here with a replacement, we had been off the air for nearly two hours."

"Can we get that recording?"

"Sure. Come on inside. I'll burn you a copy."

"No. We need the original."

"The original?"

"I'm afraid so."

"It's the only copy."

Bronson looked at Vern with no expression.

"Why do you need the original?"

"National security."

"National...seriously?"

When Bronson gave Vern the same dead look, Vern shrugged. "Okay. Come on inside."

Vern sat at the computer in the station and a minute later handed Bronson a thumb drive.

"There you go."

"May I?" Bronson pointed at the chair Vern was in.

"You want to sit here? Sure."

Vern stood and waved a hand at the chair.

"Make yourself comfortable."

Bronson sat in the chair and, using the mouse, navigated through the computer.

"What are you looking for now?" Vern asked.

"Just making sure you didn't leave a copy behind," Bronson told him.

"Really? Dude, I wouldn't do that."

"Uh huh."

Bronson handed the thumb drive to Freeman, who tucked it into his pocket, then handed Vern a business card.

"If you think of anything else, give us a call."

"Sure thing, bruh," Vern said. "Anything for national security."

Bronson and Freeman left Vern holding the card and went next door to the bait shop.

Four men, ranging in age from twenty-five to sixty-five, sat around a small TV, watching an auto race. With the exception of the oldest man, who sat in a ragged and worn swivel chair in front of a desk with a cash register on it, they sat on wooden folding chairs. The air in the room smelled of cigars and dead fish. The man in front of the desk looked up.

"Help you?"

Bronson showed his badge. "Federal agents. "Sorry to interrupt the race. Mind if we ask you a couple of questions?"

"'Bout what?" the old man asked.

"About the body found under the pier the other night."

The old man waited until Bronson had put his badge away. "Can I see that again?"

"See what?"

"Your badge. I didn't quite get a good look at it."

Bronson took the case out again, held it open for the man to see, and waited.

"Special Agent Mark Bronson. Badge number 4556. Central Intelligence Agency," the man said. "Division of Historic Significance."

"And his?" the old man said with a chin-nod toward Freeman.

Freeman held out his credentials.

"Douglas Freeman. Badge number 6187," the man read. "Well, you win that hand, Special Agent Mark Bronson."

One of the other men snickered.

"I beg your pardon?" Bronson said.

"Your badge numbers," the man said. "Yours makes a much better cribbage hand than his does. Of course, that all depends on the cut."

"Cribbage?" Bronson said.

The man pantomimed dealing cards.

"Yeah. Cribbage. Card game?" He waved Bronson off. "Never mind. What's historically significant about a body on Flagler Beach in 2019?"

Bronson and Freeman put their badges away.

"Were you here when the body was found?" Bronson asked.

"Nope."

Bronson looked at the other three men. "Any of you?"

The three of them shook their heads without taking their eyes from the television.

"So," Bronson said. "Nobody was here, and nobody saw anything."

The old man shrugged. "Looks that way. So why don't you take your badge and go back to the Division of Historic Significance?"

Bronson and the old man stared each other down. After a minute Bronson took a card from his pocket and dropped it on the desk.

"If anybody suddenly remembers their patriotic duty, call."

The old man leaned forward in his chair, picked up a trash can from under the desk and swept the card into it.

"I left my patriotic duty in Vietnam, along with my left leg." He slid the bottom of his pants leg up to show his prosthesis. "Have a nice day. Give my regards to Uncle Sam."

Bronson turned and left, followed by Freeman. At the sidewalk they turned north toward their car. Halfway there the youngest man from the bait shop trotted up to them.

"Hey," he said. "I told them I had to take a leak, so I ain't got much time, but I was out here fishing Wednesday. I saw the whole thing."

"What'd you see, son?"

"There was this loud buzzing noise, a flash of light and a big thunder boom. I was a little stunned, but I'm pretty sure something splashed down in the water a couple hundred feet from the pier."

Bronson nodded. "We're staying at the Topaz. Room 104. Come on by later and we'll talk."

"Will do." He turned on his heel and ran back toward the public restroom.

"Okay, Bronson said. "The police log said a call came in about a UFO sighting from that bar over there. Finn's. Let's check it out."

"Christ," Freeman said. "This town has 'em all, doesn't it? From Gypsy Rose Lee in the restaurant to the lost member of the Beach Boys at the radio station and the cast of bizarro-Mayberry in the bait shop."

"Could be worse," Bronson said. "We could be in Roswell."

"And did that radio station guy really call you *bruh*?"

"Welcome to Florida."

11

"Hello," Ike answered his cell phone.

"Ike, it's Richard Borque."

"Hey. What's up, Doc?"

"I thought you should know, things got a little weird after you left."

"Weird?"

"Yeah. Not too long after you two left, three guys came in, real good-ole-boy types, and demanded to know why you were here. When I wouldn't tell them, they forced me. They took the documents, knocked me out with a paperweight, and took off."

"You're kidding me."

"I wish I were. They plowed my secretary over on their way out. She found me and called 9-1-1. While the police were here doing their thing, two federal agents came in and said they were taking over the investigation, on the authority of the White House."

"That didn't take long."

"Beg your pardon?"

"Never mind. Go on, Doc."

"They took everything involved with the body, including the body itself, then they took all the video surveillance footage from the building's security system. Of course they didn't get the documents. Two more men showed up just a little while ago and took John Doe 16 off in a helicopter."

"Tell me about the three guys."

"Not much to tell. They were right out of central casting for your typical redneck type. Tank tops, baseball hats, scruffy looking. The one who did all the talking had light brown hair, blue eyes, and a tattoo of a spider on his neck. I didn't get a very good look at the other two."

"Thanks for the heads up, Doc. Take care of yourself."

"What was that all about?" Brewski asked after Ike put his phone away.

"Doc Borque. Rick and his two buddies must have been tailing us. They went into the coroner's office after we left and took the documents the Doc showed us."

"What the hell do they want with them?"

"Don't know, but not long after they left, the feds showed up and took over. The body's been taken away in a helicopter."

"Jesus. This is starting to sound like a movie."

Abraham and Eric sat on deck chairs nearby. Abraham was examining the leather case Spier had given him. When he opened it and looked inside a look of confusion crossed his face.

"What is it, Abraham?" Ike asked.

"I remember now. When Dr. Spier handed this to me. He said 'gold train' before he lost consciousness."

"Gold train?"

"Those were his exact words."

"What's inside it?"

"It is empty, except for a series of numbers embossed in the leather."

"Do you mind if I take a look?"

Abraham handed him the case. Ike read the engraving. "N47-40-30 E13-00-40. Looks like lat and long coordinates. A location of something." Ike's eyes lit up. "Jesus on a jump rope."

"What?" Brewski asked.

"Next to the Nazi Bell, the biggest legend to come out of World War II was Hitler's gold train. According to the story, Hitler had a train loaded with three hundred tons of gold, jewels, and priceless works of art, and it's buried somewhere in or near Germany. It's never been proven. There've been lots of searches, but nobody has even found any evidence of it, let alone the train itself. The most common theory is that it's buried in Poland, which was controlled by Germany during the war."

"Three hundred tons?" Brewski said.

"That's the story."

"And you think this is the location of it?"

Ike shrugged. "It could be."

"If it even exists."

"At this point, I wouldn't doubt that Santa Clause exists." He took his cell phone out. "Let's phone a friend."

Ike fed the coordinates to Bill Eldredge.

"You know," Bill said over the phone, "you could have done this just as easily as me. It's a simple matter of using Google Earth."

"That would require a computer."

"You could do it on your phone."

"Sure, and have big brother knowing everything I do? No thanks."

"Okay. Those coordinates are in the Austrian Alps. About ten kilometers southwest of Salzburg. What's special about that location?"

"Are you sitting down?"

"Yes."

"You've heard the legend of the Nazi gold train?"

"Are you...no way. This is too much."

"You got that right."

"Let me check something."

Ike heard the tapping of Bill's keyboard.

"Okay," Bill said. "Ask Abraham the name of the Nazi general who was killed in the lab."

Ike turned to Abraham and asked the question.

"He was SS Lieutenant General Hans Gruber," Abraham answered.

"He says it was SS Lieutenant General Hans Gruber," Ike relayed to Bill.

"Jesus," Bill said.

"What?"

"Guess who is listed as the man Hitler put in charge of the gold train."

"Gruber."

"On the nosey," Bill said. "And of course, his whereabouts were listed as unknown after the war. Another common theory is that he absconded with the gold after Hitler committed suicide."

"Well, we know that isn't true, at least not according to Abraham's account of the day the Russians invaded the bunker."

"Which means he didn't make off with the gold."

"So if it exists, it's still tucked away, safe and sound, wherever he left it."

"That would stand to reason."

"Okay. Thanks, Bill."

Ike tucked his phone into his pocket.

"According to Bill, these coordinates are in the Austrian Alps. That's not where the legend says the train is, but if the legend was accurate, somebody would have found it by now. Also, the man in charge of the train was none other than General Hans Gruber."

Brewski whistled.

Ike's phone rang. He pulled it out of his pocket and checked the caller ID.

"Yeah, Ralph," he answered.

"We just had a visit from two federal agents asking about the body found on the beach the other night. They were talking to the staff, anybody working that night. One of the bussers mentioned the commotion out here and you finding the two German gentlemen."

"Shit."

"They asked me what I knew about the whole affair. I told them I had no recollection of anything. They didn't buy it, of course, but there was nothing they could do about it. They left me a card in case I suddenly remember anything."

"Well played, Ralph."

"I just thought you should be aware that they would like to talk to you about your two friends."

"They'll have to find me first."

"One more thing. The police released Julio. Seems the victim decided not to press charges. And Malissa's son was released as well when the evidence against him could not be located."

"That's good news," Ike said. "I called Brian at *The Observer*. He'll be making sure the truth is known about Tiki."

"Excellent."

"You realize, of course, that once Hanson realizes his plan to smear you and The Lion has been squelched, he's liable to turn up the heat."

"Let him. I can handle all the heat that punk has got."

"And then some." Ike hung up the phone.

"What's going on?" Brewski asked.

Ike recounted the conversation.

"It started off such a boring week," Brewski said.

"I have a feeling we won't be seeing boring in the foreseeable future."

12

"I hate these damn things," Geoffrey Hanson leaned over and whispered to Stuart.

"You and me both, but these people paid two-hundred-fifty bucks apiece for a lousy chicken and macaroni meal and that is what keeps us employed."

Hanson looked at the crowd gathered in the Portuguese Club and sighed. "I tell you, this country is going to hell in a handbasket. Would you look at these mutts? Maybe twenty-five percent of them are white."

"Just get them to vote for you. We can't solve that problem unless you stay in office."

The host of the event, owner of a local car dealership, raised his hands, asking for quiet.

"Ladies and gentlemen," he spoke into the microphone at the makeshift dais. "It is now my great pleasure to introduce the man of the hour. A great businessman, a politician who works for us..."

"Not for you, I don't, spic," Hanson whispered to Stuart while maintaining his look of humility for the cameras.

"...and a true humanitarian. Please give it up for Senator Geoffrey Hanson!"

The crowd of about seventy-five people applauded wildly. Hanson stood, buttoned his suit jacket, and waved, flashing a perfect smile with the right mixture of sincerity, humility, and friendliness. Signs proclaiming the unanimous support of the room were hoisted to more cheers. Tee shirts declaring that Hanson was "Good for Florida, Good for America" were everywhere. Baseball hats embroidered with "Hanson #GFFGFA" were thrown about by Hanson's staff of volunteers, and *God Bless America* was piped over the sound system as Hanson walked slowly to the microphone, waving to the crowd and holding his hand over his heart.

He stood behind the podium, displaying a level of self-effacement that was Oscar-worthy. He continued bowing until the applause died down.

"I can't tell you," he paused and patted his heart, "how incredibly humbling it is to receive a welcome like that. My opponent can only dream of this kind of support."

More applause.

"Thank you again. Now let's talk about our mission. I spend more time in one day trying to make life better for each and every one of you—" –he pointed dramatically to random points in the crowd—"—than my opponent spends in a month. My opponent is more concerned about wasting your tax dollars on solar power and beach clean-ups. You need jobs more than a clean beach."

He allowed the audience to cheer again and did a Richard Nixon wave, complete with peace signs. When the noise level dropped, he made a show of looking at his watch.

"Unfortunately, I am unable to stay much longer."

A low moan rose from the crowd.

"I know. I'm as sorry as you are. I'd much rather eat lunch with the finest people in the country—"—he spread his hands toward the room—"—than sit in a meeting with county officials, but if I'm not at this meeting, they'll try to steal the fillings out of your teeth and then sell them back to you. Somebody has to look out for you. God bless you, God bless America, and enjoy that wonderful meal."

The crowd stood as one and applauded wildly, the signs were hoisted, and several American flags waved. Hanson waited for Stuart to take the lead then followed him toward the exit. The ovation didn't fade until after he'd disappeared through the door, shaking hands and hugging people along the way.

Stuart opened the rear door of the Chrysler 300 for him then climbed into the driver's seat.

"Get me the hell away from this sewer," Hanson said. "And where the hell is the hand sanitizer?"

Lunch on *The Great Escape* was interrupted by the ringing of Ike's cell phone. After a brief conversation, he put the phone away.

"We need to go see Bill," he said to Brewski. "Now."

"Jesus Christ," Brewski said, grabbing a slice of pizza from the box. "All right. Let's go."

"You guys stay put," Ike said to Abraham. "Help yourself to whatever food and drink you want. We should be back in an hour and a half."

"Very well," Abraham said.

"Bill says it's pretty important," Ike said as they walked along the dock.

"He couldn't tell you over the phone?"

"He could have, but he said he'd rather not."

"Really?" Brewski said through a mouthful of pizza.

"Really."

"Ike and the bald guy are leaving the boat," Rick said into his cell phone. "Really? Are you sure that's what he wants me to do?"

He held the phone away from his ear.

"All right then," he said. "You don't have to yell. I just want to make sure I got my orders right."

He disconnected and put the phone away.

"All right boys," he said to the others in the truck. "Let's go."

They climbed out of the old Ford and walked through the arched entrance of the St. Augustine Municipal Marina. Rick stopped at the beginning of the dock.

"Okay, Kip, you stay on the dock and make sure nobody bothers us. Elvin, you come in with me in case I need help. Got it?"

Kip and Elvin nodded.

"All right. Let's do it," Rick said as he started down the ramp.

When they reached *The Great Escape,* they paused and scanned the area for watching eyes. Seeing none, they climbed aboard and went into the cabin.

The two men were sitting at a table in the galley, eating pizza. Their faces showed their confusion along with a trace of fear when Rick and Elvin entered the cabin. Rick pointed his gun at the younger one; Elvin covered the other.

"You need to come with us," Rick said to the young one.

The two exchanged words in a language neither Rick nor Elvin understood.

"Hey," Rick shouted. "This is America. Speak English, damn it."

"What is this about?" the older man asked, as he stood and wiped his hands on a napkin. "Did Ike send you?"

"No. Ike didn't send us," Rick said. "You look Jewish. You Jewish?"

The man stared at Rick defiantly.

"Fine. Don't answer me. In fact, you just shut the hell up Jew, before I shut you up."

The man took a step toward Rick, but Rick wound up and delivered a punch to his face knocking him to the floor.

"Did you have to hit him?" Elvin said.

"Since when do you care about a damn heeb?"

Eric stood, knocking his chair over, and tried to make a break for the door. Rick and Elvin corralled him.

"Calm down, man," Rick said. "We're on your side. We got somebody wants to meet you."

Eric shouted something which they didn't understand.

"What'd you say?" Rick said. "What'd he say?" he said to Elvin.

"Damned if I know," Elvin said. "Let's just go. We don't know how long them two'll be gone."

"We can't just go. If he don't speak English he ain't no good to us."

Elvin pointed to the man on the floor.

"That one speaks his language."

"Mr. Hanson ain't gonna want no Jew."

"Yeah, but we need him to be a...you know, to tell us what the other one is saying."

"Interpreter, you dumb-ass."

"Yeah. That's it."

Rick thought about his options for a minute.

"Okay," he said. "You keep that one quiet. I'll grab the Jew."

Before leaving, Rick unfastened the lines securing the boat and gave it a shove with his foot. *The Great Escape* glided slowly out of its slip and moved toward the boats in the slips on the next dock.

"There," Rick said. "That's what you get for being an asshole."

They shoved the two men into the backseat of the truck and kicked up gravel on their way out of the parking lot.

Alex Grichenko opened his laptop, logged into an email account, went to the *drafts* folder, and opened the only message in it. It contained two sentences:

Agents Bronson and Freeman have been dispatched to Flagler Beach, Florida, to investigate possible sighting of Bell. Locate and initiate surveillance.

Grichenko deleted the draft and began a new one.

Understood. Will report any findings.

He logged out of the account without sending the message, then opened google maps. Flagler Beach was a little more than thirteen hours from his current location, Kecksburg, Pennsylvania. After packing, he went to the front desk.

"Checking out, Mr. Green?" the clerk asked politely.

"Yes," Grichenko answered in English devoid of any discernible accent. "Lots of moving around in my job."

He handed the clerk his American Express card and waited for his receipt.

"What business are you in?" the clerk asked while he waited for the receipt to print.

"I'm a data recovery consultant."

"Sounds impressive."

"Hardly. Most of the time I'm chasing wild geese."

The clerk chuckled and handed him the receipt. "Thanks for staying with us. Safe travels."

Grichenko nodded and smiled.

He set the GPS in his Volvo for Flagler Beach and began the trip.

When he was recruited by the Scientific Recovery Bureau, it sounded like a job he would enjoy greatly. What it was in reality was long hours of driving from one American town to another, followed by boring surveillance of American agents...all in a race for clues that added up to nothing in a hunt for something that, despite the intelligence reports from Moscow, probably didn't exist.

The hills of western Pennsylvania taunted him as they flew by outside the car windows. Each farm he passed made him envious of the people who lived there. In the seven years of this assignment, he had met very few Americans who appreciated what they had. Whereas the average Russian, those without good government jobs, knew exactly what they had...nothing.

Sometimes he wished he had never been sent to America to see that most of the stories he had been told about crime and poverty were greatly exaggerated.

So far he could find very little about life in America that did not appeal to him.

His current assignment would end in nine months. Then it would be back to Russia's perpetual winters and his robotic superiors with their blind devotion to a country which excelled only in the oppression of its citizens.

Unless he could think of a way to remain in America.

"Sit down," Bill Eldredge said.

"Sit down?" Ike said. "What the hell is this? You gonna tell me I have cancer or something?"

"No. But I think you should sit anyway."

Ike and Brewski sat.

"Okay," Ike said. "We're as ready as we'll ever be."

"Have either of you ever heard of Kim Dotcom?"

Ike and Brewski looked at each other and shrugged.

"Is that a website?" Ike asked.

"No. It's a person," Bill answered.

"Who is she?"

"She is a he. He is most famous for launching an internet sharing service called Megaupload."

"Megaupload?"

"Yeah. Remember Napster?"

"The music thing?"

"Right. Megaupload was like that. Dotcom's newest file-sharing venture is bigger and better. It's called K-dot-im, it's paired with his bitcache micropayment system using cryptocurrency."

"English, please."

Bill waved a hand.

"Never mind that stuff. Anyway, the long and the short of it is that with this new site, users don't share songs, they share information."

"What kind of information?"

"Any kind. Anything from how to make banana bread to which country has the most nuclear weapons. Health records are in especially high demand these days. Believe it or not, stolen medical information is more valuable than stolen financial data on the dark web."

"Christ," Ike said. "Sometimes I feel like there's a whole friggin' world out there that I don't even know about."

"There is," Bill said. "People will always find a way to devise new mechanisms in order to circumvent laws, pry into

133

things they shouldn't, or monitor how governments manage and process digital intelligence and citizen information."

Ike nodded. "Okay. I'm duly impressed and a little scared, but what's that got to do with us?"

"I've got an account with K.im. It's got certain markers that alert me when information of a certain type is shared."

"Such as?"

"Well, for example, any time any government entity shares something about Flagler County or Flagler Beach I get notified."

"And somebody shared something about Flagler?"

Brewski laughed. "Probably a paternity suit against you."

"Do you mind?" Ike said.

Brewski smirked and motioned for Bill to continue.

"I added a marker the other day to alert me of any chatter about the Nazi Bell. This morning I got pinged. Twice. Once for the Bell and once for Flagler Beach."

"You mean people know what's going on with the Bell, and we haven't told anybody?"

Bill shook his head and smiled. "You really don't understand the power of the internet, do you?"

"Apparently not."

"First, let's recap. It started when the coroner sent those fragments for ballistic analysis. That flagged a government agency as soon it was determined that the fragments were from a World War II era Russian grenade. Which is why you now have federal agents poking around. But what you probably don't know is that the agency those agents work for, our own CIA, is monitored by...guess who."

"The internet police?"

"Worse. The Russians."

"The Russians?"

"Of course. Remember, according to Abraham, the Russians invaded that bunker just as the Bell took off. They may not have gotten the craft itself, but they did get all the data associated with it. They also captured whatever workers survived the attack, and I'm sure they were all interrogated to within an inch of their lives."

"Or more," Ike added.

"I would imagine they sealed the bunker once they figured out what had been going on there. And you can bet your bottom dollar they're still looking for the Bell."

"Yeah," Ike said, "why should they be any different?"

Bill nodded and grinned.

"So now that the U.S. government has agents down here," Bill said, "the Russians figure there must be something worth looking for. So there's a Russian agent on his way."

"Time out," Brewski said, making a *T* sign with his hands. "If the feds and the Russians are..." he made finger quotes "...*secret agents*, how do these people on the internet know what they're doing?"

"Because people who work for government agencies are just people, and some of them don't support everything their respective governments do. So, they share some info here and there, always careful to cover their tracks. Deep down inside, people love to tell secrets they aren't supposed to. And I imagine it's the same in Russia. Maybe even worse."

"Unbelievable," Brewski said.

"Okay," Ike said. "So this Russian will most likely be tailing the two feds. Right?"

"No doubt."

"And if we know it, they probably know it, too."

"Sure. These days, intelligence work is not like it used to be. Everybody knows that everybody else is watching. It just adds an extra dimension to the job."

"So let them watch each other. They'll chase each other's tails for a while until they pack up and move on."

"That sounds good, but we're not talking about a couple of conspiracy-theory idiots poking around Area 51," Bill said. "These guys aren't going to give up after a day or two. They'll look under every rock and behind every bush until they find what they're looking for or until they're convinced it isn't here."

"Maybe we can convince them it isn't here."

"How?"

"I don't know. This is the first time I've tried to hide a Nazi time machine from two government agencies. I suppose it would be easier if we knew what they were doing."

"You want to spy on the spies?" Brewski asked.

Ike thought for a moment before answering. "You know what they say, the best defense is a good offense."

"Exactly what type of offense do you have in mind?" Bill asked.

"Right now, we have an advantage. We know about them, and their objective, but they don't know about us."

"Yet," Brewski inserted.

"Right. It's a matter of time before they figure stuff out, but if we know what they're doing, and what they're thinking, maybe we can figure out a way to convince them there's nothing here. You know? A little misdirection and maybe an accidental slip of the lip or two."

Bill nodded. "That's not a bad idea."

"We need eyes and ears on them. Can you come up with something for that?"

After some thought Bill said, "We could use a Stingray."

"A stingray?"

"A Corvette?" Brewski asked

"What's a Stingray?" Ike said.

"Besides a fast car," Brewski said.

"Basically, what a Stingray does is it spoofs a genuine mobile cell tower, then intercepts the signals in the surrounding area. All we need is the phone number of one of the agents and we can hack their data."

"How much of their data?"

"All of it. Anything on their cell phone. We can monitor and record their calls and even track their movements via the GPS in their own phones."

"Wow. You can do this without them knowing?"

Bill shrugged. "Nothing is completely undetectable, but since they're the CIA they're probably pretty confident that nobody is going to go to that extreme to listen to their phone calls."

"What about the Russians? Wouldn't they be doing the same thing?" Brewski asked.

"Possibly, but that won't affect us. It'll be like a party line."

"How do you install it?"

"I'll need a phone number and close proximity to the phone for about ten minutes."

"They left a card with Ralph. We can get the number. We could have Ralph call the agent and tell him he wants to talk."

"That should do the trick."

"All right." Ike clapped his hands. "We have a plan."

"Not to throw a wrench in your gears," Bill said, "but there are a couple of intangibles you're forgetting about."

"Abraham and Eric."

"Exactly. How do you see this thing playing out for them?"

"I really don't know."

"How about we put them in the time machine and send them on their way?" Brewski said. "Problem solved."

"I doubt either of them want to go back to Nazi Germany."

"Who says they have to go back there?" Brewski said. "It's a time machine. They can go wherever they want."

Ike and Bill looked at each other, then at Brewski.

"He's really not as dumb as he looks," Ike said to Bill.

13

Abraham paced around the small bedroom.

Although captivity was nothing new to him, his anxiety stemmed more from concern for Eric's well-being than his own.

Outside the window, rows of long narrow structures approximately the size of railroad cars, rusted and dirty with age, were like two horrific memories combined into one. Dozens of people crammed into boxcars like sardines then taken to a camp of long rows of filthy wooden buildings housing five times as many people as they should have, in the most deplorable conditions imaginable. Many didn't survive the train trip.

They were the lucky ones.

Not a day passed where Abraham didn't suffer from guilt at having been chosen to live in relative comfort simply by virtue of his education.

Maybe now he would pay his penance.

Was this the modern-day American version of the camps?

Was it his destiny to spend his life, regardless of the year, under the heel of an oppressive ruling class?

Had the passage of time not shown the world the senselessness of hatred?

Thudding footsteps were followed by the sound of the door being unlocked. Out of habit, he stood in the center of the room.

The door opened and the man who had taken them from the boat stood in the doorway.

"Your friend don't speak no English. Get your Jew ass out here and translate for the man."

Abraham followed him down a short hallway into an open space. On the left was a kitchen area that, even though it was dirty, had modern amenities the likes of which he had never seen. The rest of the space contained furniture which bore no resemblance to the sort of furniture he was used to.

A pregnant woman stood in the kitchen drinking from a green bottle. The two other men from the boat stood by windows, watching the outside. Seated on a sofa with his left leg resting across his right knee, was a muscular man with closely cropped hair. A glint of gold directed Abraham's eye to the hoop in the man's left ear. He didn't realize he was staring until he bumped into his escort, who had stopped in front of him. Standing next to the sofa was a handsome man in a very expensive-looking suit.

Eric sat in one of the other chairs looking frightened. Relief washed over his face when he saw Abraham.

Abraham's escort gave him a quick shove. "Here he is Mr. Hanson."

Abraham stood silently.

"Rick was only supposed to grab the kid," the man addressed as Mr. Hanson said, pointing at Eric, "but as usual he failed to understand his instructions. Luckily this time he actually thought something through and made a good decision. Probably pure luck, and most-likely the last time it'll ever happen, but that's neither here nor there. As you know this young man doesn't speak English and, since we don't speak German, you're going to be our translator."

"What do you want with him?" Abraham asked tentatively. "He's just a boy."

"If you don't mind, I'll be asking the questions."

Abraham nodded.

"First we're going to conduct a little experiment."

The man nodded at Rick. Rick opened the door to an adjacent room and stepped inside. When he came out he carried a staff bearing a bright red flag with a black swastika in the center.

Eric immediately stood and extended his right arm in salute.

Hanson nodded at Rick again. Rick returned the flag to the room.

"Now," Hanson said. "I'd like an explanation for that."

Abraham stood mute.

"Well, ask him." Hanson said.

Abraham and Eric had a brief conversation in German.

"He is somewhat confused why you are asking," Abraham said, "but his answer is that he was simply saluting the flag of the Fatherland."

"The Fatherland?" Hanson said. "As in Germany?"

"That is correct."

"And obviously he is from Germany."

"He is."

"Here's where I get confused. It is my understanding that it is illegal in Germany to show any sort of allegiance to the Nazi party. This includes using the Nazi salute, which he just did reflexively."

"It is illegal?" Abraham said as a glimmer of hope sprung up inside him.

"Don't mock me, Jew. Now I want to show you something. You show it to him and ask what he can tell me about it."

Hanson produced two documents and set them on the coffee table. Abraham recognized them immediately as Dr. Spier's identity papers, but he tried to temper his reaction. He spoke to Eric, then translated for the man.

"He says he does not know what they are, but they look like some old identity papers of some kind."

Hanson grinned and nodded. "So that's how it's going to be? I was hoping that he would help me understand something, and in return I would take him in and make him part of an organization in line with his beliefs."

"What is it he can help you understand?" Abraham asked. "As I said, he is just a boy."

"Not that I'm in the habit of explaining myself to Jews, but since you are my only line of communication to him I'll tell you what I want to understand. The two of you are known associates of a man named Ike. These papers belonged to a man whose body was found on the beach. Ike and his friend were at the coroner's office asking about them. The papers are obviously from Germany, and your young friend here is also from Germany. You, even though you are a Jew, speak German like a native. Even a cursory examination of those papers shows that they were used during World War II, and the bearer was a member of the Nazi party. This boy, as you refer to him, has exhibited behaviors consistent with the Nazi party. These things cannot be attributed to coincidence."

Hanson paused and paced a small circle, stopping behind the chair in which Eric sat. Eric's frightened eyes locked on Abraham, who tried to will him to remain calm. The man gripped Eric's shoulders.

"The bottom line is this. We will stay here until somebody tells me what's going on, and the longer it takes the less patient I will be."

Eric's faced grimaced as Hanson increased the grip on his shoulders.

"Do I make myself clear, Jew?"

"This ought to be fun, playing spies for a..." Brewski stopped in mid-sentence. "What the fuck?"

"What's wrong?" Ike asked, turning to face Brewski, who had stopped in his tracks as soon as they emerged from the marina's arched entrance.

Brewski pointed toward Ike's boat. "What's wrong with this picture?" he said.

Ike turned around to see *The Great Escape* nestled against a forty-foot catamaran. The two boats bobbed in unison on the gentle swells of the marina.

"What the fuck?" he said.

"I already said that," Brewski said.

Ike trotted along the dock to the catamaran's slip. Brewski followed.

"Ahoy," Ike called as a formality before stepping aboard the boat and walking to his.

There was no damage evident, other than a few superficial scuff marks where the two vessels had rubbed together.

"Did you forget to tie it up?" Brewski asked.

"Not a chance," Ike said.

Without further communication, they each pulled their guns and stepped aboard *The Great Escape*. Ike entered the cabin as Brewski walked to the bow and circled back to the stern before following Ike inside. Ike was coming out of one of the cabins, putting his gun back in his waistband.

"Nobody here," he said.

"Nobody here?" Brewski echoed. "Where the hell did they go?

"Beats me, but wherever they went, they left in mid-meal." Ike waved a hand at the table, where a pizza box and some plates with half-eaten slices still sat.

"Ahoy, Ike," a voice called.

They went to the stern deck to see Frank Silva, the harbor master, standing on the dock.

"What happened here?" Silva asked.

"I don't know, Frank," Ike answered, "but I'll take care of it."

"It must have just happened. I was out here ten or fifteen minutes ago and everything was fine."

"Thanks, Frank. Luckily, there's no damage to either boat."

"Glad everything's okay," Frank said as he walked away.

After the boat was secured in its proper slip, Ike and Brewski went to the harbor master's office.

"Frank," Ike said. "Would you mind if I took a look at the camera footage from the dock?"

"No problem, Ike. What are you looking for?"

"I really don't know. I'm just wondering how two secure lines came undone."

Frank walked them to a cabinet on the opposite wall. Inside was a video screen showing the views of the four cameras monitoring the marina.

"This one here," Ike said, pointing to the image in the lower right corner.

"Yup," Frank said, pushing buttons on the DVR below the monitor. "Camera three."

He backed the feed up until he saw himself on the screen.

"There's me, walking the docks like I do every day at that time. Your boat is there and looking fine. Can even see the line from the stern cleat secured to the dock."

He moved the footage forward until they saw the men leaving *The Great Escape*.

"What's this?" Frank said. "Never saw these guys before. There he goes, untying your lines. Is that guy pointing a gun at the other guy?"

"Thanks, Frank," Ike said as he and Brewski simultaneously turned and rushed out of the office. "I know everything I need to know."

They left their motorcycles parked at a restaurant on A1A just south of the trailer park. Circling around the restaurant and an ice cream shop, they entered the park from the rear of Constance's trailer. Ike pointed at Brewski then at the rear door of the mobile home, Brewski moved off toward the trailer.

At the front door, Ike drew his forty-five and tried the knob.

Locked.

He glanced around for witnesses, then drew his leg up and kicked the door in, charging inside. Brewski came in from the other end. The two of them stood pointing their guns at each other in the empty trailer.

"Son of a bitch," Ike said.

"Now what, Kemosabe?" Brewski asked.

Ike tucked his gun into his belt. "Your guess is as good as mine," he said.

14

"You drive," Bronson said to Freeman. "I need a break."

Freeman caught the keys and altered his course to the driver's side of the unmarked Ford.

Bronson fastened his seatbelt then took his cell phone out.

"Let's see what we've got so far," he said, consulting a government database. "The truck carrying Moe, Larry, and Curly is registered to Frederick J. Turner, 15 Milwaukee Avenue. According to the GPS, we need to go north on A1A for about eleven miles."

"Got it," Freeman said. "What do we know about Turner?"

"Our boy was born June 29, 1992. His driver's license, which is currently suspended, has him listed at five-feet-ten and a hundred-sixty-five pounds. He's a high-school dropout, registered Republican, has a credit score of 439, has never held a job for more than a year, single, no dependents, hasn't filed a tax return in six years. Parents divorced, father currently serving a thirteen-year sentence for a hate crime. Two years ago, he filed a slip and fall lawsuit against Home Depot for a broken ankle. He ended up settling for $3,800, about half the amount of his medical bills, which he never paid. He tried to enlist in the army but was declined for failing to disclose his arrest record. He's been arrested four times."

"I'm sure they were all trumped-up charges," Freeman said.

"Twice on firearms-related charges, once for assault, and once for DUI. Known associations, The Brotherhood of the Southern Cross."

"I'm sure that's a nice, wholesome church group."

"Close. Minor-league white supremacists."

"You think they wanted the papers from the coroner's office as some sort of souvenir?"

"We'll have to ask him when we see him."

Freeman turned left out of the parking lot of the hotel and headed north.

"What about the other two? The bikers."

Bronson scrolled through the notes on his phone.

"Yeah. Only one of them signed in at the coroner's office. Ike is all he wrote."

"Isn't that the guy..."

"Yup. The guy the bartender at..." He scrolled back. "The Golden Lion said we should talk to about the night of the sighting."

"Coincidence?"

Bronson snorted a laugh. "If it looks like a duck and walks like a duck..."

"Right."

"We'll stop there on the way back and see if—" –he consulted his phone again— "—Mr. Donabedian's memory has improved yet."

Freeman turned off A1A onto a narrow dirt road adjacent to a vacant A-framed building with boarded windows. The car bounced and groaned over the pot holes.

"Christ," Bronson said. "Any of these furnished trash cans have numbers on them?"

"Yeah," Freeman said. "But they're all covered by the confederate flags."

"Hold up. Is that it? Yeah. Fifteen."

Freeman pulled over in front of the trailer.

"The curtain just moved," he said to Bronson as they walked toward the steps.

"Yeah, I saw it. And the doors been kicked in."

Both agents unfastened the safety straps on their holsters. Bronson knocked on the door. It was opened almost immediately by a man who stood at least six-foot-five and weighed about two-hundred-fifty pounds. His salt-and-pepper hair was pulled back in a ponytail, and his moustache and beard were neatly trimmed to less than a quarter-inch in length. Bronson recognized him immediately from the coroner's office surveillance footage.

"Good afternoon," he said, producing his badge. "Federal agents, looking for Frederick Turner."

"I'm sorry, gentlemen," the man answered. "He doesn't seem to be here."

"Would you happen to know when he'll be home or where we can find him?"

"I'm afraid not."

Bronson nodded. "Do you live here?"

"Me? No. I'm just looking for good ole Rick too. I noticed the door was kicked in so I came in to make sure everything was okay."

"Uh-huh. Your name's Ike, isn't it?"

A brief look of surprise gave way to a grin.

"Well, yes, it is. I'll tell you, I've heard you federal agents were smart, but, damn. That was impressive."

"Funny. We'd like to talk to you, too."

Ike's eyes widened and he pointed at himself dramatically.

"Me? I can't imagine what two such important guys would want to talk to me about."

"Right. Well, you can either talk to us voluntarily and find out, or we can arrest you for breaking and entering and you can spend the weekend in jail and talk to us on Monday."

"Isn't breaking and entering a little out of your jurisdiction?"

"You'd be surprised what falls under our purview."

"Purview? Listen. If you're going to use words I don't understand, it won't be a very productive conversation."

"How long are we going to do this?"

Ike nodded. "Okay. Let's talk. But we probably shouldn't do it here. You know, in case Rick comes home."

"Fine. Where?"

"Restaurant about seven or eight miles south of here. The Golden Lion."

"Okay. We'll meet you there."

"Looking forward to it."

Bronson watched in the rearview mirror asIke and his bald friend walk away from the trailer on their way out.

"So the guy Turner was following to the coroner's office ends up breaking into Turner's trailer," he said to Freeman.

"Sure are a lot of coincidences around here."

Ike called Bill Eldredge as they walked to their motorcycles.

"Hey. Those two gentlemen from the government have agreed to meet us at The Lion in about fifteen minutes. Can you be there? Excellent. Adios."

"Mr. Hanson," Elvin said from his place by the window.

"What?"

"Ike just broke into Rick and Constance's place."

"Is that a fact?" Hanson looked at Abraham. "I wonder what he's looking for, and why he's looking there?"

Abraham spread his hands and started to speak, but Hanson held up a hand.

"Just keep quiet. We'll figure that out in good time." He pointed at Constance. "Go over there and act surprised. Tell him you're calling the police."

"The last time he was here, he pretty much laughed at Browning," Constance said. "I don't think the cops scare him."

"The last time he wasn't caught red-handed breaking in to your house."

"Hang on a minute," Elvin said. "I think the law is already here."

Hanson moved to the window.

"What the..." he said. "Those are definitely cops, but they don't look local."

"State?" Rick asked.

"Could be, but they look federal."

"Feds. At my place? What do they want with me?"

"It could be they're following Ike. That would be perfect. I couldn't ask for better luck."

"What the hell?" Rick said when the federal agents got in their car and left. "They didn't arrest him or nothing. And now Ike and his bald friend are walking away like nothing happened."

"I think I need to make a phone call," Hanson said.

Ten minutes later, he put his phone away. "I'll be damned," he said.

"What'd you find out?" Rick asked.

"Neither of my sources took credit for them. They're not state and they're not FBI."

"Well that don't make no sense. If they ain't state and they ain't feds, who are they?"

"We'll worry about that later," Hanson said, returning his attention to Abraham. "We need to get back to the matter at hand."

15

Ike stalled at the bar, talking to Tiki about a fictitious issue until Bill Eldredge showed up and sat next to him. Neither man acknowledged the other.

"They're sitting by the raw bar," Ike said without taking his eyes off Tiki, who nodded to maintain the façade. "There will be a business card taped to the bottom of the coaster Tiki will give you. It's got agent Bronson's phone number and email address on it."

Ike bumped fists with Tiki and walked away. After getting a glass of red wine and a coaster Bill moved to a table near the one occupied by Ike and the two agents.

"So how are you two liking Flagler Beach so far?" Ike asked the agents while he kept a discrete eye on Bill.

"If I was on vacation, I'd like it just fine," Bronson said.

"It's just another tourist-trap town," Freeman said. "You've seen one, you've seen 'em all."

"I don't know. I've been to a lot of towns. You couldn't pay me to live in some of them."

"We're not here to buy a house," Freeman said.

"Yeah. Speaking of that, why are you here? And why the interest in me?"

Bronson took his phone out. "You don't mind if I ask the questions, do you?"

Ike held his hands up. "No. Not at all, but what's your friend going to do?"

"Don't worry about him. Speaking of friends, where's your bald shadow?"

Ike locked eyes with Bronson. "Don't worry about him."

The stare down lasted a few seconds until Bronson pushed a few buttons on his phone and set it on the table.

"This interview will be recorded. Is that okay with you?"

Ike nodded. "Do what you gotta do," he said.

"State your name for the record, please."

"Ike."

"Jesus Christ," Freeman muttered.

Ike held up a hand and grinned. "No. Ike is fine."

"Last name?" Bronson said.

"Not important."

Bronson paused the recording. "Is this how you're going to play it? I can force you to tell me."

"Ahhh. You haff vayz of making me talk?" Ike said in his best movie-Nazi accent. "Look, I'm here voluntarily. I haven't committed a crime, and unless there's something you aren't telling me, I'm not under arrest. Either move on with the interview, or just move on."

Bronson resumed recording.

"Okay, Ike, a body was found on the beach a short distance from here Wednesday night. What can you tell us about it?"

"He was dead."

Bronson gave Ike a deadpan look. "Really?"

Ike spread his hands. "Sorry. I don't get out much."

"Were you present when the body was discovered by Officer..."

"Cabral," Freeman said.

"Officer Cabral."

"I may have been strolling by. It was a nice night for a walk on the beach."

"But you don't know anything about the body."

"Other than the fact that he was dead? No."

Bronson nodded. "Do you remember anything unusual that night?"

Ike put his hand to his chin and stroked his whiskers. "Now that you mention it, there was something odd that night."

"What was that?"

"The kitchen ran out of croutons. There was some serious panic back there."

Bronson pointed at the tattoo on the inside of Ike's left forearm; a snake wrapped around a skull, poking out through an eye socket, fangs bared. Above and below, on a ribbon, were the words *Death Before Dishonor*.

"Nice ink. You served?"

Ike gave him a curt nod.

"I was in the Air Force," Bronson said. "Freeman was a Navy man. What about you?"

"It was a long time ago."

"One American serviceman to another, how about a little cooperation?"

Ike leaned forward in his chair. "First of all, Agent Bronson, I am cooperating. I'm here, right? Second, appealing to my patriotism is going to get you exactly nowhere. Maybe if you told me what this was all about I could give you a little more, but hiding behind your aviator shades and using the straight-faced, Joe Friday, I'll-ask-the-questions approach isn't going to be very productive. You follow?"

"What were you doing at the coroner's office yesterday?"

Ike laughed. "So much for offering constructive criticism."

Over Bronson's shoulder, Bill made a circular motion with his hand, asking for more time.

"The coroner's office," Bronson said.

"That was a mistake on my part. I was looking for my dentist."

"Your dentist's office is in the County Administration Building?"

"Apparently not."

"So, it's purely coincidence that the body I asked about earlier is at the coroner's office, the only body they've gotten in the past eight days, I might add, and you just happened to show up?"

"Okay. You got me. I was trying to get a little inside info. Like I said, I was on the beach when they found him, I was curious. Is that a crime?"

"What were you doing at Mr. Turner's trailer today?"

"I told you, I was looking for Rick, saw the door kicked in and went in to investigate. Strictly as a concerned citizen."

"We have another coincidence here, Ike."

"What would that be?"

"Shortly after you left the coroner's office, Mr. Turner and a couple of his friends went in and stole government property."

"They take a stapler?"

"This is a joke to you, isn't it?"

"In fact, it is, gentleman. First of all, I don't know what agency you're associated with. You showed me a badge that could have been bought in a pawn shop. Next, you refuse to tell me why you're interested in me. And finally, you haven't told me what it is you're investigating. Surely the federal government didn't send two agents to Flagler Beach to investigate a dead body and some old papers."

Ike wished he could have taken the words back as soon as they left his mouth.

"Old papers? Nobody mentioned old papers."

Ike sighed.

"All right. You got me. I know about the papers. Like I said, I was curious."

"How did you find out about the papers?"

Ike shook his head. "Nope. Your turn."

Bronson and Freeman exchanged a look.

"Fine." Bronson handed a business card to Ike. "We're with the CIA."

"The Division of Historic Significance," Ike read the card.

"The body on the beach was that of a white male, mid-thirties. Cause of death was multiple wounds to the back from shrapnel. Ballistics testing revealed the shrapnel removed from the body was consistent with material used in Russian grenades."

"So?"

"Russian grenades manufactured before 1950."

"So, somebody's throwing old Russian hand grenades around. Still doesn't seem like a federal issue."

"How did you find out about the papers?"

"Let's just say I've got a lot of friends, and they keep me posted."

"What were you going to do with them?"

"Like I said, I just wanted to see them."

"A witness claims you met two men on the beach that night and brought them here, gave them dry clothes."

"Yeah. That's true."

"Where are those men?"

"I honestly don't know."

"Do you know their names?"

"Abraham and Eric."

"No last names?"

"That's all I got."

"Did they say anything about where they were from?"

"They spoke German, so I'm thinking Germany. Maybe."

"Did they speak English?"

"One of them did. Abraham."

"Aside from the dead body and the two German men, was there anything out of the ordinary?"

"Not that I recall."

"Nothing unusual at all?"

"Such as?"

Bronson stopped the recording.

"Thank you, Ike. How can we get in touch with you if we have any follow up questions?"

"Just leave word at the bar here, and it'll find its way to me."

Bronson nodded. "If you think of anything else, give me a call."

"Count on it."

Once the unmarked Ford drove off Ike sat next to Bill. Brewski came out of the restaurant and joined them.

"Well?" Ike said.

"Perfect," Bill said. "Check it out."

He typed a few commands and an audio program opened.

"What do you think?" Freeman asked.

"I don't know," Bronson answered. *"I definitely think he's hiding something, but I don't know what."*

"You think he knows what we're looking for?"

"I doubt it. Who knows? Maybe he just doesn't like cops and his default position is to say nothing."

"What next?"

"We'll interview the cop, Cabral. Then we'll take another crack at finding Mr. Turner."

"Is that live?" Brewski asked.

"Yeah, sort of," Bill answered. "It's like a DVR. I can go back and listen but it'll keep recording until I stop it. As long as Agent Bronson's phone is turned on, it's our own listening device. And here's a bonus. If he connects his phone to a laptop, or some other device I will have unlimited access to that equipment as well."

"You're a devious man," Ike said.

Bill waved a hand. "Awww. Stop."

"How long will this last?" Brewski asked.

"Until my laptop runs out of memory. Which is about never. Let me have your phone," he said to Ike. "I'll install the app for you so you can watch and listen as well."

"Cool," Ike said. "I'll call Butch and give him a heads up, then I think we should get back to looking for Abraham and Eric."

16

Alex Grichenko admired the small town from the crest of the bridge.

Idyllic nearly described it.

The ocean backdrop glistened in the morning sun with colors spanning the full range from pale green to dark blue. The horizon was as sharp as a razor, separating the ocean from the powder-blue sky. A lone cotton ball cloud drifted lazily over the water.

For the first time in his career, Alex told himself that if he were to die while on an assignment, he hoped it would be here.

At the intersection of State Road 100 and Route A1A, he did a mental coin toss and decided to turn right and stop at the first hotel he saw. Less than a half mile later he turned into the parking lot of a hotel called The Topaz. The parking lot was not quite full, and families of American tourists sat around the pool or walked across the street to the ocean carrying chairs, towels, and beach toys.

He stepped out of his car and took in the scene. Surfers waited on their boards for the glassy ocean to change its mind. Young girls in bathing suits that left little to the imagination strolled along the boardwalk pretending not to admire the lifeguards. Motorcycles cruised by slowly and the smell of bacon teased his nostrils.

He inhaled deeply and smiled.

Yes. This was the place where he wanted to die.

The lobby of the hotel had an old charm about it. He even liked the way it smelled. The clerk at the desk smiled as Alex approached.

"Welcome to the Topaz," he said.

Alex took in the ambience of the lobby and smiled at other guests while he waited for the clerk to register him.

"Here you go," the clerk said, handing him a card key. "Your room is number 104, Mr. Green. I hope you enjoy your stay with us."

"You can rely on that," Alex said in his best English.

The room was clean, the bed was comfortable and the view from the window was like nothing he had ever seen, nor would ever see, in Russia.

He dropped his bag on the bed and opened it. Sitting on top of his clothes was the one possession that he had brought with him from Russia; a Cold War era Makarov pistol—his father's service weapon.

On a cold winter's day in 1998, in the town of Saratov, Alex told his father of his new assignment with the Scientific Recovery Bureau – the search for the Nazi Bell. His father walked to the window and looked across the Volga River.

"During my time in the KGB I heard much talk about the Bell," his father said. "Our country has been looking for it since the end of the war. The Americans have also been searching for it. Which means this assignment is likely to take you to the United States at some point."

Yuri Grichenko shuffled to a dresser, removed a small wooden box and handed it to Alex.

"This is for you. I have no use for it anymore."

Alex knew the contents of the box for he had admired it many times as a boy. On the rare occasions when his father would return home from an assignment, Alex would watch him disassemble the Makarov, clean it with great care and reassemble it, all while carrying on a conversation with his young son.

Now, years later, the Makarov was his.

"Remember this, my son," Yuri said. "The United States was born of disloyalty to their government and built on false nobility. Do not trust the Americans."

Alex nodded, more concerned with his new possession than his father's advice.

"Thank you, father," he said.

Yuri embraced his son.

"I am proud of you," Yuri answered. "You have grown into a good man."

Alex set his laptop on the desk and logged into the email account. The draft message he had created had been deleted and another was in the folder in its place.

Agents Bronson and Freeman. Topaz Hotel. Room 108.

Alex smiled at the luck of his choosing the very same hotel as his targets. Surely it was a sign.

He picked up the phone, dialed the front desk, and asked to be connected to room 108. The phone rang several times before the call was forwarded back to the desk.

"I'm sorry, sir. There's no answer. Would you like to leave a message?"

"No. Thank you."

He hung up the phone and walked to a surf shop a block away where he purchased a swim suit, beach towel, some sunscreen, and a novel called *Blood in the Water*, written by a local author. After returning to his room and changing, he sat by the pool, positioned with an unobstructed view of room 108.

A third of the way through the novel, he was slightly disappointed when he saw the black, unmarked Ford sedan park in front of the room. The two agents climbed out and walked to the door.

Alex snickered to see them in their blue suits, striped ties and shiny shoes. They even wore matching aviator sunglasses. Americans may picture themselves as the best at everything, but they had a long way to go when it came to blending in.

He packed up his belongings and walked leisurely to the far end of the pool, admiring the view, then circled back toward his room. At the door to room 108, he dropped his novel on the ground, bent to pick it up and attached a magnetic tracking device to the underside of the Ford belonging to the American agents.

In his room, he showered and changed into clothes that didn't advertise the fact he was a government agent. When Bronson and Freeman later walked to the hotel's restaurant, he followed discretely. After he was seated he placed what looked like a ball point pen on the table and pointed it toward the two agents. On his cell phone, he activated the directional microphone app. The end of the pen lit up with a small blue light indicating the blue tooth connection was made. He plugged in his ear bud and listened.

After making some corrections for ambient noise, he set the phone down and listened while his pen picked up the conversation between the two Americans.

The seared Ahi tuna steaks, combined with the French Rosé, were perfection.

He watched with disgust as the two Americans, both of whom could stand to lose a few pounds, consumed massive hamburgers and French fries loaded with ketchup, which they washed down with cheap American beer.

In between filling their mouths with food, they foolishly discussed their progress.

"So, we talk to the cop next," one of them said. "And after that?"

"We stick with Ike and see where he leads us."

"You think he has any idea what he's into?"

"Tough to say. He knows a far sight more than he's telling us. That much I'm sure of. The key is these other two guys he talked about. We need to find them, and Ike is the only connection we have."

"What about Turner?"

The other one, who was apparently the senior agent, pondered the question as he chewed. "I'm not sure if Turner is anything more than a fly who got into the wrong ointment at the wrong time. We'll take one more shot at his trailer. If he isn't there, we may get lucky and Ike will lead us to him and we can get two birds with one stone."

For a few minutes, they ate in silence until the senior agent spoke again.

"What's wrong? You've got a look like something's bugging you."
"I'm just wondering..."
"Wondering what?"
"If this is going to be another red herring."
"It's possible, but this is a pretty strong lead. Some of the things we've found since we've been here, taken individually, could be written off as coincidence, but when you put them all together... I think we might finally be on to something."
"So you think the Bell is here?"
For the first time, the senior agent looked around the room for prying ears.
"If the dead body turns out to be the real deal, then yeah, it had to get here in the Bell. Unfortunately, Ike could be right. It could have been some idiot with an old Russian grenade."

The conversation should have given Alex great optimism. The American agent seemed fairly confident that they were, at the very least, closer than they had ever been. Which meant that Alex was also closer than he had ever been. The mention of the old Russian grenade was a concrete lead for sure.

In his pre-mission briefing he had read the after-action reports of the raid on the Malopolskie bunker. A soldier described a man in a lab coat running toward the Bell. The soldier threw a grenade. The man in the lab coat was struck but managed to make it into the vessel before it launched. Since the invasion team was under strict orders to preserve as much of the bunker as possible, the craft was allowed to launch without obstruction. Interrogations with the surviving lab workers confirmed that the controls were programmed for launch with two men aboard. It was also revealed that the presence of the wounded man would have thrown the destination calculations off, and the metal fragments from the grenade would have interfered with the electro-magnetic guidance system. It was the difference between firing a gun at a stationary target while remaining perfectly still, and firing the same gun at a moving target from a high-speed roller coaster.

In short, the Bell could have ended up anywhere on the planet, at any time.

Alex had never had total faith in the reports, since most of the information acquired from the German lab workers had been obtained with the popular Russian torture methods of the day. Such methods usually resulted in inaccurate information. It had been learned in subsequent years that a man would say whatever he thought his captors wanted to hear in order to get relief from the pain and anguish, even if only momentarily.

This new information, however, seemed to corroborate at least part of the reports. Alex realized he should feel good about things, possibly even be excited.

The senior agent made a phone call to the policeman, and they agreed to meet.

Alex paid for his lunch and left the restaurant before Bronson and Freeman. Sitting in the Volvo behind heavily tinted windows, he waited for the Americans then followed them to their meeting.

After finishing their meal, Bronson made a phone call to arrange an interview with Officer Cabral. Cabral was currently on duty, so the agents agreed to meet him at a local burrito stand and talk to him while he ate his lunch curbside.

"Thanks for meeting with us, Officer Cabral," Bronson said as he sat across from the policeman at the concrete table.

Cabral unwrapped his burrito and started eating.

"No problem. What can I do for you?"

Bronson started his recorder.

"You found a body on the beach the other night. Is that correct?"

Cabral nodded. "That's right," he said after swallowing his food.

"Can you tell us how you came to find it?"

Cabral grinned. "It was kind of funny, actually. I got a call from dispatch, said a guy called from the roof of Finn's to report a UFO sighting."

"A UFO?"

Cabral sucked on the straw in his paper cup, then nodded.

"You got it. A UFO. I thought it was weird because it was only Wednesday. Usually people don't party hard enough to see flying saucers 'til the weekend, but we do get a lot of tourists and college kids on spring break here, so..."

"Were you able to interview the caller?"

"Nope. Nobody knew who made the call, or if they did they weren't admitting it."

"Naturally. What happened next?"

"Well, the caller told the dispatcher the UFO splashed down in the water not far from the pier, so I figured I'd go down to the beach and take a look-see. You know? Just in case. I mean, it was a pretty slow night."

"And that's when you found the body?"

"Right. Under the pier behind The Funky Pelican. Well, I guess technically it was under The Funky Pelican, but you get the point."

"Right. Were you alone?"

Cabral stopped chewing, held up a finger, put the burrito down and drank some soda. "Say again?"

"I said, were you alone?"

Cabral took another bite of the burrito and nodded.

"Yeah," he said after swallowing. "Of course I was alone. We aren't a big enough department to have two officers in a car."

"I see. How's the burrito?"

"Too small. Should've gotten some onion rings."

"Do you know a man who goes by the name Ike?"

"Ike? Sure, I know him. Everybody knows Ike. He's one of those locals who seems to be everybody's friend."

"How would you describe your relationship with him?"

"Relationship? I know who he is, he knows who I am. It's a small town, you know?"

"A waitress at Finn's, who also knows him, says the two of you were talking before you found the body and he went down to the beach with you."

"Is that right? Well, he did come over to my cruiser and ask what was going on, along with about twenty other people, but that's about it. I'm afraid the waitress was mistaken about the rest of it."

Cabral took the final bite of his burrito and washed it down with the last of his soda.

"Officer Cabral, are you aware of the penalty for obstructing a federal investigation?"

Cabral stood and returned his plastic tray to the order window. On the way to his cruiser he stopped at the table. He made a show of removing his sunglasses, wiping them with a napkin and sliding them back on his face.

"If I had known you were going to accuse me of lying," Cabral said as he dropped the crumpled napkin on the table, "I'd have made you pay for my lunch. Good luck in your investigation, gentlemen."

"I'll tell you what," Freeman said after Cabral's cruiser pulled away. "I am not warming up to this town at all. Nice try with the waitress, though"

"I figured it was worth a shot."

"Should we go see if Ike and his friend are still at The Golden Lion?"

Ike and Brewski sat in a booth at an ice cream shop across the street from the burrito stand listening to Bronson and Freeman interview Butch.

"Butch handled that perfectly," Ike said.

Brewski shoveled the last of his hot-fudge sundae into his mouth. "Mm-hm. He did."

"All right. Now let's see where our federal friends go after they figure out we aren't at The Lion."

Bronson and Freeman walked to their car and headed north on A1A. A silver Volvo turned onto A1A from Fourth Street and screeched to a halt as Ike and Brewski left the ice cream shop and tried to cross the street to get to their motorcycles parked on the east side of the road.

Ike gave a wave of apology to the driver, who waved back and took off after they were clear.

17

"Okay," Hanson said, turning away from the window. "Where were we?"

He nodded to Stuart, who stood and retrieved a roll of duct tape from a drawer in the kitchen. After using it to secure Eric to the chair, he used the tape to fasten Abraham's hands behind his back.

"Please," Abraham said. "We have no information that can help you."

"We'll find out soon enough," Hanson said. "Now listen carefully."

Abraham nodded.

"As I said before, there are too many coincidences here. There is something going on and I want to know what it is. What is your association with Ike, and what is your connection to the dead man in the coroner's office?"

"We only met Ike recently. We were lost and he offered to help."

"You were lost?"

"Yes."

"Were you traveling?"

Abraham paused before answering.

"Yes."

"Where were you going?"

"We hadn't determined a final destination at that point."

"So, what? You were just wandering aimlessly?"

Abraham shrugged. "I suppose that is accurate."

"Okay. Let's try this. Where had you come from?"

Abraham paused. After several seconds Hanson nodded at Stuart, who delivered a punch to Abraham's kidney, sending Abraham to his knees.

Eric cried out in German, then turned to Hanson with eyes full of anger.

"This is odd," Hanson said. "Here we have, what appears to be a devout Nazi, yet he seems concerned for the welfare of a Jew."

Stuart hoisted Abraham to his feet.

"I'll ask you again," Hanson said. "Where had you been traveling from."

Hanson raised his eyebrows and cocked his head as he stared at Abraham. Abraham's eyes implored Hanson to stop asking the question. Hanson shrugged, then nodded to Stuart. Another blow to the kidney.

"Do you see how this is going to work, Jew? We can do this all night, but eventually you'll begin to suffer internal bleeding, and after that it won't take long for you to die."

Stuart hauled Abraham to his feet again.

"Hopefully the third time's the charm," Hanson said. "Where did you come from?"

Abraham inhaled as deeply as he could. "Germany," he answered.

"Okay. Now we're getting somewhere. Let's try the other question again now that you're more inclined to answer honestly. Where were you going?"

"As I told you, we had no specific destination. Our plans were...disrupted."

"Disrupted?"

"In a manner of speaking."

"What does that mean?"

"Our plans did not include landing in Flagler Beach."

"Landing? So, you were on a plane and it landed at the Flagler Airport?"

"No."

Hanson grunted in frustration and nodded at Stuart. Another punch. Abraham went to his knees and vomited.

Eric said something to him, to which Abraham responded weakly.

"What did he say to you?" Hanson asked.

"He told me to tell you what you want to know."

"And what did you say to him?"

"I told him I have survived much worse treatment."

"Is that right? Well, I guess it's time to raise the stakes."

Hanson waved Stuart away. Stuart moved to the back of Eric's chair.

"Clearly you have no regard for your own wellbeing, but maybe you won't be so callous with the boy's."

He nodded at Stuart. Stuart slid his hands to Eric's throat and began squeezing. Eric squirmed against the duct tape.

"Start talking, Jew."

Abraham stood in shock as Stuart increased his grip. Eric's face began to turn red.

"Stop," Abraham pleaded.

Eric shook his head trying to break Stuart's grip. He began to convulse and the redness in his face inched its way toward purple.

"Please stop. Please. You'll kill him."

"Are you going to talk?"

Eric's eyes began to bulge.

"Yes," Abraham said. "Stop. I will tell you what you want to know."

Hanson held up a hand and Stuart released his grip on Eric's throat. Eric leaned his head back and gasped.

"All right, Jew. Let's hear your explanation for this series of odd occurrences."

Abraham took a deep breath.

"This may be difficult to understand," he said.

"Try me," Hanson said.

"Very well. The boy and I, along with the man in the morgue, left Germany together. The man in the morgue was wounded before we left and he died as a result of his injuries during our...flight. Those papers were his identity papers."

"These papers here?" Hanson held the papers up.

"Yes."

Hanson looked at the papers.

"These papers belonged to a man named Spier. But they're about seventy-five years old. There's no way they belong to the dead man."

"That is the part I thought you might have difficulty understanding."

"The man these papers belonged to..." –Hanson read the name and continued– "Dr. Spier...was born in nineteen oh-seven. That would make him a very old man. Rick, how old was the corpse?"

"I don't know, Mr. Hanson," Rick said. "I didn't get a look at him."

Hanson shook his head and sighed.

"The corpse, Dr. Spier," Abraham said, "Would have looked like a forty-year-old man. As I said, he was not much older than I."

"Make up your mind. Either these papers belonged to him or they didn't."

"Those were his papers."

"But you're telling me that he was not much older than you?"

"That is what I am telling you."

"How old are you?"

"We left Germany approximately five months before my thirty-sixth birthday."

"Thirty-six? But these papers would make Spier well over one-hundred years old."

Abraham nodded. "That is correct."

Hanson shook his head. "You're not making any sense at all."

"I left out one important detail."

"What was that?"

"We left Germany in nineteen-forty-five."

There was a stunned silence in the room for several seconds.

"Did he say..." Rick started.

Hanson silenced him with a raised hand.

"What did you say?" Hanson asked Abraham.

"We left Germany on March the twenty-seventh, nineteen-forty-five."

The silence returned. Hanson stood, his mouth partially open, his brow creased, as he looked at Abraham.

"Let me see if I understand," Hanson said. "The three of you left Germany in forty-five, and you arrived here in Flagler Beach two days ago? But you didn't age in the process. How is that possible?"

"I know how it's possible," Rick said.

Hanson frowned and sighed. "Really? What is your explanation?"

"Alien abduction. They were taken up in a UFO and brought to some other planet so the aliens could probe them and stuff. Then when the aliens were done with them, they brung 'em back, but their time is different from ours. They was probably only gone for a few minutes in alien time."

Abraham tried to suppress a grin.

"Jesus Christ," Hanson said. He looked at Abraham. "That's not right. Is it?"

Abraham shook his head. "No. He is incorrect, although he did have one thing right."

"What was that?"

"Our journey did not take very long. In fact, theoretically, it should have been nearly instantaneous."

"Instantaneous?" Hanson thought briefly. "That can only mean one thing."

Abraham nodded.

"Time travel?" Hanson said.

Abraham nodded again. "Yes."

Hanson pondered the idea for a minute. The others stood in mute disbelief.

"Stuart, cut them loose," Hanson said. "Sit down," he said to Abraham. "I want to hear this story. The whole story."

Abraham recounted his experiences in the bunker, his work on the Bell, the Russian invasion, the launch, and their arrival in Flagler Beach.

Hanson shook his head.

"I'm sorry. You expect me to believe that you, a Jew, were working with members of the party on a top-secret invention that would make time travel possible?"

"I do not expect anything. It is the truth."

"That makes no sense. Why would they include you?"

"It was my education. I studied quantum physics at Cambridge."

"Sweet Jesus," Hanson said. "Time travel. It's actually possible. And naturally it was discovered by the master race."

Abraham cringed at the words.

"This is why our mission is so important." Hanson said to the others. "Do you see, now?"

"Your mission?" Abraham asked.

"Yes. Our mission to secure a world dominated by the white man. Can you imagine the advancements that could have been made if Adolph Hitler had been allowed to fulfill his plan?"

"Advancements?" Abraham asked, barely able to mask his contempt.

"That's right. Your presence here is proof that the white man is superior in every way."

"But I just told you that the Germans selected me because of my education, and forced me to assist them in their work. Me. A Jew."

Hanson waved it off. "I'm sure your contributions were nothing a German couldn't have done, but the majority of able-bodied men were fighting the war."

Abraham lowered his head and sighed.

"Now for the important question," Hanson said. "Where is this...what did you call it?"

"Die Glocke," Abraham answered. "It means *The Bell*."

"Right. So where is this bell that brought you here?"

"That, I'm afraid, I don't know."

"How can you not know?"

"As I told you, we landed in the ocean, the Bell sank. Ike and his friends retrieved it and took it someplace, but I do not know where."

"Ike," Hanson said through gritted teeth. "That guy is wearing on my last nerve."

Ike and Brewski stopped behind a large bottle-brush bush. Ike checked his phone.

"They're predictable, if nothing else," he said.

"Where are they?" Brewski asked.

"Parked on the shoulder on the other side of A1A, no doubt looking as inconspicuous as an unmarked Ford with government tags can look."

They ran from the cover of the bush to the rear of Constance's trailer.

"Let's see if we can find anything in here that'll tell us where they might have taken Abraham and Eric."

The trailer was just as they had left it.

"Doesn't look like Constance has been home much lately," Ike said.

"Doesn't look like the maid's been here this month either," Brewski said.

"You take the bedrooms I'll look out here."

Brewski came out of the bedroom ten minutes later with an envelope in his hand.

"Find anything?" Brewski asked.

"Some neo-Nazi literature, pictures of Rick and Constance, and some pictures of Constance, obviously taken by Rick during some rather personal moments. I really wish I could un-see that. Nothing that helps us find them though. You?"

"I think I may have found something that could be useful."

"Yeah?"

"In the back of the bedroom closet, under a plastic tub full of clothes, there's a hatch in the floor. Underneath, I found this..." He handed Ike the envelope.

"Quest Imaging," Ike read from the envelope.

He removed the ultra-sound images and looked them over.

"Oh, now that is interesting," he said with a wide grin.

"I also found this," Brewski unwrapped a tee shirt to reveal a Glock nine-millimeter pistol.

"Good. You never know when a gun with somebody else's prints on it will come in handy."

Ike's phone rang.

"Yeah, Ralph," he answered.

"One of Geoffrey Hanson's acquaintances just called the restaurant line. He told Tiki to get a message to you."

"What's the message?"

"Be here in thirty minutes or Abraham and Eric die."

"Shit."

He put his phone away. "Time to go," he said.

"What's up?"

"Message from Hanson. We need to get to The Lion."

Twenty minutes later they parked their motorcycles in front of The Golden Lion and took seats at Ralph's table.

"Well, here we are," Ike said to Ralph. "Now what?"

"I don't know," Ralph said. "There were no instructions other than, 'Be here.'"

"Might as well have a beer," Brewski said as he headed toward the bar.

While waiting for Tiki to get their beers, Brewski admired a pair of women as they out got out of a car on the opposite side of A1A. As the driver leaned into the back seat to retrieve a beach bag, his view was blocked by a pickup truck. His anger at the interruption momentarily prevented him from recognizing the truck. Once the passenger's door opened and a blindfolded Eric was pushed out, he forgot about the beach-going women.

"Ike," he called as he took off for the street.

The pickup turned onto Fifth Street and sped off through the neighborhood behind the restaurant.

Ike and Brewski converged on Eric and hoisted him to his feet.

"You got this?" Brewski asked.

"Yeah. Go."

Brewski ran to his bike and was off after the truck, his Harley Davidson exhaust announcing his departure.

The pickup turned onto North Flagler Avenue and raced through the quiet residential neighborhood with

Brewski in pusuit. At the intersection of North Tenth the truck turned right, nearly going up on two wheels, and sped toward A1A where it turned north without slowing. Brewski slowed enough at the stop sign to check for oncoming traffic then took off in pursuit.

The pickup passed a flatbed tow truck, barely avoiding a head-on collision with a VW bus traveling in the southbound lane.

Brewski caught up to the flatbed. Strapped down on the back was the ten-foot-tall clown head from the mini-golf course. He moved his Harley over to the double yellow line but moved back quickly to get out of the way of an RV.

The clown stared at him, laughing with its huge, red mouth.

Brewski moved out to pass again only to have three cars force him back behind the flatbed, where the clown head continued to mock him, as if to let him know this was payback for the golf ball stuck in its face.

"Third time's the charm," Brewski said as he moved to the left of the yellow line, downshifted, and shot past the flatbed.

"See ya, Bozo," he said to the clown.

The Harley reached eighty. He popped the shifter up to fifth gear and brought the speedometer to nearly ninety, closing the gap between himself and the pickup to less than one hundred feet as they entered Beverly Beach.

The window at the back of the truck's cab slid open. Brewski considered taking his out his Glock but decided he would need both hands on the handlebars at this speed. Instead, he prepared to take evasive action in case he was shot at. No shots came, but one of Rick's friends wriggled through the small opening into the bed of the truck, where he then sat up and threw something out. Brewski swerved to the right to avoid the plastic antifreeze jug. The jug was followed by a four-foot piece of lumber, then two flower pots, full of dirt. Brewski avoided them and kept pace with the truck, which was now approaching seventy miles per hour. The man shouted something through the window to the driver, then turned back around and hoisted a cardboard box over his head and launched it into Brewski's path. When it hit the road, it burst, sending articles of clothing flying in every direction. Brewski maneuvered as best he could to avoid them, but his front tire ran directly over one piece. The sweatshirt was thrown up between the tire and the fork.

"Shit," Brewski said.

He immediately released the throttle and downshifted the bike to second gear, while veering toward the grass shoulder. The bike wobbled and bucked across a nicely manicured front yard. Brewski stood on the rear brake and was able to slow the bike to about fifteen miles per hour before the sweatshirt became entangled enough in the front tire to stop it from turning. The bike stopped dead, sending Brewski over the handlebars. He tumbled to a stop inches from a BMW in the driveway.

"Mother fucker," he cursed as he did a mental inventory of himself.

The driver of the flatbed gave a couple of short bursts from his air horn as he rumbled by. Brewski looked up to see the grinning face of the clown taunting him.

"Fuck you, Bozo," he grumbled.

Not sensing any major injuries, he walked to the bike and killed the engine.

He looked at the eight-hundred-pound Harley lying on its side partially embedded in the grass.

"Mother fucker," he said again, knowing he wouldn't be able to right it by himself.

The door to the house opened and a man in his early thirties, dressed as if he was about to play tennis, came out.

"Jesus," the man said. "Are you all right?"

"I'm standing," Brewski answered. "Which is more than I can say for ole-nuts-and-bolts here. "I don't suppose you'd like to help me stand her up."

"Sure. Of course. What do I do?"

"Reach on down there and grab the seat. I'll get the handlebars. On three, lift. But be careful. Once it's upright, don't let it keep going or we'll be picking it up from the other side."

"Got it."

The man nodded when he was ready.

"One, two, lift."

Brewski moved around to the other side once it was upright and lowered the kickstand. With the bike standing on its own he examined the offending article of clothing in the fork, which turned out to be a New York Yankees sweatshirt.

"Damn Yankees," he muttered.

His attempts to remove it were fruitless.

"Christ," he said. "This thing is really wedged in there."

The homeowner disappeared into the house and returned with a pair of scissors. Brewski cut the sweatshirt apart until the front tire was free.

"Now if you can just get behind and help me push it to the driveway," he said.

They rolled the bike to the driveway, and Brewski conducted a more thorough visual inspection. He readjusted the one mirror that was still intact, yanked off what was remaining of the windshield, and removed the chunks of grass from the engine.

"I don't see any other damage," he said.

"Geez, you were lucky," the man said.

"Yeah. I got a horseshoe up my ass," he said.

He handed the man a hundred dollars.

"That should take care of the lawn," he said.

He started the bike and gave a nod to the man.

"Thanks again," he said as he pulled away and headed back to The Golden Lion.

Ike removed the blindfold from Eric's eyes and they watched Brewski roar off after the truck.

"Are you okay?" Ike asked the boy.

Eric looked at him blankly.

"Okay?" Ike tried again. "Uhh, not hurt? Damn it."

Eric handed Ike a piece of paper.

Ike,
I still have your Jew friend. I want the Bell. Do not insult my intelligence by pretending you don't know what I'm talking about. The Jew told me the whole story. You have twenty-four hours before he dies. Call this number when you are ready to turn it over. 386-555-8264.

The note wasn't signed, but Ike knew immediately who it was from.

"Son of a bitch," he muttered.

He escorted Eric to Ralph's table and sat him down.

"I think you're old enough to drink now," he said, more to himself than a bewildered Eric.

He flagged down a server and told her to bring Eric a beer. "Something German," he called after her.

While they waited, he called Bill Eldredge.

"Hey, that historian friend of yours—she said she speaks German, right? Good. Are the two of you available for an emergency consultation? I'll buy you lunch. As soon as you can. Excellent. Thank you."

He hung up the phone and raised his bottle to Eric, who had just been handed a draft beer by the server.

"Cheers," Ike said.

"Prost," the boy replied.

Brewski arrived and sat down.

"Jesus. What happened to you?" Ike asked pointing, at the clumps of grass and dirt on Brewski's leather vest and the scratches on his bare chest.

"I was doing my impression of a lawn mower," he said.

He told Ike the story, after which Ike showed him the ransom note.

"What comes after pissed?" Brewski asked. "I was pissed when the redneck was throwing shit at me from the back of the truck and I had to do the roll and tumble back there. I was even more pissed when I realized I was going to have to buy a new windshield and a mirror. Now I'm whatever-comes-next."

"Fuming?" Ike suggested. "Livid maybe? How about wrathful?"

Brewski pointed at Ike. "I like that. Wrathful. These pricks are going to feel some wrath. We're talking biblical-type stuff."

"Once Abraham is safe, you can stake Hanson to a fire-ant mound, but let's get Abraham back first."

"Hold on, Ikey," Ralph said. "You're not considering giving this sociopath the time machine, are you?"

"Not if I can avoid it. Which means we need a plan that gets Abraham out and gives Hanson nothing in return."

"Piece of baklava," Brewski said. "While we're at it, we can find Jimmy Hoffa."

The ding of a small chime came from Ike's phone.

"Hm. I forgot about those two," he said, looking at it. "The feds just parked a block over, on Sixth Street."

"When it rains, it pours," Brewski said.

"You know what?" Ike said. "I'm really not in the mood."

Ike left the courtyard, walked a block north, and approached the Ford from the rear. He tapped on the driver's window.

The window lowered and Bronson, expressionless through his aviator sunglasses, looked out at Ike.

"Agent Bronson," Ike said. "I'm getting tired of this. I've got more important things to deal with than you and your damn conspiracy theories. Why don't you two go practice waterboarding each other?"

The look of apathy on Bronson's face dissolved into anger at the level of Ike's disrespect. He opened the door, forcing Ike back two steps, and climbed out of the car.

"Bronson," Freeman said.

Bronson held a hand up to his partner. He stepped to within six inches of Ike's barrel chest and looked up to meet his eyes.

"Ike," he said. "I understand that you're a really big fish in this little pond, here, but let me explain what you're up against. I represent one tooth in the mouth of a fish that will devour you like the plankton you are. Now go back to whatever important shit you're dealing with before I think of a reason to make you vanish."

"Are you threatening me, Agent Bronson?"

"It's not a threat. It's a promise. One phone call and you'll find yourself in a CIA holding cell where they'll interrogate you until you confess to the Kennedy assassination."

"Tough talk for a guy whose worst injury in the line of duty was a paper cut."

Bronson didn't take the bait. He got back in the car and rolled the window up. Ike resisted the urge to punch the window out, drag Bronson across A1A, and drown him in the ocean. Instead, he turned and walked back to The Golden Lion. On his way, a silver Volvo drove by. Before he reached the restaurant, it passed him again.

Bill and Mabel were just sitting down when he arrived at the table. The sight of Bill triggered a connection in his mind.

"Remember the Russian you said was on his way?" he said to Bill.

"Hi," Bill said. "I'm fine. How are you?"

"Sorry. I'm a little distracted. You remember the Russian?"

"Yeah. Of course."

"I think I just saw him."

"Where?"

"He was circling the block. Bronson and Freeman are parked over on Sixth. I'll bet he's keeping tabs on them. I saw the same car earlier when Bronson and Freeman were leaving their hotel."

"So what?" Brewski asked. "The Russian is their problem, not ours. We've got enough to deal with."

"True, but you know what they say, 'the enemy of my enemy is my friend.'"

"Who are *they*?" Brewski asked.

"Everybody who's ever fought a war. We were allies with Russia during World War II. Why not try again?"

"Is this going to help get Abraham back?"

"Abraham's gone?" Bill asked. "What happened?"

Ike held up a finger. "In a minute," he said. "I have to make a quick phone call."

He stepped away from the table.

"So," Brewski said to Mabel. "Did you miss me?"

Mabel pushed a lock of blonde hair behind her ear and blushed.

"Well, I...uhh..."

"It's okay," he said. "I understand you don't want to say it in front of all these people." He threw her a wink. "We'll talk later."

She looked at Bill with a question in her eyes. Ralph laughed.

Ike returned and sat down.

"I called Bob Butler. He's going to tail the Russian. Now we can get down to business."

"Brewski already tried that," Ralph said.

"Here's the situation," Ike said. "Geoffrey Hanson and his neo-Nazi friends kidnapped Abraham and Eric. I don't know what their initial purpose was. I assumed it was for use as leverage against Ralph in Hanson's quest for The Lion. It appears that he now has a different objective. A little while ago, they returned Eric with this note."

Ike handed the note to Bill. He and Mabel read it.

"He knows?" Bill asked.

"Apparently."

"This is not good," Bill said.

"Tell me about it."

"I'm serious," Bill said. "There are only two reasons a guy like Hanson would want the Bell. The first would be to use it, which could have catastrophic results, the likes of which we can't even comprehend."

"And the second?"

"To sell it to the highest bidder. I doubt the U.S. and Russia are the only two countries that would like to get their hands on it."

"Don't worry," Ike said. "Neither of those things is going to happen. We just need a plan, but first we need some intel. Which is why I asked you to bring Mabel."

"Me?"

"We need to ask Eric about his experience with Hanson. He might know something useful."

"Okay," Mabel said. "But my German is a bit rusty."

"I'm sure it'll be good enough," Ike said.

"I'm sure it'll be more than good enough," Brewski said.

"Okay," she said. "Where do we start?"

"Just tell him to tell us everything that happened from the time he was taken until the time he was dropped off here."

Mabel relayed the question and Eric began his story.

"He says three men came to the boat and took them. Abraham tried to stop them but they punched him, and took them away in a truck. He says they went to..." she paused while Eric tried to find the right words to describe where he had been taken. "...he says it reminded him of a camp."

"A camp?" Ike asked. "Can you ask him to describe it?"

"He says there were many buildings made of metal, in rows. They were low and narrow, and I think he's trying to say rusty. Inside it was furnished like a home."

"The trailer park. We just had the wrong trailer," Ike said.

"He says they made him sit in a chair, but they put Abraham in another room. Once they realized he only spoke German they brought Abraham out to translate. Abraham told Eric, in German, not to worry and that he would take care of things. The man in charge showed them a paper," she said. "Eric refers to it as an ausweis. I'm not sure of the literal translation."

"Identity papers," Bill said.

"The ausweis belonged to one of the scientists from the bunker," she continued. "He is the one who was killed. The man wanted an explanation for the papers. At this point Abraham told Eric that he was going to say they knew nothing about them. The man didn't believe it. He had one of the other men punch Abraham several times. When Abraham refused to cooperate the man who had been punching Abraham began to strangle Eric. That is when

Abraham agreed to confess. He apologized to Eric before he did."

"Abraham talked to save Eric," Brewski said. "Isn't that ironic?"

"Ironic, yes," Ike said, "but not surprising."

"Eric says Abraham told them about the papers and they spoke at length, during which time the only word Eric understood was 'bell.' The next thing he knew they were blindfolding him and taking him out. Abraham's last words to Eric as they were leaving were to tell you not to do anything to save him. He would rather die than to let Hanson have the Bell."

"Jesus," Brewski said.

Ike shook his head. "Abraham is not going to die, and Hanson is not getting the Bell. Not if I have anything to do with it."

"What I don't understand," Ralph said, "is why did he keep Abraham? If the guy is a neo-Nazi, wouldn't you think he'd rather keep the boy instead? It's like a ready-made recruit."

There was silence at the table.

"A driver," Bill said.

"What?" Ike asked.

"He needs somebody to operate the Bell. Abraham is, quite literally, the only man alive who knows how it works."

"So, the neo-Nazi needs help from a Jew," Brewski said. "More irony."

"Yes, but you know what it means," Mabel said.

"We'll never see Abraham again," Ike said.

"True," Bill said. "It could also be a death sentence for him."

"How so?" Ike asked.

"Think about it," Bill said. "All Hanson has to do on his first trip is go back to 1944, before this all happened, find the scientists who are working on it and show them that it worked. He'll be a hero, and they won't need Abraham anymore. Hanson will be an instant rock star in Nazi

Germany, and they'll probably shoot Abraham on the spot, if he's lucky."

"And if he's not lucky?"

"They'll torture him to get any useful information and then throw him into one of the camps."

"Like I said," Ike stated, "that's not happening."

18

Alex Grichenko turned the air conditioning up in the Volvo. He adjusted the microphone settings on his phone, seated in the windshield mount, and pointed the pen/mic at the Ford. Agents Bronson and Freeman engaged in idle chatter about sports, movies, and food. Bronson asked Freeman how the kids were handling the divorce, and then the two agents exchanged observations about pedestrians walking by on A1A.

Alex sat up when a vintage, late-60s Pontiac LeMans parked on the ocean side of A1A. Classic Detroit muscle cars—another thing he loved about America.

A man and a woman got out of the car. The man took pictures of the woman, some with the Atlantic Ocean as a backdrop and others from a variety of vantage points. After a few minutes, they sat at the picnic table at the top of the dune walkover and admired the ocean.

Alex could easily see himself doing the same thing.

The topic of discussion between Bronson and Freeman changed to a man named Ike.

"You shouldn't have threatened him. We're supposed to maintain a low profile," Freeman said.

"Screw low profile, and screw Ike. For fifty cents I'd kick his ass," Bronson said. *"If he wasn't our only lead."*

"Lucky for you, he is," Freeman said with a laugh.

"Screw you, too."

"*Actually, he isn't our only lead. There's still Frederick Turner.*"

"*I told you, Turner is probably a dead end. At best, all he'll do is lead us back to Ike.*"

"*Well, sitting here is accomplishing a whole lot of nothing.*"

Bronson shook his head and sighed.

"*Fine. We'll go back to the trailer park and look for his truck. A guy like that, all we need is ten minutes with him and he'd sell out his mother. Then we'll get back to Ike.*"

"*Let's do it, but let's go back to the hotel first and grab some lunch. Watching that cop devour that burrito made me hungry.*"

Alex entered the two new leads, Ike and Frederick Turner, into his Surface Pro then followed the Americans back to the hotel.

The gold Pontiac LeMans pulled over on North Fifth Street outside the picket fence of The Golden Lion's courtyard. Bob and Lynn Butler made their way to Ralph's table.

"How'd it go?" Ike asked Bob Butler.

"No problem," he said. "He was watching the Crown Vic just like you said. After a few minutes the Ford left, and the Volvo followed. They went to The Topaz. The guys in the Ford went into room 108. The Russian guy went into room 104."

"Jesus," Ike said. "They're all staying at the same hotel?"

"Yup. They all went into the restaurant; we came back here. I got some pictures of the Russian guy if you want them."

He handed his camera to Bill, who downloaded the pictures onto Ike's phone.

Ike shook Bob Butler's hand and hugged Lynn.

"Thanks, guys."

"Any time."

The Butlers returned to the LeMans, put the convertible top down, and drove off. Ike opened the listening app on his phone and set it on the table.

"Just in case they say anything good. In the meantime, since they're eating, I say we should too."

"Let's talk this thing out," Ike said while they ate. "We know what the Russian is driving and we know what he looks like. Bronson and Freeman don't know he's here. At least not for sure. Like Bill said, they know the Russians are monitoring the situation, which means they assume they, the Russians, are not far away, if they aren't already here. But they haven't mentioned anything about it in their conversations, so they don't know for sure. Our main objective is to get Abraham back unharmed. Secondary objective is to solve the Hanson problems."

"And hopefully make him go away," Brewski added.

"If possible," Ike said.

"Don't forget the Bell," Bill said.

"How could we?" Ike said. "That's what started this whole party."

"We definitely want to keep it out of Russia's hands," Bill said.

"And we don't want the CIA to get it, either," Ike said.

"It's too big for a lawn ornament," Bill quipped.

"Here's what we do," Brewski said after washing down a mouthful of a steak sandwich with his beer. "Tonight, when the Russian is sleeping, we sneak into his room, steal his gun, shoot Hanson with it, then bring the gun back. Then we plant Hanson's body at the time machine and blow it up. We tell the CIA guys about it, and the Russian gets blamed for assassinating a U.S. Senator and, destroying a piece of history, and we get rid of a real asshole. It's win-win."

Ike, Ralph, Bill, and Mabel looked at him.

"What?" Brewski said.

"Let's see if we can't come up with something a little less violent," Ike said. "If not, we'll revisit your idea."

"Fine."

"Actually," Bill said, "the concept isn't bad."

"You see?" Brewski said, sitting back in his chair. "Thank you, Bill."

"Well, I meant the concept. Not the killing."

"What do you mean, Bill?" Ike asked.

"I mean the concept of somehow using the Russian to take the heat isn't bad."

Ike nodded. "I agree with that. But how?"

"Let's see," Bill thought out loud. "Everybody wants the time machine, right?"

"Except us," Ike said.

"Right. Hanson, the CIA guys, and the Russian, though, are all after it. We need Hanson to at least think we're giving it to him so he'll let Abraham go."

"Except he probably isn't going to do that."

"True, but he doesn't know that we know that. Now, the CIA doesn't know, for sure, that the Russian is here, but we know he's following them, and we also know they're following you two."

"All true," Ike said. "But all that guarantees is that we'll all be in the same place at the same time. I don't see how that helps us."

"Mr. Turner, I assume," came Bronson's voice over Ike's cell phone.

They all sat up and leaned closer to the phone.

"Holy shit," Ike said. "They found Rick."

Once the bald guy on the Harley was out of the picture, Rick relaxed and took the pickup's speed down to a slightly illegal sixty miles per hour.

"I gotta stop at my place on the way back," Rick said to Elvin. "I want to make sure everything's okay."

The pickup skidded to a stop in front of the trailer.

"Jesus," Rick said when he reached the front door. "Would ya look at that? That son of a bitch owes me for a new door."

After a quick walk-through, he grabbed a can of beer from the fridge.

"You know what?" he said. "I'm gonna take a quick shower while we're here."

"We got time for that?" Elvin asked.

"Shit, yeah, we got time. Just have a beer and relax. I'll be out in ten minutes."

Fifteen minutes later, Rick emerged from the bathroom with a towel around his waist, his hair dripping, and grabbed his beer from the counter.

"Just gimmee five more..."

"Mr. Turner, I assume."

Rick stopped in his tracks to see a man standing just inside the front doorway, and it didn't take a genius to figure out he was a cop. He dropped his beer and turned for the back door only to see another cop preventing his escape.

Rick put his hands up and his towel fell to the floor.

"Why don't you put that back on?" the first cop said.

Rick wrapped the towel around his waist.

"Hey, look, man. That guy was chasing us. I think he was fixin' to kill us. We had to throw that stuff at him."

"Take it easy, Mr. Turner. We just want to ask you some questions."

"About the guy on the motorcycle?"

"Just relax. Have a seat," the cop pointed to the worn sofa. "This shouldn't take long."

"Can I at least put my pants on?"

"In a minute."

Rick and Elvin sat at opposite ends of the couch. They glanced at each other nervously before Rick turned back to the cop.

"Okay. Whaddya want?"

"And you are?" the cop asked Elvin.

"Uh. I'm Elvin. Elvin Hunt."

The cop took some folded papers from the inside pocket of his jacket, opened them and looked from the paper to Elvin.

"Yes. Good. This saves us the trouble of looking for you."

He handed one of the pages to Rick.

"That's a picture of you two, and a third man, as yet unidentified, going into the coroner's office the other day."

He handed him another page.

"And here you are coming out."

A third page.

"And here's the three of you getting in your truck and taking off."

The cop looked at him with a weird grin.

"Can we agree on that?"

Rick and Elvin said nothing.

"Just say yes," the cop said.

"Yes," they said in unison.

"Good. Now, the first picture was taken just before the coroner was assaulted and robbed by three men. The second was taken just after. And the third, well, that was a couple of minutes later. Do you see the way I'm steering the boat here, Mr. Turner?"

"Boat?"

"Do you see what I'm getting at? Do you see the connection?"

Rick wasn't sure what to say. He started replaying all the cop and lawyer shows he had watched and wondered if he should plead the fifth. The problem was that he wasn't sure exactly what that meant.

"Here's the connection, Mr. Turner," the cop said. "You and your two friends hit the coroner upside his head and stole some papers. Some old papers. Where are they?"

"We ain't got 'em."

"Well, who does?"

Rick and Elvin exchanged another nervous look.

"Listen, boys," the cop said. "If you don't tell us who has the papers, we'll have to assume you're lying to us. We'll haul you in and lock you up until we find them. If it takes us too long to get them back, we might just forget where we left you. Meanwhile, whoever you're protecting gets away scot-free. That seem fair to you?"

Rick shook his head.

"Good. We finally agree on something. So, what's it going to be? Do we take you in with your towel on? I'm sure you'll make friends really fast."

Rick put his hands up.

"Okay. Okay. I did it for Mr. Hanson."

"Mr. Hanson?"

"Yeah. He told me to follow that Ike guy and that's where he went. I figured if he was interested in the papers, then Mr. Hanson would be too."

"So, this Mr. Hanson has the papers now?"

"Yeah."

"And what is his interest in them?"

"Well, at first he didn't have no interest in them. He even got real mad at me for taking them. But then he sort of figured out that there was a connection between them papers and the two fellas Ike was hiding on his boat, so he sent us to grab them."

"Grab what?"

"Not what. Who. The two guys on Ike's boat."

Elvin shot a backhanded slap to Rick's arm.

"Dude. Shut up," Elvin said

"No, man. I ain't goin' to prison for him. Everything we did was because he told us to."

"That's right," the cop said. "You're helping yourself by telling us. So, you grabbed two men from Ike's boat?"

"Yeah. One was real young, like a teenager, but he don't speak English. The other one was older. He's a Jew, but he speaks English and German. See, at first, Mr. Hanson only wanted the kid, you know, cuz he was German. But I took some initiative and grabbed the other guy because he could be a transmitter."

"Translator," Elvin said. "And the only reason you took him was 'cause I told you to."

"Shut up, Elvin."

"Okay," the cop interrupted. "Back to the two men. Where did you bring them?"

"Mr. Hanson, he's got a trailer just a few lots over. They're all over there. Waitin' on us. See, a little bit ago we dumped the kid off at The Golden Lion. Mr. Hanson wants to make a deal with Ike for the other guy."

"A deal? What kind of a deal?

"He wants..."

Elvin leaned over and whispered in Rick's ear.

Rick nodded.

"Okay. Now it's gettin' to the point where *we*," he pointed at himself and Elvin, and then at the cop. "need to talk about a deal."

"Is that right? What kind of deal did you have in mind?"

"First, let me get dressed. Then we'll talk."

The two cops exchanged a look then nodded.

"All right," the cop said. "Agent Freeman is going to check out the bedroom first. Which one is it?"

Rick pointed down the hall.

"First one on the left."

The other cop went into the bedroom and came back a minute later.

"One window. Didn't see any weapons."

"Okay, Mr. Turner," the first cop said. "Go get dressed. You have three minutes. After that your friend here gets shot."

Freeman stood next to Bronson and spoke quietly.

"He's got a Nazi flag in the bedroom and I found this on the kitchen counter."

He handed Bronson some neo-Nazi propaganda.

"Interesting," Bronson said. "I wonder if this Hanson guy is their Führer."

"I can hardly wait to meet him."

"I'll tell you something. The south may rise again, but these idiots won't be leading the charge."

Freeman chuckled.

"You better go check on him," Bronson said.

Freeman walked to the bedroom.

"You all right in there?" he called before looking in.

Rick was pulling a camouflage tee shirt over his head.

"Yeah, man. Geez. How about a break?"

Freeman escorted Rick back to the sofa.

"Feel better?" Bronson asked.

Rick nodded.

"Okay," Bronson said. "Where were we? Oh, yeah. You were about to tell us about this deal Mr. Hanson wanted to make with Ike."

Rick smiled at him and shook his head.

"No, sir. My mama didn't raise no dummy. We was about to talk about a deal between you and me."

"And me," Elvin said.

"Oh, yeah," Bronson said. "Okay. Here's what I'll do. You tell me what kind of deal Hanson wants then take me to him. Once we get there, I'll let you walk. You can disappear. We never saw you."

Rick and Elvin looked at each other.

"Do we need it in writing?" Elvin asked.

Nah," Bronson waved his hand. "You have my word."

"Your word?" Rick asked.

Bronson put his right hand up. "Hand to God," he said.

"He's a very religious man," Freeman added.

Rick inhaled deeply.

"All right." He pointed at Bronson. "I got your word."

Bronson put his hand on his heart and nodded.

"Here's the story," Rick said. "Mr. Hanson was using the older guy as a translator so he could talk to the kid. See, Mr. Hanson knew there was something special about them papers, but that Jew, he wouldn't talk, even after a few good kidney punches. So then Mr. Hanson's man, Stuart, he went over and started choking the kid. I mean this kid was about to pass out. That's when the Jew broke down and told the story."

"What story?"

Rick rubbed his hands together.

"You ain't gonna believe this shit."

"Try us."

"A time machine."

Rick grinned from ear to ear and sat back on the sofa, causing a small plume of dust to rise and hover in the shaft of sunlight making its way through the filthy window.

Bronson and Freeman exchanged a glance but maintained their poker faces.

"A time machine?" Bronson asked.

"That's right," Rick said. "See? I told you y'all wasn't gonna believe it!"

"Come on, Mr. Turner. Do you really expect us to give you a deal based on some science-fiction story?"

Rick shook his head rapidly.

"This ain't no science fiction, man. Them papers we took from the coroner? They was from World War II. One of the guys in the time machine died, and they found them papers on him. It's the truth."

"It is," Elvin added with a nod.

A cell phone on the counter vibrated then played the opening bars of Dixie. Freeman picked it up.

"Somebody named Kip calling," he said to Rick.

He pressed the button to ignore the call and put the phone back on the counter.

"He'll leave you a message," he said."

"Now you were saying," Bronson said.

"Hanson wants to trade the Jew to Ike for the time machine," Rick said.

"Ike has the time machine?"

"According to the Jew."

"How do you expect us to believe there's a time machine out there somewhere and Ike is the guy who knows where it is?"

Rick shrugged. "I don't know. But I'm telling you the truth."

"Okay. Sit tight for a minute."

Bronson motioned Freeman over and they spoke softly with their backs to Rick and Elvin.

"How should we play this?" Bronson asked.

"Drill him a little more, make sure he's consistent, but keep up the *we don't believe you* stuff. Then when he gets really frustrated, tell him we're going to need proof. Have him take us to Hanson. If Hanson's as dumb as these two, we'll turn him too. We'll tell him that they'll all go to jail if they don't get Ike to lead us to the Bell."

"Okay," Bronson said. "Looks like this assignment might be over soon."

"Let's not get our hopes up. Remember who we're dealing with. I'm surprised these idiots can even tell time, let alone lead us to a time machine."

While they sat at the table, listening to the conversation between Bronson and Rick, Ike stood up.

"Bill, can you and Mabel keep an eye on Eric for me?"

"No problem. What are you going to do?"

"We know the Russian won't be far away from Bronson and Freeman. Brewski and I are going up there, find him, and make him an offer."

"What kind of offer?" Brewski asked.

"I don't know. I'm making this up as we go."

19

Geoffrey Hanson sat in the recliner, his leg bouncing up and down keeping time to a song only he could hear. Stuart paced the room, looking at his watch every thirty seconds. Abraham sat, still and quiet, in the other chair. Kip sat on the kitchen counter, drinking beer and talking quietly to Constance.

"Where the hell are they?" Hanson asked. "They should have been back by now."

Nobody answered him.

"Christ," he said. "It was a simple assignment. I wonder if that moron took some more initiative and got himself arrested."

"Wouldn't surprise me," Stuart said.

"Call him," Hanson pointed at Kip.

Kip took out his cell phone. After a minute he spoke.

"Hey, Rick. It's Kip. Mr. Hanson wants to know where you are. Call me."

He returned the phone to his pocket.

"No answer," he told Hanson.

"Get your ass over to his trailer and see if he's there. He probably picked up a damn hooker on his way back."

"Hey," Constance said.

"Just go," Hanson said to Kip.

Alex Grichenko found a place in the shade where he could sit in his car and still watch the Americans drive into the trailer park.

They got out of their car and entered one of the mobile homes. The trailer was at least a hundred yards away. His directional mic was good for a hundred feet under ideal conditions—which the low-hanging branches of the trees and the numerous trailers between him and them did not create. In this area, he would need to be less than fifty feet away. Knowing the Americans could possibly be closing in on the Bell, Alex couldn't afford to miss anything.

Driving into the trailer park would be as bad as announcing his arrival over a megaphone. He would have to go in on foot and try to maintain a concealed position that would still allow him to monitor their conversation.

The trailer next to the one they had gone into was, by all outward appearances, abandoned. A small set of dilapidated wooden steps on the side offered him a position that allowed him to aim his microphone at an open window in the front of the other trailer.

The Americans were questioning two men.

After several minutes of this, one of the men blurted out the words *time machine.*

There were several mentions of a man named Hanson, which meant nothing to Alex, but when the man being questioned mentioned Ike, Alex knew the pieces were falling together. He repositioned himself in an attempt to get better reception, but in so doing leaned against the door immediately behind him.

The door opened and Alex rolled backward into the trailer.

The first thing to hit him was the stench of stale air, mixed with the odor of marijuana. He rolled to his knees to see five teenagers sitting on the ragged furniture passing a glass pipe between them.

Ten eyes stared at Alex, dumbfounded. Alex stared back equally surprised. Having the advantage of excellent training, and of not being stoned, he jumped to his feet.

"What's going on here?" he demanded.

A girl, sitting between two boys on a filthy sofa screamed and ran past him and out the front door. One of the boys jumped to his feet with his hands in the air.

"Don't shoot," he yelled.

Alex held a hand up, trying to quiet him before the American agents heard anything.

"Run," one of the other boys yelled.

The four kids sprinted for the front door, slamming through it and running down the dirt road, some laughing, some yelling.

Alex ducked out of sight and checked the windows of the trailer next door for signs that his cover had been blown.

After several seconds, he pointed the mic at the other trailer, keeping it close to the door jamb. The conversation was continuing. The American agents were telling the man they didn't believe his story. A textbook method to get him to expand without asking specific questions.

"How do you expect us to believe there's a time machine out there somewhere and Ike is the guy who knows where it is?"

"I don't know. But I'm telling you the truth."

Movement near the front door across from him caught his eye. A man wearing a tank top, jeans, work boots, and a baseball hat climbed the steps to the trailer where the Americans were questioning the two men. If the newcomer looked to his left, he would see the open door where Alex was standing. If he decided to investigate, things could get messy.

"Yo, Rick," the man called out. "You in there?"

Alex waited until the man was engaged in conversation with somebody inside the trailer then snuck down the steps and returned to his car as quickly as possible without attracting attention. Visual surveillance would have to suffice, at least for now.

He started the engine and turned on the air conditioning.

No sooner did he feel the cool air on his face than a motorcycle turned off the road and parked on the dirt shoulder in front of his car. The rider dismounted and approached Alex's car motioning for him to roll the window down.

"Hey," the man said. "You got a cigarette?"

Before Alex could reply, his passenger door opened and another man, much larger than the first, climbed in and closed the door. With a forty-five pointed at Alex's midsection, he said, "Hello, comrade. What do you say we have a chat?"

The two cops perked up when they heard a ruckus outside. The first one motioned for the second one to check it out.

"Just some kids running down the street."

A minute later, they heard the footsteps on the stairs outside.

"What now?" the first cop asked.

They moved toward the bedroom.

"Whoever it is," the first cop told Rick, "get rid of them or all three of you will be in jail within the hour."

"Yo, Rick," Kip called. "You in there?"

Rick got up and nervously looked around before walking to the door.

"Hey," he said, blocking Kip from entering. "What's up?"

"Hey, bro," Kip said nervously. "Hanson's about fixin' to have a shit fit. Where the hell you been?"

"No biggie, man. I stopped to grab a beer and take a shower. Tell him it's all good. I'll be there in a couple of minutes."

"All right, man. But don't keep him waiting too long. He's pissed."

"Five minutes," Rick said, closing the door.

He watched out the window to make sure Kip was out of sight.

"Damn," he said to the cops when they returned. "It's a good thing you parked behind my truck. Kip didn't notice your car. If he did, we'd all be in the shit."

"Good job," the cop said. "I almost believed you myself. Now let's get back to the time machine."

"Dude," Rick protested. "Did you hear what just happened? If I don't get back there, Hanson will come over here and cut my balls off."

"You let us worry about Hanson," the cop told him. "Tell us the story again. From the top."

Ike's first impression of the Russian was one of respect.

Here he was, sitting in his car, ostensibly minding his own business, when two men show up and threaten him with a gun.

To his credit, the Russian kept his cool, which told Ike that he had either had guns pointed at him many times or he had received some very good training. Or both.

"What's the meaning of this?" the Russian asked.

"Take it easy, Ivan. We just want to talk."

Brewski slid into the back seat, leaned over, and frisked him.

"Clean," he said to Ike.

"Who are you? What do you want?"

"Your English is pretty impressive. Midwestern, very little accent. Where you from?"

"What? I'm from Iowa. I'm on vacation."

"What's the capital of Iowa, Ivan."

"Des Moines. What is this all about? Why do you keep calling me Ivan? My name is Peter Green. Here. I'll prove it."

The Russian moved to get his wallet. Brewski rapped him on the back of the head with his Glock. "Keep your hands on the wheel."

The Russian put his hands at ten and two.

"Look," he said, "if you want money, I've got a couple hundred dollars and some credit cards in my wallet. You can have it."

"It's not about money, Ivan. We know who you are. We know why you're here, and we're hoping that if we give you what you want, you'll help us get what we want. You follow?"

The Russian glanced at Ike's forty-five then at Brewski in the rearview mirror. He sat back in his seat.

"What is it you think I want?" he asked.

"The Bell," Ike answered.

A look of surprise so brief it was barely noticeable crossed his face, followed by a slight grin.

"I assume you're Ike," he said.

"Hey. Would ya look at that?" Brewski said. "Do me next."

"And how do you know who I am, Mr. Green?"

"My name is Alex Grichenko. I am with the Scientific Recovery Bureau. A division of the KGB. You obviously know why I am here. I have been monitoring your CIA agents. I've heard your name several times. They are not happy with you."

"Story of my life."

"And now they are reasonably sure that you have possession of the Bell."

"Yeah. So I've heard."

"Explain one thing to me."

"If I can."

"If you have the Bell, surely you know its value. Both of our countries would stop at nothing to secure it. Why come to me with a deal?"

"You haven't heard the deal yet."

20

When Ike returned to The Golden Lion, he had Alex Grichenko in tow, drawing confused looks from the others.

Ike made introductions after they had sat down.

"Where's Brewski?" Bill asked.

"He's on special assignment."

"Oh, boy. This should be interesting."

A few minutes later, Brian McMillan arrived.

"For those who don't know," Ike said, "this is Brian McMillan of The Palm Coast Observer. He'll be representing the press in this affair."

"I take it you have a plan," Bill said.

"I do," Ike said. "First, I need you to set this up so I can record my next call."

Bill took the phone.

"It'll take a couple of minutes to download the app."

When it was done, he handed the phone back to Ike. "Just turn it on, and it will record every call you make until you turn it off."

"Okay. Once I make this call, we pass the point of no return."

"Who are you calling?" Bill asked.

"Hanson. I'm going to tell him he has a deal."

"What?" Bill said. "Are you serious?"

"Where's your faith?" Ike said.

"Oh, boy. Like I said. This is going to be a very interesting night."

Ike called the number on the ransom note.

"May I speak to Senator Hanson?" he said. "Senator Hanson, I'm calling about your offer. I think we can make a deal, but first I have a few conditions."

"I'm listening," Hanson said.

"First, I know you have no intention of releasing Abraham. You need him to operate the Bell."

"Very clever," Hanson said.

"It wasn't hard to figure out."

"So, what are your conditions?"

"To start, one million dollars wired to an off-shore account."

"A million dollars?"

"A million dollars. Unless you'd rather I turn it over to the real government."

Hanson was quiet for a minute.

"Fine. A million dollars."

"Excellent. I'll text the account number to you as soon as we hang up."

Ike picked up a pen and scribbled on a napkin then handed it to Bill.

"Sure," Bill muttered. "Create an off-shore account in ten minutes. Anything else?"

Ike shook his head and smiled.

"Second condition," he said to Hanson. "You forget about The Golden Lion, and every other business in Flagler Beach. Your gentrification program is over."

"Are you that concerned about blacks and Mexicans?"

"I'm concerned with people."

"Fine. You can stop me from doing good in Flagler Beach, but it's a big country. You can't police all of it."

"No, I can't. Just my corner of it."

"Whatever," Hanson said. "What's your next condition?"

"This one is more of a tip than a condition."

"Explain."

"Right now, there are two CIA agents interrogating your boy Rick in his trailer. And Rick, being the all-American idiot he is, is about to sell you down the river. If I were you,

I'd get the hell out of Dodge. I'll call you tonight at eight with further instructions, assuming the money is in my account."

Ike disconnected and handed the phone to Bill.

"Can you send the recording of that conversation to Brian?"

A minute later, Brian's phone chimed. He played the conversation back.

"Is that enough?" Ike asked.

"It's plenty," Brian told him.

"Okay, but you only use it if this thing goes south. With any luck, we won't need it."

"Got it," Brian said.

He shook Ike's hand and left.

"I'd like to be a fly on the wall in that room," Ike said to the others.

"So, what happens tonight?" Bill asked.

"I'm still trying to work out the details, but I figure if we get all the interested parties together, the CIA and Moscow can fight it out for possession of the Bell, and with any luck, Hanson will probably get arrested. Somewhere during the process, we grab Abraham away from Hanson and let the chips fall where they will."

"That's your plan?"

"I told you I haven't worked out the details yet."

Hanson stuffed his phone into his jacket pocket and turned to Kip.

"When you went to Rick's trailer, you said he was alone?"

"Well, I figured he was. He didn't exactly let me in."

"God damn it. I'm surrounded by morons. Stuart, I want you to round up as many men as you can. Make sure they're armed to the teeth. Once he tells me where the time machine is, we are going to show up in force in case he's got any cute ideas. I've had it up to my eyes with this guy."

"You got it," Stuart said.

"But right now," Hanson said, "we need to go."

"Problem?" Stuart asked.

"Federal agents. They'll be here any minute thanks to that idiot, Turner. He's becoming a liability. I want him dealt with."

"What does that mean?" Constance asked.

"This doesn't concern you."

"If y'all are talking about Rick being dealt with, it concerns me."

"Don't worry. There's plenty more where he came from, and let's face it, you're not exactly the picky type."

"Are you saying what I think you're saying?"

"Figure it out. I don't have time to explain the obvious. Come on, Stuart, we have to go." He pointed at Abraham. "Let's go. Time to move."

"Where are you going?" Constance asked.

The door slammed and she found herself alone with Kip.

"What do we do now?" Kip asked.

Constance thought for a moment while she chewed a fingernail.

"You do whatever you want," she told Kip, and spit out a piece of nail. "I'm outta here."

Bronson held up a hand to Rick.

"All right. You can stop. We believe you. Now let's go meet your friend Hanson."

"Remember," Rick said as they walked out. "I get protection."

"You got it, Bubba."

They walked four trailers over and climbed the steps.

"What the..." Rick said. "Why's the door open?"

They entered the trailer and stood in the empty living room. In the kitchen, Ike's bald friend closed the refrigerator and walked toward them, opening a beer.

"How's it going?" he said. "My name's Brewski. I hope you aren't too disappointed, but Mr. Hanson remembered a previous engagement, so he had to split."

"What's going on here?" Bronson asked. "If this was some kind of a setup," he said to Rick.

"Take it easy there, Captain America," Brewski said, dropping into the recliner. "I'm sure whatever Ricky-boy told you was true when he told it to you, but time changes things. It's the way of the world."

"What are you doing here?"

"I'm here to invite you to a special event."

"What are you talking about? What kind of event?"

"I guess you could call it an auction. Sort of."

"An auction."

"Yes. Your auctioneer will be Ike."

Brewski drank some beer and grinned.

"You realize that we are federal agents and that what you are doing is tantamount to obstruction. We could arrest you right now and ship you off to Guantanamo. Nobody would ever see you again."

Brewski drank some more beer and nodded. "Yup. You could. But I figure sending me off to Gitmo isn't going to do much to salvage your ass after you lose the Bell to the Russians, or worse, a rogue third party."

"Russians?"

"Yeah. You know—the bad guys."

"What do the Russians have to do with this? And what third party?"

"The way it's playing out is the Russians feel they're the rightful owners of the Bell. Of course, America wants it, too, because we're the good guys. Then there is another interested party who I'm sure Rick has already told you about. He's willing to pay handsomely for it, as well. So, in the interest of fair play, and all that shit, the three of you can meet at the auction block in a one-time, winner-take-all bid fest. Of course, if you're not interested..." He stood up and downed the last of the beer. "I'll just be on my way."

"Hang on." Bronson stopped him just as he reached the door. "Where and when?"

"Tonight. Be ready to move at eight. Ike will call you with the location and other details."

Brewski walked out before Bronson could reply. They heard his Harley start up and roar off into the distance.

While Ike made his phone calls, Alex strolled to the tiki bar and asked the bartender for something Americans love to drink while they're at the beach. The bartender, whose badge read *Tiki*, handed him a large margarita. He walked to the fence and gazed at the ocean. The azure surface rolled gently under the cloudless sky. The horizon was nearly seamless. A few young people played volleyball. Families splashed in the waves or dined on picnic lunches under open-sided tents. Almost on cue, a man began playing the steel drums on the bandstand in the courtyard.

For the first time in his life, Alex Grichenko felt as if he were home.

Ike was finishing a phone call when Alex returned to the table.

"I think we're good to go," Ike said to him. "One way or another you'll be done with this assignment by this time tomorrow. Then I guess it's back to Russia, or Iowa, or wherever it is you call home. Have you spoken to your people about how much they're willing to spend?"

Alex took a long sip of his margarita then looked Ike in the eye.

"Is there someplace we can talk?"

Ike led him to Ralph's office and closed the door.

"What's up?" he asked.

"I haven't spoken to Moscow about the Bell yet."

Ike spread his hands. "Why not?"

"Do you trust *your* government?"

Ike snorted a laugh.

"I thought as much," Alex said. "I feel the same way about mine, maybe more than you. So why are we going to let one of them have such a potentially dangerous piece of historic technology?"

Ike shook his head. "Well, the wheels are in motion, and there ain't no brakeman on this train."

"We don't have to stop it," Alex said. "Just alter its course slightly."

Ike and Alex came out of the office. Ike leaned over and said something to Mabel. After a brief look of confusion she nodded, took her phone out, and excused herself from the table.

Ike picked up his phone and dialed a number.

"Who are you calling now?" Bill asked.

"John Dwyer. We're going to modify the plan a bit."

"John Dwyer?" Bill asked. "The guy who owns US1 Salvage in Bunnell?"

"That's the guy."

"How does he fit in?"

"You know what they say...one man's trash is another man's treasure."

Brewski entered the courtyard of The Golden Lion and grabbed a beer at the tiki bar on his way to Ralph's table.

"Judging by that grin," Ike said to him, "I take it things went well."

"That was fun," Brewski said. "There's something really satisfying about fucking with two CIA agents and knowing they can't do anything to you."

"I knew you were the man for the job," Ike said.

"They're not happy, but they're waiting for instructions."

"Good."

"Holy shit," Brewski said, seeing Rick's pickup pull over on Fifth Street outside the courtyard. "This son of a bitch has more balls than brains. I don't know why the feds let him go, but I'm gonna go collect for a windshield and a mirror."

He swallowed some beer and slammed the bottle on the table. Ike held up a hand.

"Hold it up, there, bud," Ike said, pointing at Constance climbing down from the jacked-up truck. "This may not be what it looks like."

Constance slapped the confederate flag out of her way as she rounded the back of the truck and marched through the gate, straight to Ike.

"I need to talk to you," she said.

"Is that right?" Ike said. "What could we possibly have to talk about?"

"About the phone call you made to Geoff Hanson a little bit ago."

"What about it?"

"You sure poked the bear."

"Yeah, it's one of my favorite pastimes."

"This time it's like to get you killed."

"Is that right?"

She nodded. "As sure as I'm standing here."

"Why don't you sit down and tell me about it? Can I get you something?"

She lowered herself into a chair. "I'll take a beer."

"A beer?" Ike asked with a glance at her belly.

"Yeah. Is that a problem?"

"Apparently not."

Ike motioned to a server and ordered Constance a beer.

"Okay, Constance," he said. "Let's hear it."

"Not so fast."

"Here it comes," Brewski said.

Ike raised an eyebrow at her. "I thought you wanted to talk."

"What's it worth to you?"

"I won't know what it's worth until I hear it."

She shook her head. "I learned my lesson. I don't give anything away no more. You want to know what I know, it's gonna cost you."

Ike exhaled and shook his head. "How much?"

Constance looked at him like a mouse trying to determine if it was safe to take the cheese.

"Five hundred," she blurted.

Ike leaned back in his chair and drank some beer, looking at her with a grin. She squirmed in her seat.

"That's my price," she said. "Take it or leave it."

Ike set his beer on the table and reached into his pocket. He peeled off five hundred-dollar-bills and tore them in half. He slapped a pile of halves on the table in front of her. He held the remaining halves up.

"You get these if your story is any good."

She looked hungrily at the torn bills in front of her and took a nervous sip of beer.

"After Hanson got off the phone him and his man Stuart took off like their asses was on fire. Hanson told Stuart to round up as many men as he could. He's really tired of the way you're messing with his plans so when you tell him where to go, he's bringing a small army to make sure he's done with you."

"What about Abraham?"

"The Jew? He took him with them."

"Took him where?"

"Probably to his condo at the Aliki."

Ike nodded slowly.

"How many men do you think he'll get?"

"I don't know. He's got about ten guys that think he's the Second Coming. They'd sell out their own mothers if he told 'em to."

"And what about you? What do you think of him?"

She fought back tears. "I used to think he loved me. Now I know better. But I'd still vote for him."

"So even though he got you pregnant and he treats your boyfriend like a doormat, you'd still vote for him?"

She placed a hand on her belly. "How do you know…"

"Doesn't matter how I know. The guy has the moral code of a sewer rat, but you're loyal to him. Why?"

"Because he knows what's good for this country. He's not afraid to do what it takes to put Americans back in charge."

"By *Americans*, you mean white people?"

"Of course. We're the only real Americans."

Ike shook his head. "Unbelievable."

He handed her the remaining halves of the money.

"Get out of here, Constance," he told her. "Take your five hundred dollars and your racist ass far away. If I ever see you again, I'll put a bullet in your eye."

She looked at him with indignation. After several seconds she stuffed the bills into her pocket and stormed off.

"Christ," Ike said. "Nothing's ever easy."

21

The light inside the trailer that served as the office for US1 Salvage was growing dim. Outside, the blue sky of the day had given way to a variety of pinks and reds, which were gradually pushed away by the dark grey of dusk. The trailer door opened and Brewski stepped in.

"I think everything's ready to go," he said. "Shou
ld we get the party started?"
Ike turned to John Dwyer and handed him a roll of bills.

"Thanks, John. That's for your trouble."
"No trouble at all, Ike," Dwyer said without taking the soggy cigar stub out of his mouth. "Anything for you and Ralph."

"We appreciate it. You better get out of here before the fireworks start."

"I was never here."

Dwyer grabbed a can of beer from the dingy refrigerator and waved on his way out the door.
Ike took out his phone and activated the recording app. "Let the games begin."
"I'll go take one last look, make sure everything is set," Brewski said.
Hanson answered his phone before the first ring finished.

"Yeah," he said.

"Hello, Senator Hanson," Ike said. "Thank you for your payment. The million dollars showed up in my account, which means you are now the proud owner of the Nazi Bell."

"I hope you enjoy the money. Now where is the Bell?"

"Are you familiar with US1 Salvage in Bunnell?"

"The junk yard? Yeah. I know it."

"Be outside the gate at nine. Flash your lights twice and somebody will let you in. We'll load the Bell onto your vehicle for you. I suggest you bring a trailer or a flatbed truck."

"I'll be there."

"Remember the rest of our deal. You're finished buying businesses and property in Flagler Beach."

"Like I told you before, if you want the blacks and Mexicans to take over Flagler, you can have it."

"Better them than you."

"You'll be sorry when this country becomes a white man's worst nightmare."

"I'm a white man, Geoff, and it's people like you that are my worst nightmare. Oh. One more thing."

"What now?"

"In case you were thinking of doing anything stupid I want you to know the Bell is rigged with five pounds of C-4. I assume you're too good to drive yourself, so there better not be anybody in the vehicle but you and your gym-rat. I'll turn the Bell into a thousand pounds of scrap metal if there's so much as a plastic Jesus on the dashboard. You follow?"

"How do I know you won't blow it up anyway?"

"If I wanted to blow it up, I would have done it already and saved myself from having this conversation."

Ike disconnected the call.

"One down, one to go," he said dialing another number.

"Bronson," the agent answered.

"Okay, Bronson, I've got the Russian's bid. What is the U.S. of A. willing to pay for a piece of history that could actually change history?"

"I'm authorized to offer you two million dollars."

"Sold! To the men in black. Congratulations, Bronson. You outbid Mother Russia by a cool half-million."

"Where is it?"

"I'm going to text you an account number. Once I have confirmation of the funds, I'll call you with the location. You have fifteen minutes."

Brewski entered the trailer just as Ike disconnected the call.

"Ready to rock," he said.

"Good. Just waiting to hear from Bill."

Five minutes later, Ike's phone beeped.

"Okay. Uncle Sam came through with the cash. Let's tell him where he can pick up his prize."

He called Bronson.

"I received confirmation of your deposit," Ike said. "And they say the wheels of government turn slowly. I guess it depends on how badly the government wants something."

"Just tell me where the Bell is."

"There's a salvage yard on US1 in Bunnell, about a half mile south of the center of town. The gate'll be open. Drive in, past the office. There's a big barn at the back of the yard, just before you reach the railroad tracks. We'll be waiting for you."

"You'd better be."

"Oh, come on now. Let's not be a sore winner."

"Don't you ever worry about pissing off the wrong people?"

"Well, what fun would it be pissing off the right people?"

Ike hung up and tucked his phone in his pocket.

"Okay," he said to Brewski. "Places. It's just about show time."

The metal building rose out of the darkness as Stuart navigated the truck over the rutted dirt road past the rotting carcasses of school busses, piles of car tires and the countless crushed bodies of unrecognizable cars. A thick fog was rising from the ground.

"Jesus," Stuart said. "Looks like a nice place for a horror movie."

"Just keep your eyes open," Hanson said. "I don't trust this Jew-loving race traitor."

The truck's headlights shone through the large opening in the front of the building.

"Do you see it?" Stuart asked.

"Not yet."

Both men leaned forward. Stuart flipped on the high beams.

"There," Hanson pointed toward the ceiling. "That must be it."

Dangling from a crane twenty-five feet above the dirt floor was an object wrapped in tarps. The shape looked like it matched the general descriptions of the Bell. It swung gently on the cable. The silence was broken by a train whistle in the distance.

Stuart stopped the truck and killed the engine. The headlights lit up the operator's cab of the crane. A silhouetted figure sat at the controls.

"Now what?" Stuart asked.

Hanson peered toward the crane operator.

"I don't know. Let's get out and see what happens."

Stuart opened his door and stepped down. Hanson slid across the bench seat and climbed out, standing between Stuart and the truck.

"Hello," he called.

There was no response from the crane.

"Go check it out," Hanson ordered.

Stuart took a gun from an ankle holster and crept toward the crane.

"Hey," he called to the operator when he was within six feet.

He moved to the side and climbed onto the vehicle's massive tread. Grabbing the bar by the cab's door, he hoisted himself up. Before he had time to react to the realization that the crane operator was a mannequin, he felt a huge hand grip his ankle and yank.

"What the..." was all he managed before his face struck the tread and the world went black.

"Stuart?" Hanson called. "What's going on?"

As he prepared to take a step toward the crane, the space was lit by another set of headlights.

"Who the hell is this guy?" Bronson asked as they entered the building that could serve as a hangar for a small airport.

"It sure as hell ain't Ike," Freeman answered. "Better not be a Russian."

The man standing by the door of the truck turned toward their headlights and pulled a gun. He used his free hand to shade his eyes. Bronson stopped the truck in the doorway of the building. The man pointed the gun at them.

"I should have known it was going to be like this," Bronson said, taking out his Glock.

Freeman took his Beretta out and racked the slide.

"Ready?" he said.

Bronson nodded.

"Let's do it."

They opened the doors of the truck and stepped out, weapons pointed at the man from behind the doors.

"Federal agents," Bronson called. "Identify yourself."

Ike and Alex Grichenko crouched behind the crane next to the unconscious body of Hanson's enforcer.

"Phase one, complete," Ike whispered.

"Stuart? What's going on?" Hanson called.

The shadows in the building began to shift and move as another set of headlights appeared in the doorway.

"Right on time," Ike said.

After several seconds, he heard Bronson's voice.

"Federal agents. Identify yourself."

Ike tapped Alex on the shoulder and nodded.

"Do not trust the Americans," the words of Alex's father came back.

Alex looked into Ike's eyes. Ike met the gaze and held it. If he decided to trust Ike at this moment, he may end up in an American prison or dead, but Ike was surely risking just as much.

Alex nodded.

"I am agent Alex Grichenko of the Scientific Recovery Bureau, KGB," he shouted.

"Drop your weapon and get on your knees," Bronson yelled.

Alex pointed his Makarov pistol, the one given to him by his father, toward the ceiling and fired two shots; the first time he had fired the weapon in the line of duty. Bronson and Freeman opened fire. Hanson's body staggered backward several feet before dropping to the ground.

During the maelstrom of gunfire, Alex turned and fired a shot, point blank, at Hanson's aide.

Ike pointed at the door behind them. "Through there," he told Alex. "Brewski will get you out of here."

Alex laid the Makarov on the ground next to Ike.

"Thank you, and good luck with them," he said before he disappeared through the door into the night.

Ike pulled a bandana from his pocket and used it to pick up the Makarov.

"Agent Bronson," he called. "It's Ike. Hold your fire."

Bronson and Freeman watched Ike move out of the shadows toward them with his hands partially raised. In his right hand he held an unidentifiable object.

"Stop right there," Bronson said. "Drop whatever you're carrying."

Ike ignored the order and continued walking until he was within five feet of them, where he tossed the object to the ground at Bronson's feet.

Bronson looked down at the pistol, then at Ike.

"What the hell is going on," he asked.

Ike turned and looked at the dead body, then back at Bronson.

"Looks to me like you've got a problem," he said.

Bronson looked up at the object hanging from the crane.

"How do you figure? I've got the Bell, and I could shoot you right now for any number of reasons."

Ike chuckled. "You both emptied your weapons into our friend over there, and before you could even think about reloading to shoot me, you'd be dead. So I guess that leaves you with just that." Ike pointed toward the ceiling.

"That's enough."

Ike looked up.

"Yeah, that."

"That's really all I need to satisfy my superiors. All the rest of this bullshit is meaningless to them."

"Well then," Ike said. "Let's get it down for you."

Ike walked to the crane and started the engine. The smell of diesel fumes invaded the air. Bronson and Freeman moved forward. The tarp covered object lowered slowly and landed with a ground-shaking thud. A cloud of dust mingled with the exhaust fumes.

Freeman coughed and fanned the air.

Ike killed the engine. On his way back, he pulled a buck knife from a pouch on his belt and flicked it open. He offered it to Bronson.

"Care to do the honors?"

Bronson took the knife and grinned as he began cutting the straps holding the tarps in place. He yanked the tarp from the top down with a flourish.

"What the fuck?" Freeman said.

Bronson tossed the tarps aside and looked at the object in front of him.

The large, red ball of a nose and the wide eyes set off the clown's huge grin. A golf ball was wedged in its left cheek.

"What the hell is this?" he said.

"Before we get to that," Ike said, "let's meet our friend over here."

He stepped to the dead body and dug out the wallet.

"I don't give a good God damn about the Russian," Bronson said. "Where is the Bell?"

"Russian?" Ike said. "Hmmm. I think there's been a mistake. According to this," Ike held up the ID, "this here is United States Senator Geoffrey Hanson."

He tossed the wallet to Bronson.

Bronson examined the credentials with his mouth agape.

"What kind of shit are you pulling? Where's the Russian? And where's the Bell?"

Ike retrieved the pistol from the ground and handed it to Bronson.

"That's a 1951 Makarov pistol. Standard issue of the KGB during the Cold War. A fingerprint analysis will reveal that it belonged to KGB Agent Alex Grichenko."

Ike pointed behind the crane.

"Over there, you'll find the body of Senator Hanson's aide, killed with that very weapon."

Bronson and Freeman looked toward the crane, then at each other, and finally at Ike.

"Here's one possible scenario," Ike said. "You can take your chances telling your bosses that you lost the Bell, and then explain the death of the good senator here, killed with your weapons, I might add. Or, and I think this is a much more appealing alternative, you can look inside Bozo's mouth. You'll notice his dental work is composed of C-4. When that blows, any corpse within a hundred yards would be pretty much unidentifiable. So we walk away. You tell your bosses that in your efforts to recover the Bell, you were ambushed by the Russian, that he shot and killed Hanson's aide, then you shot him, but unfortunately he blew up the Bell to keep you from getting it, and the senator was killed in the explosion."

Bronson and Freeman looked at each other.

217

"That's the most ridiculous story I've ever heard," Bronson said.

Ike shrugged. "You're probably right. I guess you should tell the truth. You paid two million dollars for a ten-foot-tall clown head and shot a U.S. Senator in the process, all while allowing the Russians to get the Bell."

Ike nodded.

"Yeah," he said. "That'll work. Just call your families and say goodbye before you file that report, because nobody will ever see you again afterward."

Ike started walking away.

"I'd say 'see you later,' but I don't think it would be appropriate."

Bronson turned and watched him move through the light cast by the headlights of their rental truck.

"This sucks, man," Freeman said. "We can't go back with that story."

Bronson looked at his partner and exhaled deeply.

"Fuck," he said. "Ike, come back."

22

The elevator doors slid open on the twelfth floor. Ike stepped out quietly into the nicely decorated lobby, peered up and down the adjoining hallway, then motioned for the others to come out.

"All right," Ike said. "Let's have some fun."

The others followed him through the lobby into the hallway.

"You're sure about the unit number?" Ike asked Bill.

Bill looked at him with mock indignation. "Really?"

"Okay," Ike said. "Then you two know what to do? Make it convincing."

Bill and Mabel nodded.

"Should be pretty easy," Bill said. "I'll just pretend she's my ex-wife."

"That should work," Ike said. "Break a leg."

Brewski moved in front of Mabel.

"You want to kiss me goodbye?" he said. "Just in case."

She sidestepped him. "No," she said. "But thank you for the offer."

They disappeared to the left around the corner. A minute later Ike and Brewski heard Bill shout.

"Don't walk away from me!"

"Stay away from me," Mabel returned. "You make me sick. I don't ever want to see you again."

"That's our cue," Ike said.

They moved out of the lobby and took the hall to the right. When they rounded the corner approaching unit 1221, Bill and Mabel were engaged in a loud shouting match. Ike pointed at Bill and nodded. Bill threw himself at the door of the unit.

"How do you like that?" he shouted.

Mabel dropped to a knee, cradled her face in her hands and began crying. The door opened and a man stepped into the hall.

"Hey," he said. "Y'all take this shit somewhere else."

Ike slid up from behind, wrapped a huge arm around the man's neck, dragged him away from the open door and pointed his forty-five at his head.

"Good idea," Ike said. "We're going to take it right inside that condo. Is there anybody else in there?"

The man stiffened.

Ike increased the pressure on his throat.

"In about thirty seconds, you'll pass out and we'll throw your ass off the roof. So you've got about twenty seconds to talk. You follow?"

If the man considered defiance, he quickly changed his mind.

"There's two more," he croaked.

"Does that include Abraham?"

"Abra...you mean the Jew? Yeah. He's in there."

"So, including Abraham there are only two people in there?"

"No. Including the Jew there are three."

Ike frisked him, took a Glock from his belt and handed it to Bill.

"You don't mind babysitting for a minute, do you?"

Bill took the gun and nodded. "No problem."

"Remember," Ike said to Brewski. "No shooting unless absolutely necessary."

Brewski frowned. "Whatever."

They moved into the condo and crept past the kitchen, following the sound of a television coming from the opposite end of the unit. The hall opened into a spacious living and dining area with a twelve-foot sliding glass door providing a beautiful view of the ocean. A bound and gagged Abraham was seated on the sofa, guarded by a man in a recliner with his back to Ike and Brewski. The guard's attention was more focused on a baseball game on the TV, his beer, and a bowl of pretzels than on Abraham. Ike made eye contact with Abraham and held up two fingers, then pointed at the man in the chair and raised his hands in question. Abraham flicked his eyes toward a hallway. Ike motioned to Brewski to check it out. As Brewski moved off silently, Ike stepped behind the recliner and wrapped his arm around the man's neck while covering his mouth with the other hand.

"Shh," he said to the man. "Behave and you'll live long enough to talk about this."

Brewski moved down the hall with his gun drawn. There were three doors; two stood open to dark rooms; the third was closed with light coming from beneath. The bathroom exhaust fan was the only sound.

Brewski stepped in front of the door and kicked it in, then charged forward, gun leading.

The bathroom was huge.

He saw himself in the full-length mirror immediately in front of him. To his right was a walk-in shower big enough for eight people. Next to that was a single shower stall. A six-foot vanity with double sinks ran along the wall.

"What the hell, Johnny?" came a voice from behind the door to his left.

Brewski yanked the door open as the man on the toilet dropped his copy of *Bait and Tackle* and stood, trying to pull his pants up.

Brewski sent a kick to the man's genitals. The man grunted and fell backward, arms flailing, trying to maintain his balance. Using one hand to hold his pants above his knees and the other to push off the wall, he lunged at Brewski with his shoulder lowered. The two men stumbled backward onto the floor of the bathroom. Brewski's gun slid across the marble and came to rest in front of the group shower stall. The man climbed on top of Brewski and drew a fist back to punch him. Brewski drove his knee up, again connecting with the man's groin, sending him flying into the shower door. The glass exploded and showered over him.

Brewski spotted his gun at the man's feet.

When the man bent to pick it up, Brewski picked up a two-foot-tall ceramic pelican and threw it. It knocked the man into the shower stall. Brewski charged in and kicked him between the legs again. The man growled and lunged. With his arms around Brewski's waist, he drove him backward. They landed on the floor in front of the vanity. As the man drew his arm back to punch, Brewski opened the vanity door and grabbed the first thing he saw.

He drove the plunger into the man's face and pushed him off. Grabbing a bath towel from the bar, he wrapped it around the man's face and head, and drew it tight from behind.

"Let's go, mother fucker," Brewski said. "You need to cool off."

He dragged the man to the toilet closet and pushed his face into the unflushed bowl. He dropped the lid on top of the man's head and knelt on it until the man stopped fighting.

"How do you like that shit?" he asked.

He retrieved his gun and returned to the living room where everybody, including the other two guards, who were now bound and gagged, sat waiting.

"Did you have fun?" Ike asked.

"Where the hell were you?" he said.

"I didn't think you'd need help with one guy on the john."

"That son-of-a-bitch put up a hell of a fight. I think his balls are made of titanium."

Ike grinned. "Good to know."

"Is there a beer in this place?" Brewski asked.

23

"Hey, I think our federal friends are leaving," Ike said, setting his phone on the table and turned the speaker on.

"What a God-damned soup-sandwich this turned out to be," Bronson complained.

"Yeah, but at least we've got a plausible story," Freeman said, *"thanks to Ike."*

"Ike? If it wasn't for that asshole, we wouldn't need a plausible story."

"That's not the point. The operation went south and we were looking at who-knows-what kind of shit storm. At least now we can blame it on the Russians."

"Just drive," Bronson said. *"Get me the hell out of this hell hole."*

"Hell hole?" Freeman said. *"I don't know. It kind of grows on you."*

"Yeah, like a cold sore."

"Asshole?" Ike said after closing the app. "After all I did for him?"

"Some people are just ungrateful," Brewski said.

A server arrived at the table with a tray and delivered their lunch.

Abraham and Eric smiled as they enjoyed their meals and cocktails, their faces finally beginning to show genuine relaxation.

Brewski raised his steak sandwich but stopped inches from his wide-open mouth.

"Good morning, little schoolgirl," he said looking toward the courtyard entrance.

Ike turned to see Bill and Mabel, followed by a young woman.

Ike waved to the server once they sat down.

"Good afternoon," Brewski said to Mabel. "And may I say you look lovely in this light?"

"I think I'm getting too much sun," she said.

"Moving along," Ike said. "Did you have any luck?"

"I did," she said. "I found a non-profit, scientific research group in Canada. They have no government affiliations and are completely funded by independent donors and sponsors from around the world. Their only goal is the furthering of education and understanding."

"That sounds like the group we want. Have you contacted them?"

"Indeed, I have. Needless to say, they are extremely excited at the prospect of acquiring the Bell."

"Good. They can have it."

"It should be destroyed," Abraham said.

"I understand your position," Mabel said. "But something of such significance is too valuable to destroy. This group has no political agenda. They are interested in the science and the ways it can benefit mankind."

"That is my point," Abraham said. "This device has no benefit to mankind, because there are too many men who would stop at nothing to use it for their own nefarious desires."

"We just have to keep it away from such men," Mabel said.

"You are a historian," Abraham said. "You, of all people, should know what I am talking about. As long as that device exists, there are men full of hate, and consumed with their own personal agenda, who will want to take advantage of it. I have seen it first hand, and even now, seventy-five years after its conception, I see that such men still exist. Time marches on, but the darkness within men remains unchanged."

"That doesn't mean we should stop trying."

"You are welcome to try, but I, for one, will be content to watch the passage of time from, I believe the expression is, the sidelines."

"On a much happier note," Mabel said. "Abraham, I'd like you to meet somebody."

Mabel motioned to the woman sitting next to her.

"This is..."

Abraham looked at the woman with a furrowed brow. Her large, brown eyes, curly, shoulder-length hair and the shape of her mouth were instantly recognizable. His mouth moved soundlessly and he shook his head slowly.

"Sarah?" he finally managed.

"No," Mabel said. "It's not Sarah. This is Ellen. Ellen Rosen. Your great-granddaughter."

Abraham's eyes were immediately flooded with tears.

"How?"

"I took it upon myself to do some research," Mabel told him. "It seems that the night you were captured, Sarah wasn't killed, as you had assumed. She, along with the woman from the Underground, eluded the Germans. She eventually made it to Switzerland."

Abraham put his hand over his heart and smiled.

"Sarah is alive? In Switzerland?"

"Why don't we let Ellen tell the story," Mabel said.

The young woman held back tears of her own.

"I don't know where to begin. I've always been told you died in the camps."

Abraham shook his head.

"This is...and you are so young," Ellen continued.

"That is a very long story," he said with a sad smile. "Tell me about Sarah."

"Great grandmother lived out the war in Switzerland, as Mabel said. When the war ended, she returned to Poland in hopes of finding you, but, of course, she had no luck.

Germany and Poland were in total shambles after the war, and with the discovery of the camps, it was assumed that anybody who was unaccounted for had..." she choked back the words.

"Yes," Abraham said. "Go on."

"Her son," Ellen continued. "Your son, Abraham Rosen, was born in August of 1945. Together they sought asylum in the United States. They settled in Rhode Island, a small state about one-thousand miles north of here. Grandfather attended the University of Rhode Island and later graduated from the Massachusetts Institute of Technology. He was an engineer."

Abraham smiled and nodded.

"He worked for a company called DuPont where he helped to develop materials that make up some of the products which we use every day. He was very gifted. In 1962 his son, my father, Aaron Rosen was born on the Fourth of July. Great grandmother lived to see him graduate from high school, but she developed a heart condition and passed away in 1983, five years before I was born. After she passed, father took a job in Florida. I was born here in 1988. In 2010, mother and father drove to Rhode Island to bring grandfather back to Florida. His health was failing and they wanted him to be nearer to us in his final years. On the way back, in Washington DC, their car was hit from behind on a bridge. The car was forced off the bridge into the Potomac River. They were all killed in the crash."

Abraham's head sank.

Ellen reached out and took his hand in hers.

"I'm so sorry to be the one to deliver all of this bad news."

Abraham shook his head and smiled at her.

"It is not bad news," he said. "Sarah lived. She survived the war. She raised our son, which led to your birth and this moment. To know all of that happened, while I thought she had died that night, is the best news I could receive. And to meet you is a joy beyond all expectations."

Ike cleared his throat.

"Sorry to interrupt," he said, "but maybe the rest of us could meet Abraham's sole heir?"

"Of course," Ellen said. "I apologize."

She introduced herself to Ike and Brewski.

"Bill and Mabel told me what has happened. I have to admit, at first I was quite skeptical. I mean...a time machine? But Bill showed me a picture on the internet of Great Grandfather from his days at Cambridge, then another taken last week. I confess, I'm still in shock at all of it, but..."

She looked at Abraham and smiled, fighting back tears at the same time.

Abraham patted her hand gently.

"I'd like you to meet Eric," Abraham said to her. "This young man and I have been through quite a bit in the past week."

Ellen said hello to Eric. He greeted her in German, to which she responded in kind.

"You speak German?" Abraham asked.

"Yes. Great grandmother insisted grandfather learn Yiddish and German, and he, in turn taught father, who taught me."

Abraham and Eric spoke to each other, in German.

"He wanted me to explain to him who Ellen was," Abraham told the group.

"That's got to be a bit confusing," Brewski said.

Abraham smiled at Eric.

"He's a very bright boy. Considering all he's been through in his short life, he is handling things very well."

"Good afternoon," Ralph called.

The group looked to see Ralph approaching the table, his wheelchair being pushed by Alex Grichenko.

"I would like you all to meet Mr. Peter Green."

Alex waved and smiled at them. "It's a pleasure to meet you all. Again!"

"Peter is a Flagler Beach native," Ralph said, "according to his birth certificate."

Ralph produced an envelope from the side pocket of his wheelchair and pulled out a birth certificate, followed by assorted other documents.

"He also has a passport, a Florida driver's license, a social security card and a credit card."

"Not to mention an Amazon Prime account," Peter added.

"So what's next, Mr. Green?" Ike asked. "You've got a cool million dollars, compliments of your new Uncle Sam. Going to do some traveling? See the country?"

"I've seen quite a bit of the country already," he said. "I think I'll settle down here and establish some roots."

"It's a nice place to settle," Ike said.

"Speaking of cool millions," Ike said. "The two million donated by the CIA is all yours Abraham. You can use it to catch that train."

"Train?" Abraham said.

"Yeah. You know? The one in Salzburg."

"Yes. The train," he said.

"Train?" Ellen asked.

"Yes," he said to her. "How would you like to visit Austria?"

24

Ike and Brewski watched Bill, Mabel, and another woman enter the courtyard of The Golden Lion. The trio was dressed for the beach, but Bill had a laptop with him.

"Jesus," Brewski said to Bill. "You take your damn laptop to the beach?"

"Not quite," Bill answered. "I've got something to share with you."

Brewski hopped off his stool and offered it to Mabel.

"I knew you couldn't stay away from me," he said.

Mabel declined the seat, instead letting the other woman have it.

"What have you got, Bill?" Ike said.

Bill opened the laptop and set it on the bar.

"I got an email from Ellen, Abraham's great-granddaughter."

"Wow. What's it been? Six months?"

"Something like that."

"Time flies, huh?"

"Go ahead," Bill said. "Read it."

Ike read the email aloud;

Dear Bill,
Great-Grandfather, Eric, and I have been in Salzburg for several months now. The climate isn't as nice as Florida, but it is a beautiful country. We were a bit worried about the identification papers and passports provided by Mr.

Donabedian, but they never drew a single bit of scrutiny. *WHEW!*

To avoid confusion in our encounters with people, we have decided that Great Grandfather and I will introduce ourselves as brother and sister. We aren't sure if the world is ready for the real story!

Eric is doing well. He is a wonderful boy, and I have decided to adopt him. Naturally he is thrilled with the idea, as is Abraham!

We have toured the countryside extensively. The changes wrought by the passage of time were difficult for Abraham to comprehend, since, in his mind, he was here only a few months ago, but he has dealt with it quite well. After seeing the camp memorials, he and Eric were able to find the location of the bunker in which this whole adventure began. Time has all but forgotten it. It was buried deep in the forest, and only somebody who had been there could have even found it. The only thing remaining was the decayed remnants of a small structure, which to an uninformed observer would appear to be an ancient outhouse.

Using the money given to us by Ike, we purchased a piece of land in the mountains outside of Salzburg. With the help of some local laborers, we have been working around the clock using the information you provided to us.

Yesterday, our efforts were rewarded beyond all expectations (see attached photo).

Naturally, Abraham will return any stolen artifacts to the heirs of the rightful owners. If proper heirs cannot be located, he will see that they go to museums or memorials. With the gold he plans to make restitution wherever possible, but even after that is done, the amount of wealth in this train is unimaginable. Abraham is already talking about scholarships, programs to help the poor, and every other conceivable charitable cause.

He insists that he will not allow time to erase the memory of what this train represents.

Thank you again for all of your help. Please convey our thanks and love to all involved, especially Ike.

Much love,

Ellen, Abraham, and Eric Rosen

Bill reached over Ike's shoulder and opened the photograph.

In the photo's backdrop of a dimly lit cave, they could make out a locomotive. On its nose was the instantly recognizable symbol of the Third Reich. Behind it, boxcars faded back into the darkness. Several men stood on the locomotive with shovels in hand and all cheering wildly. In front of the scene, Abraham stood between Ellen and Eric, his arms wrapped around them, their faces lit with joy.

"Wow," Ike said. "They actually found it."

Brewski counted the boxcars.

"There's five cars visible and who knows how many more," he said. "I think it's safe to say that they've hit the motherload."

"Judging by the looks on their faces," Ike said, "they've found something a lot more valuable than the train."

Bill closed the laptop.

"Okay," he said. "We're off to the beach. You guys have a wonderful day."

"Are you coming back for a cocktail later?" Brewski asked Mabel.

Mabel looked at the other woman. "What do you think?" she asked.

The woman leaned in and kissed Mabel. "Whatever you want, Love."

Mabel looked at Brewski.

"We'll see," she said with a smile.

Brewski watched in shock as they walked away arm-in-arm.

"Are you kidding me?" he said.

"Hey," Ike said to him. "Don't judge."

Epilogue

It was like travelling in another time.

"I guess this is how they did it back in the old days," Rob Danford said as he closed the road atlas.

He eased the truck out of the rest area and followed the signs to Route 5 toward Buffalo and Canada.

Driving a big rig for the Yellow Line Network for over twenty years, mostly for private clients who preferred to keep things below the radar, he thought he had seen just about everything a driver could see, but this job was one for the books.

Maybe he should have listened to Elise and turned the job down, but the money was just too nice...even with its bizarre conditions.

Over the years he had learned not to question his clients. It was common for him to be kept in the dark about what he was hauling, and he never got nosey when the cargo was being loaded or unloaded. Truth was, the money he was being paid was more than enough to squelch his curiosity.

This job was different.

Right from Jump Street...when he was contacted with the job offer.

Two weeks earlier, on his way home to Palm Coast after a long haul to South Dakota he stopped for breakfast at a Waffle House in Tennessee. While he enjoyed his omelet one of the waitresses came inside from a smoke break and walked to his table with an envelope in her hand.

"Man in the Mercedes says this is for you," she said to him.

Rob looked up at her with confusion.

"Me?" he said after swallowing his food.

"That's what he said. 'Give this to the man sitting by the cash register.'" She pointed at the register. "There's the cash register, and you the only man near it."

She shook the envelope at him. "C'mon, I gotta get back to work."

He took it reluctantly.

"Who did you say told you to give it to me?"

She jerked a thumb over her shoulder.

"Man out there in the blue Mercedes."

Rob looked around her and scanned the parking lot.

"I don't see a blue Mercedes."

She turned around and looked.

"Huh. I guess he left."

She walked away, leaving Rob with the thick envelope.

After glancing around the nearly empty restaurant, he pulled the envelope open and peered into it at a one-inch-thick stack of fifty-dollar bills. He pulled out the business card attached to the cash with a paper clip.

Augustine Lusignan – Scientific Research Institute – Moose Factory, Toronto, Canada.

On the back of the card was a handwritten request.

"Job offer. Hampton Inn lobby if interested. If not keep the cash and have a nice day."

He set the envelope down and finished his breakfast. Using one of the fifties to pay his bill, he carefully watched the waitress as she swiped it with the special marker to confirm its legitimacy. Once she had slid it beneath the cash drawer, he quietly told her to keep the change.

Outside, he walked across the parking lot to the Hampton Inn next door. At the side of the building sat a blue Mercedes with Canadian tags.

Rob removed his sunglasses when he entered the lobby and looked around. An older man sat in a chair, reading a newspaper. Somehow sensing Rob's presence, he folded the newspaper, set it on the table next to his chair, and motioned discretely to Rob.

"Mr. Lusignan?" Rob said, consulting the business card.

The man stood and offered a hand.

"Yes. Augustine Lusignan," he said. "Please call me Frank."

"Pleased to meet you, Frank. Call me Rob."

"Sit down, Rob," Lusignan said, indicating the chair to his right. "I'd like to talk to you about a job."

"Before you start, may I ask how you got my name?"

Lusignan grinned.

"Of course. The Institute for which I work often conducts research in highly sensitive areas. Discretion is always our first priority. We reached out to some friends in the U.S. who have found a network of drivers who are always on the right side of the yellow line."

Rob nodded. Lusignan's use of the words *network* and *yellow line* were all he needed to hear. Whoever Mr. Lusignan was, he'd been vetted and cleared.

"Okay," Rob said. "What's your job?"

"We need something transported from Flagler Beach, Florida, to the Canadian border."

"And when do you need this *something* delivered?"

"As soon as you're available."

"I'll be available the day after tomorrow."

"Excellent, but before you accept the job, I feel you should know the conditions."

"There are always conditions."

"These may be different from what you're used to."

Rob grinned.

"Let me see if I can guess," he said. "Don't ask what the package is. Don't watch when it's loaded, and don't watch when it's unloaded. That about sum it up?"

"Not quite."

"There's more?"

Lusignan nodded.

"Okay," Rob said. "Let's hear it."

"It's our understanding that you own a 1997 Peterbilt 357."

"That's true, but I don't drive it very often."

"We need you to drive it for this job."

"Why is that?"

"Because it is exempt from using electronic trucking-log devices by the grandfather clause."

"I see. Okay. I'll use the 357. Is that it?"

"No. This delivery must be kept as far under the radar as possible. Therefore, you cannot use the interstates."

"That's a bit extreme, don't you think?"

"No. We don't," Lusignan said. "Are you still interested?"

"Sure. You paid enough money for me to listen. I'll hear you out."

"Is your truck equipped with a satellite navigation system?"

"Sure. It's got a Qualcomm."

"You'll have to disable it."

"Disable it?"

"I'm afraid so. You'll have to navigate the old-fashioned way. Using maps and atlases."

"Wow. I can't use the interstate or a GPS. I assume you're not looking for a fast run."

"Time is not a factor on this job"—Lusignan smiled, as if at some sort of private joke—"as it were. Also, we will require you to drive completely legally. No more than eleven hours of driving at a time and ten hours of break afterward, and keep your speed to no more than five miles per hour over the posted speed limit."

"Damn," Rob said.

"Finally..." Lusignan said.

"There's more?"

"One last thing. You won't be allowed to carry your personal cell phone with you. If you need to contact someone," Lusignan handed him a flip phone and another business card. "Use this phone to call the number on this card and you'll be connected to whatever number you'd like to call. You can use your CB radio for normal driving related communication, but under no circumstances are you to divulge your location...to anybody."

Rob looked at the card.

"Archie's Flower Shop?" he said.

Lusignan nodded. "You'll be patched through to whoever you want to talk to."

Rob sat back in his chair.

"Well, Mr. Lusignan, these conditions of yours are a bit unusual, even for the network. Not to mention costly. Driving the speed limit on surface streets will take more time and use more fuel."

"You'll be paid five dollars per mile, plus two hundred fifty dollars per day for expenses. Half in advance."

Rob's eyes widened.

"Five dollars?"

"That's right."

Rob sat silently for a moment.

"Are you interested?" Lusignan asked.

After a brief hesitation, Rob nodded. "You've got yourself a driver."

"Excellent," Lusignan said.

"Where do I pick up the load?"

"Are you familiar with a restaurant in Flagler Beach called The Golden Lion?"

"Sure. I've been there a few times."

"Go there and ask to speak with a man named Ike. Show him my business card, and he will take you to the cargo."

Rob wrote on the back of the business card. *Golden Lion. Ike.* "Got it."

Lusignan opened the briefcase at his feet and took out an envelope.

"Five thousand dollars and your drop-off location. The balance will be paid when you deliver the cargo."

Rob took a quick look inside the envelope.

"Count it if you like," Lusignan said.

"That's okay. I trust you."

Lusignan offered a hand; Rob shook it.

"Good luck, Mr. Danford."

"Hey," Rob said with a chuckle. "I'm driving a truck, not going to war."

Lusignan walked away without a response.

The meeting with Ike and the pickup of the load was simple enough. Whatever he was delivering was inside a huge wooden crate and strapped to a flatbed. The only markings on the crate were the very innocuous *Restaurant Supply Warehouse—Palm Beach, Florida*, followed by a phone number.

Rob had been half-tempted to call the number but decided against it. Anybody who went to such lengths to have this item delivered fifteen hundred miles in complete secrecy would surely have a ghost answering service at the other end of the phone number.

Once the flatbed was hooked to his tractor, he set off on US-1 heading north.

In a way, traveling old school was a nice change. By the time Route 219 took him from Pennsylvania into New York, he was enjoying the relaxing pace. He used the flip phone to call Elise twice from the road. She didn't like not knowing where he was, but she didn't press the issue.

The final leg of his journey went through Buffalo in a rainstorm, the first bad weather he'd run into. As per his instructions, he called Archie's Flower Shop and told the person at the other end that he was one hour out. He was instructed to park at the Buffalo Museum of Science and wait to be contacted.

He exited Route 219 and took Ridge Road.

With less than three miles to Route 5, he saw flashing lights ahead.

"Now what?" he said.

As he approached the scene, a lighted message board directed him into an empty Home Depot parking lot.

"You've got to be kidding me. At two o'clock in the morning?"

Squinting through the rain, he read the flashing message board.

Mobile weigh station—all commercial vehicles.

"I thought they weren't allowed to put these things on private property," he wondered aloud.

Navigating through the cones, he guided the truck onto the scale. With his log sheets in hand, he rolled his window down and waited for the Department of Transportation officer.

"These guys sure ain't in a hurry," he said to himself, watching the officer and the two D.O.T. workers talking to each other and pointing at his truck.

Movement in the passenger's side mirror caught his attention. He glanced over to see two men shutting down the message board and moving it off the road. Two other men gathered the cones and stacked them next to the message board.

"What the hell?" he said.

When the officer approached his door, Rob leaned out the window and smiled.

"Hey, are you guys packing up? Timing is everything, I guess. I should have gotten here a few minutes later," he said with a chuckle.

"Sir, could you step out of the vehicle?" the officer said.

"Is something wrong?" Rob asked as he climbed down. "I got all my paperwork here."

The officer took the paperwork from Rob and stuffed it into his pocket.

"I'm going to need those," Rob said.

The officer glanced at something behind Rob. Rob turned his head to follow the officer's gaze in time to see the two D.O.T. workers approaching quickly. His mind processed the scene in a flash, but his body didn't have time to react.

The left breast of the bright-green vests worn by the two men were stenciled with *Delaware D.O.T.* What were they doing in upstate New York? One of them had a syringe in his hand, and the other carried a black piece of cloth. Rob instinctively backed up, but he was blocked by the officer, who restrained him by twisting his arm behind his back and putting him in a choke hold. The syringe was jabbed into his thigh, and the black cloth was pulled over his head.

Time slowed to a crawl. Before he lost consciousness, he heard muffled voices speaking in slow motion.

"He'll be out for about two hours. Put him behind the message board. Barnes, you drive the truck. They'll be expecting him at the border soon, so let's get going before they realize something's wrong."

Through the woven fabric covering his face, the lights of Route 5 swirled and danced. He heard the familiar sound of his truck engine in the distance. By the time he was dropped onto the wet grass, he was losing the ability to form cohesive thoughts.

Before he slipped completely into the darkness, he told himself one last thing.

Right place...wrong time.

A few words from the author:

First and foremost, I would like to thank you, the reader, for choosing my book when you have a virtually unlimited number of options. It truly means a lot to me.

Second, some who have read my other works may have noticed Ike has a new boat, which he cryptically explains away in this book. For a detailed explanation of what happened to *The Knight's Mare*, I invite you to read the novel **Blood Dawn**, written by my friend Chris DiBella, in which Ike, and his boat, play a prominent role.

Next, I would like to thank some people who have graciously loaned their names to characters in the story you have just read:

Adam Morley
Becky Pourchot
Brian McMillan – *Palm Coast Observer*
Captain Matt Doughney – Flagler Beach Police Dept
Elise Danford
Ellen Meyer
"Fizz" Ed Velasco
Richard Bourque
Rob Danford
Vern Shank
Vincent Lyon

Finally, a word about a couple of key elements in the story.

<u>The Nazi Bell</u> is the subject of a great deal of speculation. Reports of its existence began when a Polish author claimed to have seen transcripts of a post-war interview with a former SS officer in which The Bell was described. The author claims he was not allowed to make copies of the transcripts, which detracts from the credibility of his story. Also, no concrete evidence of the Bell's existence has ever been found. Regardless, many still believe it to be real.

The exact function of the Bell, if it existed, is also a matter of debate. The two most common theories are that it was either a secret weapon or a device for space travel. To my knowledge, there is no theory suggesting it was a time machine. I took that liberty myself.

<u>The Nazi Gold Train</u> is also a bit of a legend. Reportedly the train, loaded with there hundred tons of gold, treasure, art, and weapons, was buried somewhere in Poland, then Germany, at the end of World War II. Despite many searches, it has never been found, leading many to believe it is a myth. Again, for the purposes of this story, it exists.

Once again—thank you for reading ***Doomed to Repeat***, and if I could ask one last favor: I would be grateful if you would take a few minutes of your time to leave a review on Amazon. Even if it is only a few short words.

Reviews are independent authors' most valuable means of spreading awareness for our books.

I understand if you would rather not leave a review. Perhaps, if you enjoyed the book, you could recommend it (or any of my other books) to a family member, friend, or co-worker.

You are an invaluable means of communication for me and all authors.

Peace

Turn the page to read the first chapter of my next book Rising Tide. A fast paced crime story involving a piece of art Abraham recovered from the Gold Train and donated to Ike for as a token of appreciation.
Enjoy!

RISING TIDE

Chapter One

Things were about to go from bad to worse, and Lee Denton was out of ideas.

Standing in his doorway, blocking most of the daylight with his six-foot-six, two-hundred-seventy-five-pound frame, Ike grinned at Lee.

Not the kind of grin that signals fun and happiness, it was more like the kind of grin that told Lee he was about to have a bad day.

"Come on in, Ike," he said.

He stepped aside to let Ike in and glanced at the two Harleys in the driveway. There was no sign of Ike's right-hand man, Brewski, but Lee knew he wasn't far away.

"Can I get you anything? Beer?" Lee said.

"I'm not here to socialize," Ike said.

"Yeah, I know," Lee said. "I just figured...yeah, never mind."

He closed the door. Ike stood in the foyer like a cigar-store Indian.

"Ike, listen," Lee started.

Ike held up a hand to cut him off.

"You know how many times I've heard that?"

Lee shook his head as if the question required an answer.

"And every time I hear it," Ike continued, "it's usually followed by one lame excuse or another. And let me tell you, I've heard them all."

Lee's eyes went to the floor. He was silent for a moment or two.

"All right," Ike said. "Let's hear it."

Lee looked at him inquisitively. Ike motioned with his hand.

"Come on. I don't have all day."

Lee felt a wave of relief. Surely his explanation would buy him a temporary stay. Even if it were only a few days. He just needed time to figure out what to do.

"It's my sister, Ike."

Ike frowned.

"Your sister? Don't tell me. She needs an operation. That's not..."

"Her husband beats her. She's in the hospital. She doesn't have any medical insurance, and she needs to get away from him before he kills her, or her son, or both of them. She doesn't have any money. I was trying to scrape up enough to pay the hospital and get her the hell out of that house."

Ike looked down and pinched the bridge of his nose, then let out a long sigh.

"Jesus Christ, Lee. You were trying to raise money to rescue your sister by making bets on long-shots?"

Lee could feel his eyes beginning to water.

"I didn't know what else to do."

Ike took another deep breath and shook his head.

"How old is the kid?"

"He's nine. He's autistic. Smart as all hell, but, you know, different."

"Yeah. I know what autistic is."

"Her husband's an asshole. If I could, I'd give him a taste of his own medicine, but he's crazier than a shit-house rat."

Ike looked past Lee to the sliding glass door at the rear of the kitchen and made a waving motion. Lee turned to see Brewski, who had been sitting on the patio in a lawn chair, get up and walk toward the front of the house.

"What's your sister's name?" Ike asked.

"Dianna," Lee said. "Dianna Summers."

"What hospital she in?"

"Flagler. On 100."

"Husband's name?"

Brewski entered the foyer.

"What's up?" he asked.

Ike held up a finger, then motioned to Lee to answer the question.

"Ron. Ron Summers."

"Ron Summers?" Brewski said. "Why are we talking about that scumbag?"

"Your sister is married to Ron Summers?" Ike asked.

"You know him?"

"Yeah. I know him."

Brewski nodded in agreement.

"Then you know what a jerk he is."

"Jerk is being too nice. But, yeah. You don't have to explain. Where's he live?"

Lee gave Ike the address. Ike recognized the location. A trailer park off of State Road 100 in Bunnell.

"Where's the kid?"

"In school," Lee said. "I have to pick him up in an hour. He's staying here with me until Dianna is out. Then she's coming here, too. I'm not letting her go back there."

Ike nodded.

"Here's what we're going to do, Lee," he said. "The five grand you lost on those bets just became a loan. You now owe Ralph six, and you have two weeks. After two weeks it becomes sixty-five. After four it's seven. You follow?"

Lee nodded enthusiastically.

"Yeah. I got it, Ike. I can't thank you enough. Thank you."

Ike held up a hand.

"Don't thank me yet. If you don't pay up, I'll be back, then you'll be going from the frying pan into the fire."

"I know. I just need a little time, that's all."

Ike turned and opened the door, then looked back at Lee.

"That's exactly what you got. A little time."

Ike moved aside to let Brewski leave then closed the door on his way out without another word.

Lee watched his nephew's face light up as it did every time he came out of the school and saw Lee's maroon Sentra. Whenever Lee had to pick Ronny up at school, which was becoming more and more frequent, Ronny would tear his hand away from the teacher's aide who escorted him out of the building and run to the car as if he hadn't seen his uncle in years.

Lee reached across the seat, opened the door and gave a wave to the aide while Ronny climbed into the car and automatically fastened his seatbelt.

"Safety first," he said to no one in particular.

Lee closed the door then tussled the boy's curly, brown hair.

"That's right, kiddo," he said.

"Where are we going?" Ronny asked, as though they were headed out on an adventure.

"First, we're going to the hospital to see your mom, then we'll go to my house and play a little Donkey Kong. How's that sound?"

The game was older than Ronny by about twenty-five years, but every time they played, it was like the first time for him, and he loved it. Lee was glad he hadn't thrown it away and that it still worked.

"Wait 'til you see what I got," Ronny announced.

Lee pulled out of the school lot and headed for home.

"What do you got?" he asked.

Ronny held up his cell phone.

"Is that a new phone?" Lee asked.

"No. It's not. It's my iPhone six. Mom can't afford a new one yet, but that's okay."

"So, what do you have?"

"A new app. It's on the phone. It's called *Bug Your Neighbor*. I got it from the dark web. I'm not supposed to know about the dark web, but I do. Don't tell mom. Okay?"

"Mum's the word," Lee said. "Now you have an app to bug your neighbor? When I was a kid we just rang the doorbell and split, or toilet-papered the house. Stuff like that."

Ronny gave him a sideways look. "Not bug, like bother. Bug, like listen," he said with a bit of annoyance.

They were sitting at the traffic signal at the intersection of US1 and State Road 100. The four corners of the intersection were occupied by a pizza place, a gas station, a bar, and a bail bond office. Ronny did something to his phone, put it to his ear and listened for a second before handing the phone to Lee.

"Here. Listen."

Lee put the phone to his ear and heard a woman and a man talking.

"*His name is Arturo Hernandez. His bond was twenty-five thousand.*"

She gave a last known address.

"*Twenty-five thousand,*" the man said. "*I'll have Arturo in a county cell before midnight. You can have my twenty-five hundred in cash if it's easier.*"

"*You'll get a check, like you do every other time.*"

The callers hung up as the light turned green. Lee handed the phone back to Ronny.

"I'm not sure your mom would like it if she knew about that," he said.

"You said you wouldn't tell her. I heard you."

"That was before I knew what you were doing."

Ronny looked at Lee like with disapproval.

"You said you wouldn't tell."

"All right. I won't tell. But you shouldn't listen to other people's conversations."

"Why not?"

"Because they might not want you to hear what they say. It's private."

Ronny looked off into the sky as though privacy was a foreign concept.

Before Lee could continue with his life lesson, a whirlwind of thoughts converged in his head.

He owed Ralph Donabedian lots of money.

He needed lots more money to pay for Dianna's medical bills and get her out of Ron's house.

He had no way to get this money in the available time.

Bail jumpers were wanted fugitives, as he had learned from watching *Dog*.

With Ronny's app he had just learned of the address of one such wanted fugitive.

If he could get to said fugitive before the bounty hunter, he could bring him in and collect the reward himself.

"Ronny," he said. "Can you install that app on my phone?"

Ronny laughed.

"Of course I could. But you said it wasn't nice to listen to other people's conversations."

Lee gave him a playful shove on the shoulder.

"I was just kidding with you."

"Are you sure?"

Lee pulled his cell phone out and handed it to his nephew.

"Sure, I'm sure," he said. "Come on. Hook me up."

Ronny took the phone and went to work.

At the hospital, Ronny ran to his mother's bedside and pulled up short to avoid hurting her with his hug.

"Sorry, Mom," he said. "I can't hug you. I might hurt you again."

Dianna reached and touched his cheek.

"Hi, baby," she said.

"Mom," Ronny dropped his hands to his sides and looked at the ceiling. "Don't call me baby. I'm not a baby."

"I'm sorry, ba...Ronny."

Lee stepped to the bedside and leaned in to kiss his sister's cheek.

"How you doing?" he asked.

"I'm fine. Doctor says I had some internal bleeding, but it's all set now. I just need to rest for a couple of days. You know."

Lee nodded.

"Okay. Well, listen. I've got a few things to take care of, so I'm gonna leave Ronny here and take off for a couple of hours. That okay?'

"Sure. He can tell me all about his day. Can't you, Ronny?"

"Sure, Mom," Ronny said as he put his phone to his ear.

~ ~ ~ ~ ~

Lee parked along the train tracks to the west of the bail bond office, activated the app and waited. A man walked by, talking on his phone.

"Come on, man. You said it would be ready tonight."

"You can't wait 'til tomorrow?"

"What time tomorrow?"

"If I get the parts before ten, it'll be ready by noon."

"It better be or else..."

The conversation fizzled out as the man got further away.

"Hmm," Lee said. "Looks like I have to be pretty close to the phone to hear anything."

He got out of his car and walked to the front of the bond office. There was a concrete bench to the right of the entrance. He took a seat and waited. After fifteen minutes, the lights from inside went off and a woman came out. She locked the door and walked away, giving Lee a polite smile as she passed.

"That's it for the night, I guess," Lee said.

He put his phone away and walked to his car.

"There's always tomorrow," he said as he drove away.

Ron and Dianna Summers shared a double-wide in a trailer park that had seen much better days.

Ike and Brewski sat on their motorcycles in the parking lot of a storage facility on the other side of State Road 100. The setting sun on the opposite side of the building put them in the shadows. Ike watched the trailer through a monocular.

"I've driven by this place a thousand times," Brewski said. "I never gave it a second look. Tell you the truth, I thought it was abandoned."

"It should have been bulldozed twenty years ago," Ike said. "Even if they put up a 7-Eleven, it would be an improvement."

"What did Ralph find out?"

"The trailer is actually owned by Dianna. Her first husband cleaned her out when he split. This was the only thing she could afford. Ron has no claim to it at all, so we're going to serve an eviction notice."

"Not that I have anything against ruining this guy's day," Brewski said. "But this seems a bit above and beyond. Even for you."

"I've never liked Summers, and I've never had any reason to cross paths with him, but he's like a cockroach—most of the time, you don't even know he's there. But eventually a light is turned on and you see him, and it reminds you that he's there and needs to be dealt with. Lee turned on the light; now we're going to deal with him."

Brewski nodded.

"All right. I'm good with that. Let's go."

"A few more minutes," Ike said. "Let it get a little darker."

Once the sun was completely below the horizon, they crossed SR100 and approached the trailer. Ike climbed the steps to the front door while Brewski went to the rear. Through the door he could hear the sounds of the television. After giving Brewski a minute to get into position, Ike knocked on the door.

When the door opened, Ike pushed Summers back into the trailer and followed him in, pushing the door closed behind him. Summers looked at Ike with confusion.

"What the..."

Ike closed the distance between them, grabbed the backpedaling Summers by the throat, and pushed him all the way across the room until he slammed into the far wall.

Summers' eyes widened as his confusion morphed into fear.

On the television, the cast of *Duck Dynasty* discussed various strategies for nighttime frog hunting.

Brewski came in through the back door and stood in the kitchen.

"What do you want?" Summers asked, glancing from Ike to Brewski, then back to Ike. "I don't have nothin'. No money, drugs, nothin'."

"It's not about what we want, Ron."

At the use of his name, Summers studied Ike's face.

"I know you," he said.

"Good," Ike said. "Then we don't need to bother with introductions."

"What do you want?" Summers asked again.

"Like I said, it's not what we want. It's what you want, Ron."

Summers shook his head rapidly and furrowed his brow.

"What I want?"

"That's right. What do you want, Ron?"

Summers continued looking at Ike as though Ike had asked him to explain nuclear physics.

"Let me make it simple," Ike said. "Do you want to spend the rest of your life eating your meals through a straw and having nurses change your diapers every day because you can't walk to the head?"

Summers was too baffled to answer.

"Not simple enough for you?" Ike said. "Let's approach it from another angle. I'm going to come back tomorrow night at the same time. If you're still here, your days of walking upright are over. You follow?"

Ron swallowed.

"Why?" was all Ron could manage.

"Let's put it this way, Ron. You're not the only one who can put people in the hospital. Difference is, when you go into the hospital, you won't leave under your own power."

Brewski came into the living room and turned off the TV.

"I can't stand those dumb, redneck assholes," he said.

Ike released his grip on Ron's throat.

"So, let's go over it again, Ron. You have twenty-four hours to get your ass as far away from Dianna and Ronny as possible. Like maybe Seattle. You leave, and you never look back. As far as you're concerned, Florida has a *Do Not Enter* sign at the border. Are you with me?"

Ron nodded. "I got it," he said.

Ike pointed at him.

"Twenty-four hours," he said. "Gone."

Ike turned and walked to the door. Brewski tossed the remote to Ron. While the remote was in the air, Brewski made a fake lunge at Ron as though he were going to punch him. Ron covered his head with his arms and let out a small yelp. The remote hit him in the chest and fell to the floor.

"See ya, tough guy," Brewski said as he followed Ike out the door.

Acknowledgments

I would like to extend my sincere thanks to the following people for their instrumental help in the creation of this book:

Cover creation – **Keri Knutson**

Editing – **Karin Nicely**

Design and Layout – **Becky Pourchot**

For reading and critiquing an early draft –**Susan Toy, Dennis Ference, Susan Nicholls, Greg Nicholls, Bill Eldredge, Mary Kronenberg, Becky Pourchot, and my brothers, Joe & Ted**.

For technical advice on computer related technology – **Bill Eldredge***

For technical advice on trucking – **Rob Danford***

For technical advice on weapons – **Tony Walker***; (www.tonywalkerbooks.com)

*If there are any inaccuracies in any of these areas the fault is mine. Certain technical "adjustments" may have been made to suit the story.

41584966R00156

Made in the USA
Lexington, KY
08 June 2019